NO PLACE
FOR A *Lady*

HEART
of the WEST ✲ 1

NO PLACE FOR A *Lady*

A NOVEL

MAGGIE BRENDAN

Revell

a division of Baker Publishing Group
Grand Rapids, Michigan

Published by Revell
a division of Baker Publishing Group
P.O. Box 6287, Grand Rapids, MI 49516-6287
www.revellbooks.com

Printed in the United States of America

Library of Congress Cataloging-in-Publication Data
Brendan, Maggie, 1949–
    No place for a lady : a novel / Maggie Brendan.
      p. cm. — (Heart of the West ; bk. 1)
    ISBN 978-0-8007-3335-3 (pbk.)
    I. Title.
PS3602.R4485N6 2009
813'.6—dc22   2008032933

09 10 11 12 13 14 15   11 10 9 8 7 6 5

In memory of Jerry O'Neal, aka Jess McCreede, better known as Gary to me—my mentor, dearest brother, and friend. Not a day goes by that you don't cross my mind.

Acknowledgments

I'd like to express my deep appreciation to my best friend and critique partner, Kelly Long. There are no words to articulate what you mean to me, especially as my friend, and what your support of my writing, your prayers, and your encouragement mean. Many thanks to Caroline Friday for her encouragement, friendship, and humor. You've kept me laughing!

I must acknowledge the ACFW (American Christian Fiction Writers). In the last four years I've learned so much from them and the two fantastic conferences that I attended. The talent and support of the ACFW writer's loop is just incredible, and I'm proud to be a part of it. I'm grateful to DiAnn Mills for her consideration of me when I missed my first critique appointment at the Denver conference, and her critique guidance. A warm thanks to Brandilyn Collins, my conference mentor who prayed over me, and Colleen Coble, who told me to dream big!

Many thanks to Jennifer Schuchmann, a talented writer in her own right, who convinced me to submit my writing and urged me to attend writer's workshops. Thank you, Jen.

A special thanks to my agent, Tamela Hancock Murray, who believed in my book; Revell Books for allowing my story to come to life; and my insightful editors, Andrea Doering and Jessica Miles.

Lots of hugs to Dottie, Barbara, and Sarah Sue of The Bookmark at Johnson Ferry Baptist Church for their love, prayers, and encouragement. Also, sincere thanks to Jan Tilton, the Johnson Ferry Prayer Room, and my friends of the JFBC sanctuary choir. You're the greatest!

I'm so grateful for my children, Sheri and Jared, who told me that I can do just about anything that I set my mind to! Their amazing feedback and belief in me was extremely important. I love you both. My dear daughter-in-law, Amy, made each writing week sweeter by bringing little Sarah for visits to keep me in the "real" world. You're both precious to me.

A heartfelt thanks to my husband, Bruce, who believed that I could do it and kept the technical side running smoothly for me. Thank you for telling me again and again what a good writer I am.

Sylvia, thanks for telling me to reach for the stars and for reminding me that Jess would be proud. And to my dear niece, Halle, you know what your encouragement means to me. I love you. Without your dad's support throughout my life, I don't know where I would be today. My gratitude knows no bounds when it comes to him, and I miss him deeply.

A special thanks to my O'Neal family, my grandchildren, and all my incredible extended family. What a blessing all of you are to me.

I couldn't end this without acknowledging the gift of writing that God has blessed me with. I'm amazed that You love me!

"For I know the plans I have for you," declares the Lord, "plans to give you hope and a future."

Jeremiah 29:11 (NIV)

1

June 1892
The Yampa Valley, Colorado

Crystal Clark gripped the side of the bouncing buckboard to keep from tumbling onto the rocky roadbed below. From the first moment she'd left home she'd been wondering if she'd done the right thing by coming to Colorado. Maybe she should have remained in Georgia. At least there she knew what to expect. Out here the only person she knew was her aunt. Crystal had once thought her life was almost perfect, but in an instant, her father's death had changed everything that she thought secure.

Rusty, her aunt's driver, had been waiting in Steamboat Springs when she stepped off the stage. Now he pulled hard on the reins and stopped the horses on a rise that overlooked the Yampa Valley. "Thought you might want to take a minute, enjoy the view up here."

Crystal gazed at the unfolding vista resplendent with flaming Indian paintbrush and chickweed. Mountains loomed ahead. "What a breathtaking sight," she said, coughing as dust filled her throat and nostrils. Sweat ran in tiny rivulets down her back beneath her fitted corset and slithered its way down her clinging stockings into her snug-fitting heels. Despite these momentary inconveniences, Crystal could only think about her heartache.

"It's mighty pretty from up on this here rise." He grinned. "I knew the minute Kate sent me to fetch you that you were gonna like it here, ma'am."

Like it here? she thought.

Still, Crystal felt her lips turn up at the edges. Despite everything she'd been through, Rusty seemed to have the ability to make her smile.

"Kate said you're coming here to stay," he added.

Crystal frowned. She didn't know what she would be doing with her future, but in truth, she felt she had no alternative but to stay.

"I don't know about staying . . . That depends on a lot of things." Crystal thought the old-timer a bit nosy for all his charm.

"So, missy, what'd ya think of the mountains? Ain't they somethin'?"

"They are so majestic, Rusty. God made beauty everywhere, didn't He?"

"For a fact, ma'am. He did, He sure did." He scratched his scruffy beard with his free hand. "It'll be mighty nice to have a young person of the female persuasion around for a change. Being with cowboys all the time can wear on a man after a while." He chuckled.

"Right now, I'm afraid that I'm just tired and looking forward to a good night's sleep."

12

"I hear you're from Georgia. When'd you start out?" Rusty asked.

Crystal sighed. "Nearly two weeks ago." Thinking back on it made her appreciate the settlers who had first come to this wild land years ago. "At Kansas I boarded the Rio Grande, which took me to Denver. From there I took the Colorado Central and Pacific narrow gauge railroad to Central City. Believe me, I was leaning as far back in my seat as possible when the engine hugged the edge of the mountains to start down. From Central City, I had to travel the rest of the way by stagecoach." Crystal closed her eyes and thought back to how scared she had been when the stagecoach crossed over the Continental Divide and then labored over Rabbit Ears Pass. "I had trouble breathing up there and had a headache as well."

"I know what you mean, missy."

Inspired by the vastness of the beautiful valley nestled below the majestic snowcapped Rocky Mountains, Crystal soon forgot about her aching and stiff muscles. "Aunt Kate's description of Colorado was accurate. This is very different from what I'm used to."

"So tell me, what is it like in Georgia? I've never traveled farther south than Denver," Rusty said.

"Well, it's heaven on earth to me. But you might find it strange. It's not wide open like it is here, and we have lots of beautiful trees. Magnolias, dogwoods, oaks, and a variety of azaleas. Throw in humidity and you'll get an idea of what it's like."

"What are azaleas?"

"They're bushes that bloom in early spring. Some are white, some are pink. Underneath the dogwood trees, they make a very pleasing picture."

She felt hot tears spring behind her eyelids. Just talking about home made her chest tight. The day she had to sign the deed over to the bank, Crystal thought her heart would break. No one, not even Drew, had stepped in to help straighten out her finances.

Although Drew wanted to marry her, something in her heart told Crystal that she did not feel as deeply for him as he did for her. Maybe time apart from Drew would give her a chance to know for sure what God had planned for her.

The old-timer interrupted her meditations as his strong, capable hands flicked the reins and guided the horses into the valley floor. "It sounds beautiful."

Crystal couldn't bear to keep talking about Georgia, and she changed the subject. "It's been so long since I've seen Aunt Kate. But I have so many fond memories of her visits to Georgia. When she wrote, asking me to come for a visit, I wired her the same day and packed my bags. But I wasn't sure what to expect."

"Well, good for you. We'll do our best to see you have a fine visit. Not much longer now, missy. And it won't always be this hot and dry, either. Reckon this is a shore sign of frost. Snow flies in September, sometimes late August here in the valley. Soon the pass will close."

Crystal glanced at the man's profile. Lines crinkled around his mouth on his weather-beaten face. He smiled at her, removed his hat, and mopped his brow with a handkerchief. His thick red hair swirled around his head like a flame whipped by the wind. Rusty replaced his hat and stuffed his handkerchief into his shirt pocket.

Crystal smiled back weakly and sighed. "The closest thing to snow I've seen in Georgia was flurries before a January ice storm. Tell me about the snow here. What's it like?"

"The winters here can be long and hard, especially on the livestock. I remember the blizzard of '87 that me and Kate weathered together. Your uncle had died two years before, you know. We had very little supplies to see us through. For ten days the world stood still, and the snow was six feet deep in places. Drifts reached to the roof of the house. That year most of the cattle either froze or starved to death." He paused in his ruminating, and Crystal watched his face soften as he looked into the distance.

"The cattle got lean because of the drought during the summer . . . So weak and defenseless, they didn't have much of a chance. The snow so deep that our cowhands couldn't reach 'em. We hadn't counted on a summer drought with bitter snowfall on its heels. Our thermometer broke when it got thirty below. Kate read later on in the *Steamboat Pilot* that Montana recorded a minus forty-six degrees. Not sure what it was here."

Crystal shuddered. "Why in heaven's name would a person stay way out here, away from civilization, with a bunch of cows during a snowstorm in the first place?"

Rusty chuckled. "Maybe you'll change your mind after you're here a spell. This here is God's country."

"Sounds perfectly miserable to me." Crystal twirled her parasol, fanning her hot cheeks with a white lacy handkerchief. As far as she knew, the entire world was God's country, but she understood what he meant. Crystal felt that way about Georgia. *Oh well, it will just be a visit until I can figure out what I need to do.*

Late afternoon sun filtered through the ponderosa pine, lending a dappling effect to the surrounding junipers, sagebrush, and violet alpine asters.

"There's Aspengold. Your aunt's ranch was named after those shimmering trees in that grove to the rear of the house." Rusty pointed to a rustic, sprawling ranch house.

Crystal followed the direction of his finger. The ranch was nothing like she expected. Unlike her father's beautiful cotton plantation home with its huge white columns framed by giant oak trees, Aspengold was a low, almost flat log house with a porch running its full length. Not far from the house were corrals, a barn, and a smaller version of the main house, which Crystal guessed must be the bunkhouse from her aunt's descriptive letters. The trees of white bark laden with black boles were nestled near the porch. The small, quaking leaves seeming to wave their greeting in the afternoon sunlight.

"Carmen's spotted us." Rusty flicked the reins on the horses' rumps, and they snapped into a trot toward the ranch. In the distance, dogs started barking at the sound of the wagon rumbling down the dirt road.

Crystal saw a woman in a full red skirt run back into the house, then reappear with another woman whom she recognized as her aunt Kate. Crystal felt her chest tighten again. How in the world was she going to fit in with these folks and their simple life? Maybe it wouldn't be for long—and maybe she'd think again about Drew.

As Rusty brought the wagon to a standstill in front of the veranda, the dogs yapped, and several cowboys appeared and swept off their hats in greeting. The tallest cowboy reached up to lift

Crystal down, and she felt herself swing to the ground as though she were nothing more than a child. The cowboy towered above Crystal. She glimpsed confederate-blue eyes underneath dark eyebrows and thin lips below a thick moustache. For the briefest moment, their eyes held, and Crystal felt strange at the warmth of his hands holding her waist. Releasing her, he bowed with a ridiculous grin on his face.

Kate grabbed her niece and kissed her on the cheek. "Crystal, it sure is good to see you. You're a sight for sore eyes, girl." Kate pulled back. "Let me get a good look at you. I declare! You've grown up on me. The spittin' image of your ma."

Crystal felt her face turning pink. "It's so wonderful to see you too. It's been too long, hasn't it?" Crystal smoothed the wrinkles of her skirt. "After that long, dirty ride, I must look a mess." She pushed a few loose strands of dark, wavy hair back, knowing her face was dirt-streaked.

She looked up into Kate's soft and full face, with hair grayer than she remembered four years ago. Kate Morgan was in her late forties, a strong, determined woman whose tall frame and husky voice made her appear almost mannish. But Crystal knew that there wasn't a bigger heart in all of Colorado than her aunt's.

Pulling Crystal forward by the elbow, Kate beamed with pride and announced, "This is my niece, Crystal Clark, and I want all of you to make her feel welcome." Kate gestured toward the tall cowboy who had helped Crystal down from the wagon. "Meet Luke Weber—he's my foreman."

"Ma'am." Luke touched the brim of his hat for a split second.

Crystal noticed that he did not remove his hat. *So ungentlemanly.* She stood straight and prim. "I'm glad to make your acquaintance." Crystal lowered her voice to a softer pitch, tilting her head up to look at Luke. She felt a little uneasy under his steady gaze but returned it with her own.

Standing well over six foot, Luke's tall, lean frame belied his well-developed muscles suggesting years of working outdoors. A red bandana was knotted around his neck, and a blue chambray shirt reflected the color of his eyes. Dusty black boots, a little the worse for wear, held spurs at the heel, making a slight jingling noise each time he shifted his weight.

"And these here boys are Curly, Jube, and Kurt, the best ranch hands in these parts," Kate said.

Crystal turned to greet Curly, who was obviously named for his head of tight golden curls. Curly wiped his hands on his large bandana before he stepped toward her. He smiled. "Howdy."

Crystal smiled back. "Hello."

Jube kicked at a rock with the toe of his boot and, without looking directly at her, muttered hello, blushing to the roots of his scalp.

Kurt nudged between the two of them and took Crystal's hand to kiss it. "A real pleasure, ma'am," he said without releasing her hand, "to meet a Southern belle, and a most exquisite one at that."

Crystal noted his obvious good manners and Eastern accent, but she pulled her hand away from his. "It's my pleasure to meet y'all." They were quite a grubby band of boyish riders to her way of thinking, and she couldn't help but notice that they all wore spurs. What a racket.

"What y'all gawking at?" Kate gestured with her arms and fanned herself with her apron. "Rusty, get those bags in. Carmen, please bring us a glass of cool lemonade as soon as Crystal's freshened up a bit. I'm sure she's about to parch. Crystal, this is Carmen." Kate pulled forward a lovely Mexican girl, who flashed a suspicious look from her brooding dark eyes. Her large silver earrings glinted in the sunlight.

"Sí, señora." Carmen turned on her bare feet to do Kate's bidding.

Jube stepped up to help Rusty unload Crystal's suitcases. Curly and Kurt carried them to the porch, and the worn planks creaked under their weight. Luke stared at the big trunk and threw Rusty a quizzical look, but Rusty just rolled his eyes upward.

Kate laughed. "Well, I see you didn't bring enough change of clothes."

"That trunk has my gowns, what's left of them. Y'all *do* have parties out here, don't you?"

Jube looked at Curly, who reached down to pick up an odd-shaped case, and then over to Luke, who shrugged his shoulders.

"We have a barn dance every now and then," Kate replied.

"Oh . . ." Disappointment sounded in her voice, but she wore her brightest smile. "I guess we'll have to do something about that then, won't we?"

Curly slammed her black case down, and Crystal rushed toward him. "Land sakes! Please be careful with that. It's my Autoharp, and it's easy to damage."

"Your *what*?" Curly's face turned the color of a southwestern sunset as he shuffled his feet.

Crystal immediately set him at ease. "You couldn't have known."

19

She lifted the case and patted it. "It's a musical instrument. I promise to play it for y'all sometime, Curly. How would that be?"

"That's a deal." Curly smiled and pulled the last suitcase to the door.

The drovers just about fell all over themselves in an attempt to help with her baggage. A faint trace of gardenia hung in the air as Crystal moved past the cowboys. Rusty and Luke just stood back and leaned against the fence to watch.

Crystal supposed she should be flattered by all the attention, but now she didn't think there would be much stimulating conversation or many parties way out here without neighbors for miles. And the dust. She hated it along with the dry heat. Luke, who looked amused by her very presence, was not what one would call sociable. He didn't seem to want to be bothered with her any more than she wanted to be in this part of the world.

Crystal fanned herself with her lace handkerchief and followed her aunt into the ranch house. *Lord, what have I gotten myself into? What did I expect?*

The cool water felt refreshing on her face and neck and revived Crystal's tired, dusty body. Patting herself dry with a thin towel, she noticed the room's simplicity. A small fireplace stood opposite the bed with a crude rocker placed to one side. On the ancient, scarred, cherrywood bed were piled several colorful patchwork quilts, and atop the dresser was a pitcher cradled in a cracked rose bowl. A small lady's desk sat beneath the window. Blue gingham curtains fluttered against the window frame. Someone had picked wild columbines and placed them on the nightstand, but now their petals drooped. Though different from her normal surroundings, she decided somehow this room seemed rather cozy.

She was determined to make the best of the situation. This was better than having everyone back home feel sorry for her.

She missed Lilly, and tears threatened to fall. No more Lilly pulling the covers back and laying out her nightgown. Crystal had begged her to come along, but Lilly wouldn't think of leaving the South and her family. All of a sudden, Crystal felt homesick. She sighed deeply then and wandered out into the narrow hallway.

The large front room was decorated with fine Indian pottery. Beautiful colored blankets adorned the walls, while an enormous fireplace of fieldstone boasted a huge elk head mounted above. Wood floors gleamed as afternoon sunlight spilled through spacious windows. Delicious smells wafted through the house and made her aware of her rumbling stomach.

By the time Crystal stepped out onto the porch, just Kate and Carmen were sitting in rocking chairs. The ranch hands apparently had gone back to their respective chores. She assured her aunt that she felt human once again.

Carmen stood and offered her a tall glass of lemonade. "Thank you." She took the glass and smiled at Carmen, but the Mexican girl lowered her head. Crystal wasn't sure if the dark-haired beauty was bashful or just couldn't speak English.

Carmen took a chair nearby, but Crystal felt her dark stare and sensed Carmen's discomfort. Crystal smoothed her blue cotton skirt with its fitted shirtwaist. She noticed Carmen's hurried movement to tuck her bare feet underneath her skirt. Crystal bent down to give her aunt a brief hug with her free arm before taking her own seat.

"I see you've changed your traveling clothes to something a bit more comfortable," Kate commented.

"Yes, I did. It was pretty dusty on the trail coming here." Crystal felt much cooler in the light-blue sprigged cotton dress.

The lemonade was delicious, and the conversation grew animated as Crystal told Kate of her excursion from Atlanta through the Rocky Mountains.

"I have to admit, Aunt Kate, the mountains are even more beautiful than I could have ever imagined."

"I tried to tell you, Crystal. They are indeed incredible. Wait until you've had a chance to explore them."

After Carmen slipped back inside the house, the conversation turned serious. Crystal learned that since her uncle's death, Kate was struggling to hold on to the ranch.

"Last year was a hard one with low beef prices, and rustlers were stealing my cattle, trying to add to their own herd. I lost a few head to drought, because there wasn't enough grass to fatten 'em up."

"I'm sorry, Aunt Kate. I didn't know."

"Without Rusty's support and hard work from my ranch hands, and the good Lord . . . " She sighed. "Honey, last year might have been a very bleak one indeed. I'm sorry. I didn't mean to start up complaining." Kate gazed out into the front yard. Her shoulders slumped forward. Her stern face softened a bit, and she looked worn out. Crystal reached over to hold her hand.

"Problems always appear to be larger than they are, especially when they're *your* problems." Crystal remembered her own burden of straightening out her father's bills and dealing with the creditors. "The hardest thing I ever had to do was sell the family home, and I certainly didn't want pity. My parents taught me that God has a purpose in our lives, and I'd like to believe that. I'm just not sure what that purpose is yet."

"You're just like your mother, never down for too long. It is such a pity that her life was shortened by cholera—and you just ten years old. You are just like her." A shadow crossed Kate's worn face briefly, but then she straightened, and her face lit up. "With that attitude, you're gonna be good for me, dear. I know it was hard for you to leave, but perhaps in time you will grow to like it here, Crystal. I'd love for you to stay. To tell you the truth, from your pa's letters before he died, I thought you would be settling down with Andrew Franklin, unless I missed my guess."

Crystal rocked the chair back and forth in agitation. "Drew did propose, but I just couldn't give him an answer. Not yet. I'm still not sure if I want to spend the rest of my life with him, let alone have his mother dictate our every move."

"You would be set for life, Crystal. His family wields a lot of power in Georgia, although a political lifestyle would not be my choosing."

"Comfort *is* important," she said, not looking straight into her aunt's eyes. "But, Aunt Kate, I've never been interested in power. Although I care for Drew, I'm not sure it's the kind of love that will last forever. I worry sometimes that he is too involved in himself to be devoted to anything but his career. Perhaps time apart will answer many questions in my mind and his. I want to follow God's leading for my future, and quite honestly, I don't know if Drew figures into that plan."

"I'm glad to hear you say that. You have matured in more

23

ways than one, and I know that my sister wanted a secure future for you, sweetie. Now, I'm gonna see to it that your future is brighter."

Crystal's heart warmed with her aunt's comments, and she was glad that she had someone to count on. It felt good not to be alone anymore, despite the new surroundings.

2

The bunkhouse was bustling with excitement at the arrival of the newest unmarried female within a twenty-five-mile radius. Luke watched the rest of the cowpokes with a taciturn yawn. He leaned back in his chair, stretched out his long legs, and propped them up on a nearby bunk. He began whittling on a piece of wood as he listened to the raucous cowhands. They seemed unaware that they had the chance of a columbine in a hailstorm, yet they were busy comparing notes on how to win Crystal's affections. Luke wondered if she had even noticed the columbines that he'd placed on her bureau. Now he felt foolish that he had put them there at all. Surely she was used to exquisite roses—at the very least.

"Well, you saw how she took to me right off, being the friendliest." Curly lay in his bunk, chewed on a piece of hay, and folded his arms under his head to gaze at nothing in particular.

Kurt strolled over to the cracked mirror, examined his rugged good looks, and smoothed back his thick hair. He twirled the ends of his handlebar moustache, impeccably groomed, between his forefinger and thumb.

"My dear boys, a lady of her upbringing bristles at such friendliness. However, she will all but swoon at the display of charming good manners." Kurt squared his shoulders, tugging at his vest. "I should know."

"Aw, cut it out, you two! I hear she has a beau back in Georgia. I bet more'n one," Jube said, dusting his hat off against his leg. "I overheard Kate and Rusty talkin', and I don't 'spect she'll stay too long."

"Way I hear it, she doesn't have a home to go to. Had to sell out because of debts her father left behind when he died. No lady reared in a fine lifestyle is gonna have nothin' to do with the likes of us," Curly informed them.

"What do you think, Luke?" Jube asked. Luke knew they valued his opinion in just about everything from calf branding to selecting prime horseflesh.

Luke set down the wood he was whittling. He pushed back his chair, grabbed his hat, and in two short strides was at the bunkhouse door. "What I think is that we have better things to do than chew the fat 'bout some blasted female that's got her nose in the air and whose deepest thought is whether or not she'll get to wear her ball gowns. Go back to your card games and quit wasting your time. See ya back at the main house for supper." The door slammed behind him. He heard Curly ask the punchers, "What's eatin' him?"

Waning sunlight reflected its beauty against the silvery aspens, in sharp contrast to the sapphire-blue sky. The summer breeze sighed and sent a gentle shiver through the cinquefoil, a reminder that fall was on its way, and the alpine buttercups nodded in agreement. Luke breathed in deeply, savoring the pungent fragrance of spruce and fir. He walked through the woods and away from the noisy bunkhouse, where a game of cards was taking place.

He reflected on the past ten years of hard work. He'd scraped every bit of pay to lay aside for the day he'd buy his own spread. He already had his eye on a section south that had fertile land fed by the Blue River along the Gore Range. One day it would be his.

Not that he was complaining about the work. Kate was not just his employer but his friend as well. She treated him like the son she was never able to have. She'd taken him in when he was fourteen, right after his parents died of typhoid fever. Since then, there had been laughter and love to replace his sadness as a young boy.

Realizing he had walked farther than he intended, Luke headed back to the house. In the distance he could see Carmen lighting the lamps. His stomach told him it was time for supper.

"Around here, we don't dress for supper except on special occasions," Kate told Crystal as they made their way toward a sizable dining room. Crystal admired a well-polished oak table that could seat twelve people with ease.

"I'm a very informal person, and my ranch hands dine with us, since we are small in number." Kate's blue eyes twinkled. "It makes life much more interesting, and I can keep better track of things. Go on over and sit down. The others will be along soon. Carmen has just about got everything ready."

"It smells wonderful, and I'm hungry," Crystal said, seeing the food on the table. *Looks like a fried pancake stuffed with something from the pasture*, she thought. She just smiled.

"Once you've tried Mexican food, you'll wonder how you lived without it," Rusty declared, hurrying to her side and pulling out a chair for her. He had washed up and changed his shirt to a red-checkered one that emphasized his freckles, and he'd slicked down his thick, unruly hair, which plastered his head like a wet red dishcloth. Crystal grinned and thought it sweet that he would try to impress her.

As soon as she was seated, there was a mad scramble and scraping of chairs as the rest of the hands appeared. Kurt and Curly grabbed the chairs on either side of her. Jube sat across from her and helped himself to a plate of enchiladas. His fresh-scrubbed, boyish face and bashful look made him appear young. Rusty, she noted, sat at the opposite end of the table from Kate. Suddenly the room became quiet as Kate blessed the food and the hands that had prepared it.

"Here, Miss Crystal, try these enchiladas. Carmen makes the best in the West." She wondered at the wink Kurt gave everyone as he passed the dish to her.

"Sí, es verdad. And these are tostados, made with beans, chilies, and corn tortillas," Carmen said, while casting a look at Luke.

The look did not go unnoticed by Crystal. She watched Luke stroll in and sit at the farthest end of the table with his hat slung low over his forehead. It had a slight roll at the sides, blocking the view of his eyes. *You don't have anything to worry about from me*, she wanted to say aloud to Carmen.

Crystal figured that Luke wore his hat low on purpose. That

way no one knew if he was staring. And he was staring—at her. She wondered what he was thinking. She brought a forkful of the enchilada to her mouth in dainty fashion. Carmen paused with her serving and watched Crystal's face.

"Well, whaddya think?" Curly's Adam's apple bobbed when he spoke.

Everyone in the room looked at Crystal. "Mmm," she managed while chewing. Then tears stung her eyes as she swallowed and choked and gasped, "*Water, please!*" She could feel her face turning bright red.

Kurt hurried to her side and offered her water that she managed to gulp down. Laughter exploded all around her from everyone except Kate.

"Carmen! I thought I asked you to prepare a plate made with mild chilies just for Crystal," Kate said, her voice rising.

"Sí, señora." She scurried off toward the kitchen. "I was just getting them."

"It's my fault," Kurt said, trying to keep from laughing. "I should've known not to pass those to her."

"Crystal, are you all right?" Kate's face showed concern. She passed Crystal the sugar bowl. "Here, put a little of this on your tongue. It'll stop the burning directly."

Crystal placed the sugar on her tongue. "I'll be fine," she said with more assurance than she felt. "Those were very hot. I guess I'm just used to fried chicken and biscuits."

"Perhaps you'd like to treat us to your specialty sometime." Luke spoke for the first time since he'd walked in. "I've heard lots about Southern cooking. Maybe you could give us a sample." He was shoveling in food like it was his last meal. He paused to wipe milk foam from his moustache and to give her a quick wink.

Crystal flashed him an annoyed look. Was Luke flirting with her? Probably not.

"Good idea," Kate agreed. "It's been too long since I've tasted any."

"I guess I could do that," she said, helping herself to the special batch of enchiladas that Carmen held out for her. *I'll never pull that one off. Was that lying?* Crystal knew she'd never be able to whip up a full-course meal with the Mexican girl's ease. She wasn't even sure she knew how to make the batter for fried chicken.

Lifting her glass, she drank deeply, allowing the water to ease the mild burning in her throat, and looked around the table. With the exception of Kate, they were all eating like starved dogs. Table manners, apparently, were not high on their agenda.

Crystal had a captive audience during the rest of the meal. She saw Kate look down at the end of the table and wink at Rusty, and he smiled back at her, rubbing his thumb back and forth across his beard.

Kate pushed back her chair. "We're going to have a party on Friday in your honor, Crystal, so you can meet our neighboring ranchers."

"That would be wonderful," Crystal replied. "A party sounds like fun. I want to know about your lives here. The countryside is so vast and different from Georgia. I can't wait to get a better look."

"Do you ride?" Luke asked, with one raised eyebrow.

"A little."

"Be ready at seven, then." Luke stood up and doffed his hat.

"Oh, and by the way, better ask Kate if she will loan you some of her britches. Those full skirts won't do out here. Then I'll show you a little piece of God's country."

Crystal squirmed in her chair. He'd just assumed she'd want to go riding with him. "Why so early?"

"Well, we wouldn't want you to get sunburned the first day here, now would we? We like to treat greenhorns special. Besides, the days start at dawn and end at dusk around here."

"Oh, I see now, Mr. Weber. In other words, you go to bed with the chickens," she teased. The cowboys around the table laughed at their banter.

Luke ignored her comment and walked toward the door. "Thanks for those delicious enchiladas, Carmen."

Crystal thought that though Luke never appeared to be in a hurry, his long legs crossed the room in just a few strides. Abruptly the door closed behind him.

The rest of the cowpunchers took their cue from him, it seemed, and in less than a minute they were heading back to the bunkhouse. That was it. No after-dinner conversation and retiring to the parlor for coffee. Crystal already missed home—even Drew. How in the world would she ever get up and be ready at daylight? Before Papa died, she was used to sleeping until nine and having breakfast with him. It was apparent to her that she'd have to fit into their crude environment if she decided to stay. *Oh, Papa, why did you leave me all alone?* her heart cried.

After Kate said good night, Crystal changed into her gown and hopped under the quilts. She lay in the dark for a long time, listening to the silence and thinking about the cowboys and Carmen. She had to chuckle as she remembered the hot enchiladas. It was all done in fun. They meant no harm. Life would definitely be different here.

She slipped out of bed and walked to the desk. She pulled out some paper and dipped her pen in ink to start a letter to Drew. She told him that she had arrived safely, described the long ride to the ranch and a few details of her aunt and the cowboys, and ended with missing home and him. *Does he miss me too?* she wondered as she folded the letter and addressed an envelope.

Briefly she held the letter in her hand and stared at it as if it were written in a foreign language. She'd mail it in the morning and deal with her feelings later. She was really too tired to think about them now.

Crawling back under the quilts, she closed her eyes and thanked God for her safe trip over the treacherous mountains. She prayed that He would give her a willingness to learn this new way of life and a heart to listen for His guidance.

Morning light spilled through the thin curtains, sending warmth across Crystal's face. She felt a gentle nudge on her shoulder. For a moment she thought she was dreaming.

"Honey, there's no sleeping in 'round here," Kate said in her usual cheery but gruff voice. "Time you got up. Breakfast is on the sideboard. I brought you some britches. I'm afraid they'll be a mite too big, you bein' so thin. And here's a flannel shirt you can tuck in and belt. There're hats by the door, take your pick." She was a burst of energy, bustling around the room with such force that the floor creaked with her weight. "And here's warm water for you to wash up with."

Crystal could barely get her eyes focused. "Is it really morning already?"

"Sorry, dear. Rusty and me are riding over to Stillwater to look at some horses. Enjoy your day and don't get overheated now, you hear?" With a kiss on Crystal's cheek, Kate was already out the door before Crystal could murmur her thanks.

Crystal yawned and stretched, then swung her legs over the side of the bed. She could hear the dogs barking in the distance as the buckboard rattled down the drive. Crystal had seen the tender look Rusty had given her aunt last night at supper. *Something's going on with the two of them, or my name's not Crystal Clark.*

She gingerly put her foot on the cold floor and shuddered. The mornings were quite a bit colder than she had expected. She skipped across the floor to keep her feet from touching the cold pine boards any longer than necessary and pulled the curtain back from the window. Kurt and Jube were leading horses out to the corral, and Kurt waved as he saw her. She waved back and quickly dropped the curtain. Kurt certainly was handsome, but Crystal was not interested in cowboys at all. No matter how good-looking.

By the time Crystal got to the dining room, everyone else had already eaten. The sideboard held fried ham and something that resembled scrambled eggs with green things in them. "Guess Mexican food is all that Carmen can cook," she said under her breath. She chuckled as she remembered Luke's taunt about her cooking up a Southern meal. *Have to stall for time on that one.* She could cook delectable pies and decent biscuits—that was about it.

She helped herself to a cup of very strong coffee. How she would love a bowl of grits or a stack of hot pancakes.

Carmen came in carrying a huge tray and began clearing the sideboard. "I was waiting for you to come and eat." She slammed the dishes onto the tray.

"Oh. Please, come and sit here with me and have a cup of coffee while I finish. I'd enjoy the company."

Carmen cast her a suspicious look but set the tray down. "Only for un momento. I have much to do."

"I won't mince my words," Crystal drawled. "I believe that you purposely made sure that I would eat those hot enchiladas." When Carmen's face flushed red, Crystal held up her hand. "Never mind apologizing, I just wanted to let you know I may be a greenhorn, but I catch on fast. I don't intend to get in your way here. Besides, I'm here for only a short time, and I don't need any enemies. Do you think we could just try to be friends and start over?"

"Sí, señorita. I am sorry. It was just a little joke." Carmen looked down at her bare toes sticking out of her sandals.

"Good." Crystal sighed with relief. "Please call me Crystal."

Carmen's wide, flashing grin was her response.

3

Early morning, before the rest of the world was stirring, was Luke's favorite time of day. He'd been up a while already, puttering around the tack room. He liked things neat and tidy. The cowboys didn't always put things back in their respective places, even though they'd all been warned to.

Thoughts of the trail drive in the not-too-distant future filled his mind. He'd have to hire a few more hands to move the cattle to Denver. Unlike last year, the pastures were rich and high. He could either let the herd fatten up a little more, which could raise the price per pound but risk the market falling, or go ahead to make plans to ship them from Denver to Chicago. He'd have to talk it over with Kate and Rusty.

He saddled two sorrels and was just leading them out of the barn when he noticed Crystal walking toward him. He patted Buck's muscular neck to control his laughter as his eyes took in Crystal's wide, baggy britches, which seemed to swallow her small frame. They were cinched at the waist, defying them to fall down. Her plaid flannel shirt, open at the throat, exposed a slender, white neck. The long sleeves had been clumsily rolled at the cuff just above her delicate wrists. To ward off the sun's strong rays, Crystal had chosen a wide straw sombrero that almost hid her eyes from view. She was swinging a knapsack that held their lunches. There was something awfully sweet and innocent about Crystal that was reflected in her countenance. *Careful, Luke. Don't let those wide eyes fool you.*

"What are you staring at?" she asked. She tilted the oversized hat back to look up into his face.

"Mornin', ma'am. Don't you think you'd better lace those shoes a bit tighter?" He struggled to keep his face somber.

Crystal looked down at the brogans she'd borrowed from Kate and frowned. "They are a little on the big side, aren't they? Besides, they have very little style."

"They're not meant to. Kate uses those for hiking and working in the garden." Luke slipped the bridle over the horse's head and the bit into her mouth. "This is Bess. You'll like her. She's real gentle and knows her way around these parts by heart. Buck here is a mite feisty with certain folk, ain't that right, fella?"

Buck stamped his hoof, tossed his beautiful mane, and snorted. Luke watched as Crystal let Bess nuzzle her hand, looking for a treat.

"Hello there, girl." Her low voice was as smooth as warm honey as she ran her hand down the horse's cinnamon-brown side. "You're a real beauty," she cooed, patting the ripple of muscles on Bess's side. Gathering the reins in her left hand and placing her left foot in the stirrup, Crystal reached for the pommel with her right hand and pulled herself into the saddle before Luke could offer assistance.

"You seem to know a little about horses." Luke raised a dark brow in surprise.

Crystal smiled down at him and then explained, "My father *did* have some fine riding horses once. He taught me a little. We didn't just sit on the front porch all day fanning ourselves, you know." She threw her head back, and rich, silvery laughter bubbled out.

From where Crystal sat she could see Luke's shiny black hair, fine and straight across a deep forehead looking naked without his hat. His shoulders were as broad as a mule's back, and he was small hipped. Without a doubt, he had the longest legs she had ever seen, and large hands and feet. Those hands, despite their size, stroked Buck's withers with affection. She couldn't help but compare him to Drew, whose slight frame was always impeccably dressed for whatever occasion—from his clipped, groomed hair and neat, clean fingernails all the way down to his shiny black shoes. Two totally different people, Drew and Luke. Now why was she even comparing? Luke meant nothing to her, and—she'd wait for God's direction on Drew.

Realizing that she was staring, Crystal nudged Bess out of the corral with a poke of her heel.

Plucking his hat from the fence post, Luke mounted Buck and came abreast. "We'll ride down to the lower pasture and let you get a look at some prime beef, and then back along the Blue River. If you get tired, just say so, and we'll take a rest and have that lunch Carmen packed for us."

He led the way down the drive and away from the house, following a trail lined with thick aspens, their leaves rustling on the early morning breeze. Columbines of violet blue were scattered in their wild fashion, and chipmunks scurried across the rocks. The trail widened, and Luke spurred Buck into a light canter across the valley floor, glancing over his shoulder at Crystal. She knew he was surprised at her riding skills by the look on his face.

The flat trail gave way to a narrow, rocky incline as Luke slowed Buck to a walk. They were climbing now, and Bess picked her way among the rocks for sure footing. Crystal figured Bess knew the trail so well she could have been blindfolded, and she realized she would be safe on the horse's broad back anywhere.

Luke stopped in a sheltered thicket of spruce trees, swung off his mount, and turned to help Crystal down.

"Come along, I want to show you something." He grabbed her hand and pulled her partway up to the rocky ledge. "Watch your step now."

The rock-strewn pathway eventually led them above the timberline. Crystal was panting as they reached the top of the ridge. The altitude made it difficult for her to catch her breath. From this vantage point she could see the mountains to her left, craggy and purple with their snow-capped peaks. On the other side, tall spruces and firs surrounded a wide, deep canyon. Water rushed below, spilling over rocks worn flat and shiny by its never-ending flow. It was so quiet with just the stirring wind lifting the pine boughs with its gentle rustle. In the distance, a hawk soared with ease and grace with the crystal blue sky as its backdrop.

"It's so beautiful." Crystal stood transfixed. Luke's face reflected such peace as he looked out over the canyon that Crystal sensed his true love of this beautiful land. Up here the wind was so strong that she had to use one hand to hold her blowing hair out of her line of vision and the other hand to hold her hat in place. A small thrill pricked her soul. Ah . . . God was so big, and His handiwork displayed His nature. Everything seemed well in the world today.

"This is where I'll have my own place someday. It has fertile pasture land just perfect for raising cattle," Luke said.

"Who owns it now?"

"Jim McBride, but I'm pretty sure he'll sell to me. I've been saving for a long time . . . Shoot! What's a few measly acres to him when he owns hundreds? You'll meet his family at the party Friday night." Luke stepped closer to the ridge and gazed out at the grand landscape before him. His conscience pricked him about the conversation he'd had with McBride concerning his daughter's hand in marriage and the parcel of land.

Luke propped one foot on a huge rock and placed an elbow on his knee. "Yep, this time next year, I'll have me a snug cabin nestled in those pines and a few head of cattle to boot." His jaw was set with a determined angle as his heavy dark brows knitted together in thought.

"How about a wife and children? Do they figure in your *ideal* picture?"

"Yessiree, they do. But it will take a strong and determined woman who would have to make sacrifices till we get on our feet. What I need, Miss Clark, is a partner."

"Sounds like you want a workhorse to me." Her eyes flashed.

"Afraid of hard work? Listen, little missy, this part of the country was founded on hardworking men and women. They had big dreams. Some didn't make it, but I intend to. It's pure struggle against the elements and nature just to survive, but that's part of the challenge, and I like a challenge."

Luke thought of his parents, who had worked so hard to

scrape out a meager living but never owned much before typhoid took them. How or why Luke had survived, he wasn't sure.

"Is that why you brought me up here? Proposing already? And we don't even know each other," she teased with a lopsided smile.

Luke became flustered. "Why, heck no. I . . . just wanted to show you what I have in mind someday."

She turned to face him but in her haste tripped over her large shoes. She fell hard against Luke and sent them both sprawling in the underbrush.

"What—" Luke muttered under his breath while he stared into Crystal's emerald eyes. Her weight atop him was light and soft. She struggled to untangle her legs from his.

"I'm so sorry." Crystal's face flamed red.

Luke continued to hold her against him. He could feel the outline of her legs through her britches. Luke knew he smelled of leather and horses mixed with soap, and he wondered if Crystal considered the smell offensive. She, on the other hand, smelled fresh with a light fragrance he couldn't place.

"It's all right, greenhorn. Guess Kate's shoes are real hard to fill." The corners of his moustache twitched as he chuckled, and for one long moment they assessed one another. Her eyes were large and sparkled such that Luke had a hard time dragging his own eyes away. Crystal's nearness was somehow unsettling. He released her and helped her to her feet. He retrieved her sombrero and slammed it none too gently on her head. Dusting off his own hat, he headed to where they had tied the horses. "Better get moving, if I'm gonna show you the ranch."

Crystal plodded behind Luke, thinking about what he'd just told her. One would think he already had someone who wanted to share his life by now. She wasn't good at guessing his age. No matter. She'd never be anybody's workhorse.

The ride to the summer pasture was a long but beautiful one. Crystal loved the smell of the spruces and the quietness that surrounded them, but the fragrance was soon replaced by the smell and sound of bawling cattle long before they came into view.

Crystal saw Curly acknowledge them as he spurred his horse forward, reining in alongside them on the edge of the pasture. He mopped his freckled face with his bandana, spat a stream of tobacco, and crossed his wrists over the pommel of the saddle, grinning at Crystal. "So, what do you think of Aspengold so far, Miss Clark?"

"I'm impressed, Curly. But please, don't be so formal. You can call me Miss Crystal." Her voice was cheerful.

"Be my pleasure, ma'am." He tipped his hat, then turned to Luke. "I've been rounding up strays. They're getting purty fat. Reckon we'll get a good price for these steers in Denver?"

Crystal saw the admiration in Curly's eyes and how he hung on to everything Luke said as they talked. It seemed that Luke affected everyone that way. Kate had told her that the cowpunchers admired and respected him. He had a way of conveying to even the youngest and most unskilled hands that they were all worth something to him.

Coming from the other side of the pasture, Kurt waved his

hat in greeting at Crystal. Luke's eyes narrowed, and he said, "I better get you out of their sight, Crystal, or I'll never get a lick of work out of 'em."

"See ya at supper, Miss Crystal," Curly said. He doffed his hat and quickly galloped off, leaving dust in his wake.

Crystal and Luke stopped in an aspen grove and had lunch. She had never seen so many wildflowers blooming in one spot. As they munched on thick slices of roast with hearty chunks of bread, Luke told her the names of the flowers—lupines, mountain laurels, columbines, and asters. He surprised her at his knowledge. Crystal was pleased that he would bother to learn them and figured he must have a tender side. After sweet strawberries for dessert, Crystal complained of a headache.

"Altitude affects most people that way until their body gets used to breathing thinner air." Luke didn't act concerned about it. "It might take a few weeks for you to adjust."

The way she was feeling, Crystal wasn't sure she ever would.

By late afternoon they were back at the ranch, and Crystal felt like her head was going to split in half. She was hot, tired, and thirsty. Luke had to help her down from Bess's back and half carry her to the porch.

"Miss Crystal! Can't you stand up? I reckon this fine Colorado air just don't agree with Southern gentility."

The sarcasm in his voice was just enough to set Crystal's teeth on edge. "Go ahead! Just leave me alone to die right here on the porch." She could still hear him laughing as he left the porch and led the horses to the barn.

Over his shoulder he yelled, "Carmen will take care of you!"

Carmen scurried out to help Crystal inside to her bedroom, took off the brogans, and loosened her shirt. "You just lie right there, and I'll bring you something cool to drink and something for that headache. Poor thing."

When Crystal didn't appear at supper, Luke and the other hands were disappointed. Kate explained to all of them that they'd have to remember that Crystal was not used to the altitude.

"Tenderfoot, all right," Luke commented. "Just gonna get in the way here with the trail drive an' all."

Kate shot him a quizzical look. "Crystal is strong, like my sister Anne was, in spite of all her fluff and outward appearance, I'll have you know."

Luke felt a little rebuffed by Kate. It rankled him that it even mattered to him in the first place, and he tried to put Crystal out of his mind. He had too many things to think about to let a female get in his way.

4

The morning light bathed Crystal's face in warmth, waking her to the realization that she must have slept through the night. Carmen had left a glass of water next to the bed for her. The headache was gone, but she was still very thirsty. She stretched and reached for her wrap, groaning as every muscle protested with soreness. What must the others be thinking? *Lazy Southern belle used to sleeping late and whiling away the hours.* Crystal smiled. Actually, that wasn't too far from the truth. She washed her face and pinned her long hair up. She was determined that she would earn their respect, but how, she wasn't sure.

Life in Georgia had been rather dull, she admitted. There were the same faces, same humdrum dinner parties with no real direction in her life. Flirting with the most eligible bachelors in Atlanta had been fun. The men had vied for her attention, but Drew had all but told her they would have a life together. She cared for Drew, but there was no real passion, no inner spark that made her look forward to their next meeting. Maybe those were just dreams of what love was supposed to be like.

She wanted the same kind of love that her parents had had.

Her heart grew heavy when she thought about them, but she remembered God's promise that she would see them again. She took great comfort in that, and it gave her peace of mind. Without it, she knew she had no hope at all.

Crystal donned a full skirt the color of a ripened peach, trimmed with gray piping, and a pristine white pleated blouse. She grimaced at her reflection in the mirror. She wished she were tall like Kate.

The jingling of spurs drew her attention to the front porch, and she pulled back the curtain just as Kate and Luke walked into the yard, talking about the trail drive.

"We should plan on movin' 'em out in the next few weeks, while the weather is in our favor," Luke told Kate as he rolled his lariat into a neat spiral.

"Better hire on a few more hands then. I'm going to Steamboat. Why don't you come along and see who you can find?" Kate turned in time to see Crystal at the window and waved at her to join them.

Crystal threw her wrap around her shoulders and went outside. Luke turned, shifting his weight to one side with his hand on his hip. She couldn't see his face and was glad that his hat was slung low.

"Mornin', glory," Luke said with a lopsided smile. "Did you get your beauty rest?"

Crystal controlled the urge to snap back at him. "Yes, I did. I feel refreshed and ready to tackle the day."

"Good." Kate shaded her eyes from the sun with one hand. "How 'bout riding with us to Steamboat for supplies this morning?"

"I'd love to."

Crystal could see Luke's moustache twitching at the corner of his mouth. She felt sure her answer had surprised him.

"All right then. Better hustle and grab some grub. Rusty's hitching the buckboard." Kate motioned in the direction of the barn. "We'll be there waiting for you."

Crystal hurried back inside to eat a biscuit and wash it down with a quick cup of coffee, then dashed back out to meet them.

The ride to Steamboat Springs seemed to take much less time than Crystal's first ride from town. It was a crystal clear morning with a cloudless sky. Thimbleberry shrubs grew profusely along the road, their white flowers giving rise to red berries. Indian paintbrush dotted the summer landscape, and asters prospered.

They bumped and rattled their way up the trail, but Crystal didn't mind because she was going to town. Since the train depot was on the edge of Steamboat, Crystal hadn't gotten a good look at the shops the day she first arrived. She looked over at Luke, who was riding alongside the wagon on his horse, Buck. Even in the saddle he was tall. He held the reins in his hand, clicked through his teeth to Buck, and guided him with gentle pressure on the reins. She stared at his profile. His thin, pointed nose; his dark, trimmed moustache; and his worn hat, curled at the sides with a sloping crease at the crown, created a pleasing image for Crystal. Today he had chosen a black leather tight-fitting vest, unbuttoned, and a red chambray shirt that complemented his dark good looks.

Luke must have felt her eyes boring holes through him because he turned to look at her. She forced herself to look away.

To Luke's way of thinking, her choice of clothing wasn't practical, with her stiff white blouse and dainty slippers of gray to match the trim of her dress. In place of her lace parasol, she wore a hat the size of a boulder with wide peach sashes that dwarfed her slight frame. A gold locket hanging from her delicate neck nestled on her ample bosom and winked up at Luke while the sun's heat beat down. If she thought those *things* on her feet would carry her through the muddy streets of Steamboat, she was in for a surprise.

"I'm glad I'm not a woman trying to impress the opposite sex," Luke grunted.

Kate shot him a quizzical look. Luke responded with one of his incongruous grins.

The first things Crystal noticed about Steamboat were the activity, the bustle of wagons, the riders on horseback, and the muddy streets. The hastily built frame shops were plain, their wood and paint now bleached a dull gray from the harsh chinook winds and blizzards. Her heart sank. Shopping here was not going to be like shopping in Atlanta. She tried to hide her disappointment when Kate told her that the general store stocked everything a body could want.

When they pulled up in front of Franklin's Mercantile, Kate climbed down from the wagon. "Luke, me and Crystal will meet you for lunch in one hour at Flo's Café." She turned and called out to the owner, John Franklin, who was sweeping the porch of the store, and with hurried steps made her way toward him.

Luke looped the reins over a hitching post and gave Buck a treat, nuzzled his neck, then continued on down the street, apparently engaged in his own world. He left Crystal standing in the wagon, waiting to be helped down. He hadn't even looked back. He needed to be taught a few lessons in manners. What was his hurry? Hurrying was so undignified anyway.

She fretted with her heavy petticoats, which were hung up in the brake of the wagon.

"Here, let me help you with that before you topple," a voice called out from the store's porch.

Crystal stretched out her gloved hand to the stranger while he unhooked her dress from the brake with great care so as not to tear the peach-colored material. He helped her down from the wagon.

"I'm Josh McBride. You must be Kate Morgan's niece from Georgia." He was heavyset, and his light brown eyes smiled back at her from his clean-shaven face. His jeans were brand-new. Not a spec of dust showed on his brown boots. His brown Stetson hat, in the same shade of brown, had been steamed and rolled with care. "I've heard all about you."

"You're too kind." Crystal said, flustered by his frank, appraising look. He continued to hold her hand in his big one. She could feel the strength of his fingers through her gloves. "I'm Crystal Clark."

"I'm very glad to make your acquaintance."

Kate stuck her head out of the dry goods store, and the bell clanged loudly. "Come on in, Crystal. Oh, I see you've met Josh. Are your parents in town?" she asked him.

"No, ma'am," he replied. "I'm here with my sister, April. She's browsing around in the store today. Doggoned if I know what for." He chuckled and turned again to Crystal. "Good day, ma'am." He touched his fingertip to the brim of his hat, clearly admiring her.

Crystal felt two hot spots stain her cheeks, and she hurriedly moved inside the dry goods store.

"See you at the party Friday night, Josh?" Kate asked.

"We wouldn't miss it!" he called back over his shoulder as he started down the boardwalk.

"Josh." Kate tapped him on the shoulder. "Can I speak with you a minute?"

Josh paused. "Sure. What's up?"

"You go on in, honey. I'll be there in two shakes of a lamb's tail," Kate instructed her niece.

Franklin's Mercantile was the center of daily life for the bustling inhabitants of Steamboat. It also served as the US Post Office and the "place to find it all under one roof."

The practice of merchandising had served as a vital element to the prosperity of John Franklin and his family. His success had carved him a prominent place in the community. He was a fair but shrewd businessman, knowing when to extend credit and when to withhold it.

For the townsfolk, the mercantile store was more than just a mere store. In the winter, it served as a meeting place to exchange bits of news while many a yarn was told around the warmth of its huge potbellied stove. In the summer, its shady porch provided a good excuse to stop and gossip or talk about the weather, which was the normal topic of discussion. It had a unique odor of its own, mingling leather, wood, apples, and tobacco.

Crystal gaped in amazement at the tall bolts of material stacked precariously and at row upon row of canned foods and other sundry items. Leather harnesses, tack, and the like were on one side of the store, and clumsily built racks near the back held molasses and whiskey in large barrels. Another wall held tonics, herbs, shaving cream, and soaps.

She strolled over to the shelves. *Perhaps some new toilet water for Friday night?*

Two young women, heads bent together, were examining a length of ribbon against blue calico, but when they saw Crystal looking at them, they stopped. One of them walked toward Crystal.

"May I be of assistance?" she said. She was older than Crystal had first thought as she drew closer. Her hair was pulled back into a severe chignon, not one strand of hair escaping, and her black heels rang out like pistol shots when she crossed the hardwood floor.

"I'm Mary Franklin." When she smiled, her dark brown eyes twinkled, as though she found everything in life amusing. She moved with enthusiasm while straightening the fabric bolts, pausing long enough to push her spectacles back up over her long, thin nose.

"How do you do, Mrs. Franklin? I'm Crystal Clark, Kate Morgan's niece." She shook the proffered hand. "I'm just browsing."

"My, my. All the way up from Georgia, I hear. I hope you enjoy your visit out West. Kate and I are good friends, and she's told me

50

all about you." She turned and motioned for the blonde to join her. "April, meet Crystal, Kate's visiting niece."

Crystal watched as the tall girl carried her willowy frame with self-assurance to Mrs. Franklin's side. Her beautiful, cascading curls hung almost to her waist and were held back off her high cheekbones with a blue gingham ribbon. A brown felt hat hung down her slim back. Her enormous blue eyes raked over Crystal with an icy gaze, though her lips were smiling.

"Kinda outta your territory a bit, aren't you?" Her greeting was uttered in a cool, detached voice.

Friendliness in the South was as common as flies on a water-melon rind, so April's rudeness took Crystal quite by surprise. She squared her shoulders, stood as erect as her five foot two inches would allow, and answered in her most courteous manner.

"Maybe so, but clothes can be changed to suit the occasion, unlike temperaments and attitudes, which require much more control." Crystal stared at April's jodhpurs and black riding boots, hoping her meaning was obvious to the pretty girl. "Besides," she drawled, "I think I'm beginning to like these mountains and the wide-open spaces."

"Crystal, what a beautiful hat," Mrs. Franklin exclaimed, reaching out to touch the ribbons adorning Crystal's hat. "Isn't it, April?"

"Why, yes. But more suited to garden parties in the South than out here in the West." Her eyes rested on Crystal's bosom. April was tall and graceful even in riding clothes, but she would never forgive God for not endowing her with an hourglass figure. Whenever April complained about her bosom, her mother would say she wished hers were no bigger than a hickory nut. Alice told her daughter that having a décolletage was a nuisance. But that did little to improve April's desire for a shapelier figure.

Crystal felt rebuffed and, as April implied, a bit overdressed. But she tossed her head back and laughed as though April's words didn't affect her at all. She turned to pick up a pair of pants and said, "Mrs. Franklin, might you have these in my size? And, oh yes, I'll need a pair of good, sturdy shoes. I'm afraid that I shall ruin these before the day is out." She glanced down at her own kid slippers. They were more suited for indoors, but she didn't need that tall beanpole with blonde hair telling her what to wear and when.

She chuckled under her breath as April stormed off. "Is she always so nice?" she asked Mary.

"Goodness, don't mind her! She's so spoiled by that father of hers. I declare. She was just miffed because you're a sight for sore eyes and unmarried, therefore her enemy. You are one of the few brave enough to put her in her place."

Kate returned from her conversation outside with Josh. The floorboards squeaked as she joined them. "All set, Crystal? John has everything loaded, so we can go on over to Flo's and have a bite to eat."

"I just need to wrap these britches up. We are out of anything small enough to fit her feet, but I'll send off an order right away." Mary folded the pants.

"Just put it on my account, Mary," Kate said.

"I have money, Aunt Kate." Crystal groped in her handbag.

"Nonsense," Kate said. "A few more dollars one way or the other won't break me."

"Well, if you insist. Thank you."

Kate looked down at Crystal. "Having you here, girl, is thanks enough. Mary, I'll be seeing you out at the party come Friday night."

Mary waved and then winked conspiratorially to Crystal. Crystal liked the kind older lady. Josh was just driving his wagon off as the women emerged from the store. He grinned and looked as though he was about to slow the wagon to a stop, but April scowled at him and said they must be hurrying.

Flo's Café wasn't much to look at from the outside. But inside, the homey atmosphere and delicious smells invited its patrons to settle down at any one of its numerous tables covered in bright red tablecloths. The same red-checked material adorned the gleaming windows, allowing the customers to view the activities of the bustling cow town.

Crystal and Kate had been waiting for almost a half hour for Luke to arrive. "Where in tarnation is he?" Kate asked to no one in particular. "Let's go on and order our lunch, Crystal. He must have stopped off to chew the fat with Lars, our local smithy." Kate motioned for Flo, who lumbered over to their table.

Flo's gray hair was twisted into a knot on top of her head, and the heat of the kitchen kept a constant flush on her round cheeks. Her starched white apron was loosely tied around her ample waist. She stood next to the table, arms akimbo.

"What can I serve up for ya today, Kate? We got steak and gravy simmered in onions or vegetable stew." Flo turned to Crystal. "And who might this young lady be?" she bellowed, causing the other patrons to stare at Crystal.

"This here is my niece, Crystal, from Georgia." Kate beamed, tilting her head upward to smile at Flo.

"Pleased to make your acquaintance, Crystal. Now, what'll it be today?"

Both of them decided on the vegetable stew, which was served with slices of thick, crusty bread. Crystal drank several glasses of water. "My throat has been dry since the day I arrived," she said to Kate.

"That's because the air is so dry out here. You'll get used to it."

Their conversation soon turned to ranching and Crystal's future.

"I'd like it if you would stay on here for good, Crystal. You are such a bright light in my life right now. Besides, I always wanted children." Kate looked at her with so much affection that Crystal wasn't sure what to say.

"Thank you. I do like what I've seen so far, and I'm looking forward to meeting new people at the party that you are being so gracious to give for me."

They chatted about the trail drive and community affairs.

"Aunt Kate, why will you take the cattle to Denver to sell?"

"Because we'll get a better price per head in Denver, although a wealthy banker by the name of Henry Gebhard is in the process of building a slaughterhouse in Steamboat as we speak. Besides, since the railroad isn't yet opened up into Wyoming, and we live south of Steamboat in the valley, it just makes better sense."

"I can't wait to take you to church so you can meet everyone in the community," Kate said. "You'll like Reverend Alden. He preaches the Word, pure and simple, and he's not married."

Crystal giggled and assured Kate that she wasn't looking for anyone. They finished up the delicious stew and bread.

Flo had convinced them to have a slice of apple pie with their coffee when Luke pulled up a chair and sat across from Crystal. Pushing his hat back, he grabbed Flo by her thick hand and said, "I'll have the steak and gravy, and you might as well go ahead and bring me that pie with it. Nobody can beat your cooking, darlin'."

"Oh, go on with you! I'm used to being charmed by the likes of you!" Flo laughed with obvious affection.

Kate seemed more interested in the reason they had come to Steamboat in the first place. "What kept you, Luke? Did you sign on anyone for the trail drive?"

"Yes, ma'am, I did. Five to be exact. Up from Durango most of 'em, looking for work. Sorry, I didn't mean to hold you ladies up." He looked at Crystal.

"Manners don't seem to be your strong suit, Mr. Weber," Crystal said. "A gentleman always removes his hat indoors, and he doesn't keep a lady waiting."

"Is that a fact, Miss Georgia Cracker? Maybe a gentleman does, but not a cowboy. The only time a *real* cowboy removes his hat is for a funeral, a wedding, or church. A cowboy likes to keep his hat close by in case he needs to get out in a real hurry. That thing you call a hat on your head is big enough for two barnyard owls to roost in."

Crystal felt her face burn at his reprimand and glanced at Kate, who looked amused at the two of them arguing. Before Crystal could think of an appropriate retort, Kate looked at Luke and nodded to him, indicating that he'd better remove his hat. Grinning at her, he flipped it over the back of the empty chair.

Talk centered on the particulars of the trail drive, and both women watched in amazement as Luke wolfed down the steak and gravy and polished it off with two large pieces of pie and what seemed a gallon of coffee.

The afternoon ride back to the ranch proved to be very hot. Not even a breeze obliged them, and the ranch with its few cottonwoods surrounding the porch was a welcome sight. Kurt waved his hat in greeting as they rode past the corral, where Jube was breaking in a new mare. Crystal waved back, and Kurt hurried over to help her down.

"Afternoon, Miss Crystal." He beamed at her.

"Hello, Kurt." She wrinkled her nose at the smell of horseflesh intermingled with perspiration from the heat. He was covered with dust, which he attempted to brush off his britches.

He seemed pleased that she would allow him the privilege of assisting her. Jube joined them and helped unload the supplies they would be using on the trail drive. He was quiet and seemed to be a man of few words, especially around womenfolk.

"Those things there go in the kitchen to Carmen," Kate said, pointing to the last of the supplies. "They're for the party Friday night."

Luke stood near the barn, talking to Rusty about the hands he'd just signed on, but out of the corner of his eye he watched Crystal conversing with Kate, Kurt, and Jube. She seemed unaware of the effect she had on either of them.

"Save a dance for me now," Kurt was saying.

"Uh . . . and one for me too," Jube stammered.

"Be careful how many you promise, Crystal." Kate laughed. "It's been a while since we've had a shindig. They could dance your legs right off."

Luke knew from Crystal's reaction that she wasn't crazy about dancing with the cowboys. But most of them could dance, so her feet would be spared.

"Better get washed up for supper, boys, before Carmen rings the dinner bell," Kate reminded them. She walked over to where Rusty stood smiling in open admiration for the tall, husky woman.

Crystal excused herself to wash up. Luke noticed the two cowboys gazing at the gentle sway of her hips.

"Well, I'll be switched!" Kurt exclaimed. "What a woman, huh, Jube?"

"Yep. She's too pretty for the likes of us, though," Jube said.

"Never sell yourself short where the ladies are concerned, dear boy." Kurt smoothed back his dark hair.

Two days before the party for Crystal, Aspengold was in a merry flurry of activity. Any excuse to take a couple of days off work and socialize with surrounding ranchers was a blessed relief from the June heat. Knowing that the trail drive was a few weeks away, with many long days in the saddle, the drovers were rowdier than usual with the anticipation of partying, dancing, and flirting with the women. Although Kate ran a tight group with strict moral codes, sometimes the cowboys could get a little raucous.

Carmen was busy preparing the needed food, and their delicious smells wafted throughout the house. Kate and Crystal lent a hand in baking the desserts. Carmen looked at Crystal, her eyebrows arched in question. "You can cook?"

"If there's one thing a Southern girl must learn beside manners, it's baking pies," Crystal remarked as she rolled up her sleeves. "Now, just hand me an apron so I can get started. Where's the fruit? How many pie pans do you have?"

Kate watched as Crystal sifted flour onto a muslin cloth and began making piecrusts in a large bowl with the hand of an experienced cook. Carmen hurried to gather pans, sugar, and the dried apples she had put up from the last year's crop.

After a few moments, Kate slipped out the kitchen door, leaving the two young ladies humming with fervor in their mutual endeavor.

Crystal looked out the kitchen window as she kneaded the pie dough. She watched as Kate walked over to the porch where Curly, Jube, and Kurt awaited instruction on how to set up for the party.

"Swept out the barn yet, Jube?"

"Yes, ma'am," he answered in a respectful tone.

"Curly, you and Kurt go ahead and get the spit set up over the coals for Carmen. Jube, find some two-by-fours and throw together a few tables to hold the food. We don't have near enough tables." She issued orders in her no-nonsense fashion, and they scrambled to do her bidding.

Rusty and Luke were cleaning up the oil lamps they would need and discussing the trail drive when Kate joined them. "Luke, I'm pleased to hear that you hired Sourdough as the cook again. Carmen's uncle and the cowhands regard him as the best cookie west of the Colorado River. That'll make for a happy crew."

"Glad that you approve. Ready for the party?" Luke poured the oil into the last lamp.

"Gettin' there." Kate stood close to Rusty, watching every move he made.

"Wear that blue dress that matches your eyes," Rusty said affectionately, gazing back at her.

"Now why would I want to do a thing like that?" she teased just like a girl with the first blush of love.

Luke got the distinct feeling they wanted to be alone and made up some imaginary chore that needed seeing to. He stopped by the bunkhouse to retrieve a small brown bag that he tucked into his vest pocket, then headed to the house. Wonderful smells assaulted his nostrils, and he took a deep breath and stepped through the back kitchen door.

"Carmen, I declare you're outdoing—" He stopped short as Crystal, with her back to him, bent over the stove and muttered to herself, "A few minutes more . . ."

Carmen was nowhere to be seen. Several pies, cooling in the breeze, lined the windows. When Crystal turned she jumped. "Oh! I didn't hear you come in," she said, wiping her brow with a flour-covered hand. Her hair, damp from the heat of the stove, curled against the nape of her neck and at her temples. Her face was flushed a rosy pink, making her green eyes stand out under their thick lashes. She looked utterly domestic and feminine. She stood there fanning herself with the bottom corners of her spattered apron.

"If you're looking for Carmen, I told her to take a rest. She's been up since dawn cooking," she said, dropping her apron. She walked over to the sink, sunk her arms up to the elbows in hot suds, and began washing pans.

"No, I wasn't looking for Carmen." He took a knife from the table and helped himself to a chunk of apple pie. It was delectable.

Crystal glanced over her shoulder, then flung the dishrag into the sink, sending suds and bubbles flying.

"What do you think you're doing?" she yelled as his tongue flicked around his moustache, reaching for the remains of the pie. He gave her one of his incongruous grins, showing rows of small, even teeth.

"Carmen always lets me sample her fine cookin'. Boy! Every pie she cooks is better than the last one."

He would have reached for another helping had Crystal allowed him to, but she popped him on the forearm with a dish towel and said, "Not another bite, Mr. Weber! Those are for the party, and since I'm in charge of the kitchen right now, I suggest you take your big paw off that pie."

Luke spun around and caught her arm. "Since when did you start giving orders?" His arm stung from the dish towel. He wasn't sure he liked this new Crystal.

"Since I started doing the dishes," she retorted. He was standing so close that he could smell her lilac perfume, and he stared into her green eyes. She yanked her arm from his grasp, and he stepped aside to let her pass back to the stove, where black smoke was billowing out.

"Oh no! Now see what you made me do," she cried as she flung open the oven door. With the end of her apron, she pulled the blackened pie out and howled as the heat went right through her apron. The pie fell to the floor, and she dropped in a heap next to it.

Luke leaned back his head and roared with laughter. "Seems the kitchen just isn't your cup of tea. Here, let me help." He reached down and took her hand. It was red and already forming a blister. It was so small and soft.

"Ouch!" She groaned and bit her bottom lip. She pulled her hand from his. "I can take care of it myself, Mr. Weber."

"Call me Luke. Mr. Weber sounds too formal, kind of like your upbringing."

"There's nothing wrong with my upbringing," Crystal said through clenched teeth.

"Well, I'll bet you learned how to pour tea but not how to make it," he teased her.

"I couldn't care less what you think. It doesn't affect me one way or the other."

She got up and stepped to the pantry for a piece of muslin and a mop and bucket. Luke leaned against the table with his arms crossed and his hat pushed back. Did he have to watch her? He always thought everything was funny. His dumb grin infuriated her. She wrapped the muslin around her hand and began scooping up the remains of the pie into the slop bucket. And still he watched, saying nothing.

"Mr. Weber, if you have nothing better to do than to stand around, maybe you'd like to take this out for me." She thrust the slop bucket into his hand.

"I don't do women's work, but I guess that makes two of us." He laughed, took the bucket, and strode from the room, his spurs jingling across the hardwood floor. Crystal attacked the floor with fury, muttering under her breath. Something about him made her feel inadequate. She wasn't sure why. His manners were deplorable, yet he made her feel silly. She heard footsteps approaching again and steeled herself for his taunting.

The door opened and Kurt stuck his head in. "Mornin', Miss Crystal." Crystal straightened up, smoothed back her hair, and wiped her hands on her apron.

"Hello. I was just cleaning the floor. Seems I had a minor

accident and burned my hand. Is there something I can do for you?"

Kurt looked at her with a twinkle in his eye and said, "Smells too good in here. Let me see your hand. What happened?" He reached for her hand, and she protested.

"It's nothing, I guess. Just a little burn." Ignoring her protest, he unwrapped her hand gingerly to see it anyway.

"At least it's not very big, but I've got just the thing for it. I'll go get it. You stay put." He guided her to a kitchen chair and eased her into it.

Luke emptied the slop bucket and remembered the reason he went to the house in the first place. He made his way back across the yard to the kitchen door. He paused as he saw Kurt's head bent over Crystal's. She was smiling up at him and laughed as he held her hand and brushed her fingertips with a slight kiss.

Luke cleared his throat. "Don't let me interrupt. These are for you, Miss Clark." He tossed a small brown bag that landed in Crystal's lap.

"What's this?" Her brows knitted together with skepticism.

"It's peppermint. Suck on it for that dry throat of yours."

"If I didn't know better, I'd say you're trying to be nice for a change." Crystal peered inside the bag and withdrew a piece of peppermint.

"Even a cow needs a salt lick."

Crystal sputtered, "So now you are comparing me to a cow?" She jumped out of her chair and tapped her toe, her arms crossed defiantly.

Luke ignored her outburst and turned to Kurt. "Did you mend the fence I told you about?"

"Already done." Kurt stuck his hands in his pants pockets and rocked back on his heels.

When Luke continued to stare at him, Kurt said, "Just going to run and get a little salve to put on that burn."

"Don't bother. I have something to put on it, but thank you, Kurt. You are most kind." Crystal's eyes rested on his dark ones.

Luke started back out. "You comin', Kurt?"

"I'm right behind you," he answered. He backed out of the room, still smiling at Crystal.

By the time Friday afternoon rolled around, everyone was filled with the excitement of having a good time just seeing their neighbors and catching up on the latest gossip. Carmen had hams slowly roasting on the spits and had explained to Crystal that they must cook for several hours. Curly had set up a few crude tables on one side of the barn and reserved the largest area for the dancing that would come later on.

Crystal walked down to Kate's room to ask if there were any details they might have overlooked before getting dressed. After a thoughtful look, Kate shook her head no, but she wanted Crystal's opinion on which dress to wear.

"I don't wear too many dresses, so the pickin' is slim." She laughed, her eyes twinkling.

Crystal nudged her aunt aside to peer into the big wardrobe. After rummaging around, she came up with a blue gown trimmed in cream lace at the throat and wrists.

"This is pretty and would bring out the blue in your eyes, Aunt Kate."

"Funny, Rusty said as much the other day." She took the dress off its hanger. "It's been a long time since a man complimented me, and a long time since I even cared." Her voice became softer, and Crystal followed her eyes to a framed daguerreotype of her uncle on top of the dresser.

Sensing the sadness that came over her aunt, Crystal remarked, "And about time too! It's been more than six years since Uncle John's death. You're still a fine-looking woman with a lot of zip left in your step. Now slip this dress on and let me do your hair."

Crystal prattled on and fussed over Kate's thick hair. She pulled it into a soft bun at the top of her head, leaving a few curls dangling from her temples and the nape of her neck. Standing back to admire her handiwork, she admitted that Kate looked years younger. Crystal hurried to her room and brought back rouge that she applied to Kate's cheeks, finishing with a sprinkling of powder.

"Rusty won't recognize me." Kate stared at her reflection in the mirror. Crystal leaned over and gave her aunt a hug, and they giggled conspiratorially.

"You'd better get changed, love," Kate said. "Our guests will be arriving soon. I need to be there on the porch to greet them. Now scat! And thanks for your help."

Crystal spent more time on her toilette than she had intended. There was a giddy feeling in the pit of her stomach. She wanted to impress Kate's friends and wanted them to accept her. The sounds of wagon wheels and loud greetings told her she'd wasted enough time. She took one last look in the mirror and wiped her moist palms on the moss-colored gown.

"Miss Crystal, Kate sent me in to get you. Everyone wants to meet you." Carmen stood at the doorway dressed in a festive red Mexican skirt trimmed in black ruffles with a matching top that hung off her shoulders. "You look beautiful. I have never owned a dress as fine as this." She said in awe while fingering the luxurious material.

"Bless you. Maybe you'd like to borrow it sometime?"

"Oh, I couldn't do that."

"Sure you could. I wouldn't mind at all. The color would be perfect with your dark complexion, although I love what you are wearing," Crystal said.

Carmen's eyes shone in admiration for her new friend. Crystal hooked her arm through Carmen's elbow and said, "Shall we go?"

It was now dusk, and the lamps had been lit in the barn, casting a soft glow and transforming its surrounding lofts and stalls into a wide dance hall. Carmen's culinary delights lined the tables alongside Crystal's pies. A huge bowl of strawberry punch threatened to spill over.

Several people had already helped themselves to the punch and now stood about talking. Curly and Jube were the first in line to eat, as usual. They talked in soft tones about the available young women who stood in a close-knit group and pretended to ignore the men's bashful glances.

Kurt stood talking with Rusty, whose arm was around Kate's waist. Rusty listened, but he was busy watching Kate. "There's Jim and Alice," he interrupted.

Jim McBride escorted Alice to their side, followed by his son, Josh, and daughter, April. "My, you're looking prettier than ever, Kate," McBride said.

Kate greeted them with enthusiasm. "And both of you are looking fit as fiddles."

"Evening, Rusty." McBride stretched out his hand. It was obvious that Rusty had no kinship with McBride, but he stuck his hand out to him. McBride was one of the biggest cattle barons and was still trying to add more to his vast empire.

McBride let his hand fall to his waistcoat. Alice turned to admire Kate's hair and inquire of Crystal. Alice was tall like her daughter, with the same fine, delicate features. April politely excused herself from the group of adults and headed in the direction of her friends.

"I wonder what's keeping Crystal," Kate said to no one in particular.

Kurt waved his hand in the direction of the barn's entrance. "There she is," he said, starting toward Crystal and Carmen.

Crystal paused at the doorway. She was unaware of the admiring looks from the cowhands and the envious looks of the women. She was a picture of loveliness in the moss-colored gown, with her beautiful hair piled high and trailing curls touching her slender white shoulders.

As Crystal looked around for her aunt, the size of the party surprised her. The cowboys were cleaned up in their best pants and shirts, with boots shining. A place near the back had been cleared, and Rusty, along with a couple of older men she didn't recognize, proceeded to set up their instruments for the evening's music. Rusty picked up a fiddle and plunked out a fast-paced tune, while the others joined in with a guitar, harmonica, and a washboard. This was a side to Rusty that no one had told her about, and it tickled her heart. She stood tapping her toe to the beat, and he caught her eye, smiled back at her, and mouthed, "Thank you." It was evident that he was pleased with Kate's transformation tonight.

Jube swept up Carmen in the dance, and other couples entered the fun. Crystal felt a touch at her elbow, and Kurt led her into the midst of the dancers. He was a good dancer, much to her surprise.

He pulled her close to him and whispered, "You look ravishing, Miss Crystal."

"Why, thank you." She felt herself blushing.

"How's the hand?"

"Much better, thank you," she answered. She tried to keep her distance, but he pulled her closer. She was relieved when Josh tapped Kurt's shoulder to cut in.

"You dance quite well, Miss Crystal. I've been watching you." Josh's brown eyes roamed over her and lingered below her neck. His stocky frame, hard as a rock, leaned closer to her until she could feel his legs pressing against her dress. It had been a long time since she had danced.

When she looked into his eyes, she had a funny feeling in the pit of her stomach. He wasn't at all like the cowhands in manner or dress. He was very good-looking, his square jaw clean-cut. Without his hat he appeared shorter.

"I hope you're going to like it here and perhaps stay." He squeezed her hand.

"I haven't decided yet." She took a step back to create a space between them.

When they had circled the floor a few times, he suggested they get some punch, to which Crystal readily agreed. Laughing and out of breath, they headed toward the punch table.

Kate joined them and introduced her to Bill Alden, the minister of the local church. He was tall and thin in his dark suit, and he appeared to be in need of a few good meals. He took Crystal's proffered hand. "Your dress nearly matches the color of your eyes," he said. He led her into a waltz, leaving Josh holding two cups of punch with obvious disdain.

"Thank you, Reverend. How large is your church membership?"

"We're small. Around one hundred twenty-five, but attendance varies depending on the weather." He smiled. "Do you sing?"

"Yes, a little, but I can play piano better."

"Wonderful! Maybe you'd be inclined to play for us some time?"

"I'd be happy to," she said as they swayed to the music.

Bill seemed delighted with this bit of news.

Crystal feigned attention as he talked on, but she scanned the room for signs of Luke out of the corner of her eye. She saw him almost the minute he entered the barn. His tall frame embodied the litheness of a cougar, and every woman in the room stared while he strolled toward the tables. She saw that April wasted no time engaging him in conversation and hooked her arm through his elbow.

Luke must have felt Crystal's gaze, and he turned around to look straight at her with a hard, piercing stare. She felt confused. Was he miffed at her? She turned her attention to Bill and smiled up at the pastor, pretending rapt interest in his words.

Crystal danced again with Kurt and Josh, then another waltz with Bill. She realized she hadn't eaten and suggested they sit the next one out, and Bill seemed eager to please. They made their way to the heavy-laden tables, while Bill heaped his plate so high that she was afraid it would dump on his lap.

Weaving their way through the crowd, they found chairs outside where the cool night air fanned their warm faces. They could hear giggling and voices whispering, then April's voice came across loud and clear. "Did you see her frumpish silk dress, with her bosom almost falling out for everyone to see?" She snickered. "You'd think she was at a War Between the States ball."

The group of young girls stood clustered near the opening of the door, apparently unaware of Crystal just outside. The laughter continued.

"I think she's beautiful, and so is her dress, although a bit too elegant for a barn dance. What's the matter, April, afraid she'll steal your thunder?" one girl asked.

"Not at all," April said. "I just think she looks and acts like a floozy, and she's throwing herself at the men!"

"Well, I just think all of you are being a little unfair," spoke a quieter voice.

"Oh, Emily, grow up!" April said. "She doesn't know the difference between a pancake and an enchilada. I'll be glad when she's gone." The talking diminished as they walked out of earshot.

Bill swallowed hard as Crystal's face crumpled with hurt. "I'm sorry you heard that, Crystal." In the light glow of the lamps Crystal saw his face turn scarlet. "They didn't mean anything by that. Perhaps when they get to know you, they'll feel differently," he soothed.

"They are indeed lacking in hospitality," she said, swallowing the lump in her throat. She sounded stronger than she felt, and she could feel her eyes burning. She had lost her appetite.

Later, Crystal stood talking with Charles and Sara Johnson, whom she liked on the spot. They were simple homesteaders, and she could sense their genuineness. Their daughters, Emily and Beth, were two rather plain-looking young girls she recognized as the ones she'd overheard earlier. Beth eyed her openly, but Emily was sweet and struck up a conversation with her. Out of the corner of her eye, Crystal watched as Luke encircled April's waist and hugged her to his hipbone while they stood watching others dancing. Jube sauntered over to where she and Emily stood.

"Would you care to dance, Emily?" He shifted nervously, not looking at her.

"Well . . . I can't dance too good." She had a soft smile, and Crystal thought she was prettier when her smile reached her blue eyes.

"What you don't know, Jube can teach you," she said. She pushed Emily in his direction and smiled inwardly. *What a sweet couple they would make.*

By now, Crystal had a gnawing feeling in her stomach. She was a bit giddy with excitement from all the fun and gaiety. She supposed she should eat something, but that was soon forgotten as Luke ambled in her direction.

"Care to dance, or have you worn yourself out?"

"Tired? Me? I'm used to dancing," she responded a little louder than she intended. Luke chuckled and led her to the floor. Rusty was calling a square dance, and before she knew it she was being whirled and sashayed from one partner to another until she ended back up in Luke's strong arms, but not before she saw April place a possessive hand on his arm. Crystal looked away. Then, out of nowhere, Luke was at her side, pulling her off the dance floor.

"Follow me!" Luke said as she tried to keep up with his long strides. He steered her to the door and outside into the cool night air.

"I believe you need to get some fresh air." They strolled toward the corral.

"I feel mighty fine. I don't need air," Crystal said, but Luke put a protective arm around her.

Her rib cage is so small. Why, my two hands could span her waist. He remembered how she looked as Bill whirled her around on the dance floor. The bodice had a low neckline, narrowing to her waist, where white ruffles peeked out from the pleated folds of her skirt. He thought she couldn't have looked lovelier with her chestnut hair pinned with velvet ribbons hanging down her back. He'd felt a strange pull inside as he'd watched her giving rapt attention to the pastor.

"I just haven't eaten anything yet. That's all that's wrong with me." She looked up at him, her eyes sparkling like diamonds as they filled with tears. "Luke, some of the girls don't like me." She leaned against the corral railing. "They think my dress is gaudy and the neckline too low and . . . " Her voice trailed off, and she started crying.

Luke felt a tug at his heart and pulled the small form to him. "Shh . . . you are just imagining they think that." He stroked her head as he would a child. Her hair smelled so sweet.

"No, I heard them." She pulled away, wiping her face with the back of her hand.

"You sure do stick out like a sore thumb. But you know, that's jealous females for you. Always comparing." His eyes swept over her with admiration.

"Stick out? Blast you!" Her green eyes snapped.

"What? I didn't mean what you think—"

"Luke Weber, are all cowboys so thick between the ears? Don't you ever think before you blurt things out?" she yelled. "You have the manners of a warthog!" She turned and picked up her skirts to go.

Luke stung as though he had been slapped. What had he done? "And you, Crystal, have been reminding me ever since you arrived!"

"Better go back inside to your *darling* April, who's been milking you all night. Because she can split wood, round up horses, and fire a gun faster than lightning." Crystal snapped her fingers for emphasis.

It was Luke's turn to be angry. "I think I'll do just that, Miss Fancy Pants!" He whirled around and stalked back to the barn, leaving her alone. *Blasted little piece of fluff! What did she expect, wearing a gown that only accentuates her amazing figure? Every man in the place was ogling over her!*

He walked straight to Rusty and scowled. "Rusty? Play a fast one, ol' man." Luke knew he was barking orders at his good friend and was sorry immediately.

"What's nettled you?" Rusty cocked his head in Luke's direction.

"Nothing."

"It's the little things that get tangled in your spurs that trip you up, Luke." Rusty slapped him on his shoulder.

Luke frowned. "Now what's that supposed to mean?"

Rusty just shook his head and rosined up his bow for the next set. Luke walked off in a huff and pulled April back out onto the dance floor.

The remainder of the evening was a blur in Crystal's memory. After Luke had stormed off, Josh had come looking for her and claimed she was the best dancer there. Crystal let him lead her back to the party. She felt Luke's eyes on her and deliberately flirted with Josh, who seemed pleased as punch with her direct attention. He seemed to be one of the few men here with manners and breeding. Besides, she liked his kind brown eyes.

"Crystal . . ." Josh spoke in an unabashed manner. "Would it be all right if I called on you next week?"

"I'd like that very much, Josh." Crystal smiled up at him, knowing full well Luke's gaze was on her while he danced with April right next to them.

It was well after midnight as Kate and Crystal bade their guests good night. In a flurry of good-byes and promises to have Crystal over soon, everyone waved, tired but contented to make their way home under a bright, full moon.

Autumn was a distant thought as the morning sun sent its scorching rays on the Sabbath day. It was apparent that Sunday church was always observed in Kate's household.

Crystal shook and fluffed out her Sunday finery. It was a rust taffeta shirtwaist with tiny tucks and a full skirt in the same rich color, trimmed in cream velvet with panels of voile inserts. She frowned. The outfit was a little worn, but on close scrutiny, one could tell it had been finely stitched and was once the height of fashion. She would have to purchase some material for a new one and mend the others that hung in her wardrobe.

She twisted her thick hair to the top of her head and secured it with pins. With a jab of a mother-of-pearl hat pin, she placed a straight-brimmed hat on her head and raised it jauntily on one side over a bandeau of rust rosettes.

If Crystal had been surprised at the cowhands' fresh attire at the party, she was even more astonished at their dark suits and stiff white collars on Sunday. The womenfolk rode in the buckboard, and the men followed on horseback. Kate was perspiring profusely beneath her black bombazine but seemed very pleased that her "extended family" indulged her in their church attendance.

Crystal's face warmed slightly when Luke's cool gaze caught hers. It was hard to figure out what he was thinking. She felt like she'd made a complete fool of herself Friday night and had avoided his presence whenever she could by tending to chores.

As the white steeple of the church came into view, Kate guided the horses beneath a stand of spruces alongside some other buggies in the shade. Rusty and Kurt assisted the ladies down, and they all walked toward the group of people who were milling around outside the church steps. Children ran around the adults and played hide-and-seek behind their mothers' wide skirts.

"Yoo-hoo!" Mary Franklin called out to them as they approached.

Crystal waved and started in her direction and was met by Emily Johnson, who smiled shyly at Jube as he was tying up the horses.

"Ma wants to know if you can come to dinner after church. Please say you'll come," she said to Crystal.

Crystal glanced at Kate, who nodded, and she turned back to Emily. "I would love to."

"Great. See you right after service then." Emily turned to join her family inside the church.

"She's such a sweet young lady," Mary commented to Crystal and Kate. "And I can see that she's taken an instant liking to you, Crystal."

"I like her too."

"By the way, your shoes should be in by the middle of the week," Mary said.

"Good. I'll be in to collect them."

"Come early and I'll make us some fine imported tea, and you can tell me all about the South. I've always wanted to visit there." Mary smiled at her.

The sharp peal of the church bell rang out, indicating the service would soon begin. Crystal watched as April waited on the steps of the church for Luke, who took her arm and guided her to the pew where her family was seated. Taking a seat next to Kate and Rusty, Crystal kept her eyes straight ahead when Reverend Alden approached the pulpit. Kurt sat on her left with Curly and Jube behind them.

The reverend smiled directly at her. Kurt gave her a sideways look, and she squirmed under his scrutiny and reached for a hymnal as Bill stood. He opened his hymnal and said, "Let's all stand and sing 'To God Be the Glory,' found on page fifty-seven in your hymnal."

The congregation raised their voices in unison under the reverend's direction. His voice rang out loud and clear. Crystal was amazed that such a rich baritone emitted from his string-bean body.

While Bill preached, Crystal looked over the congregation. The majority of the folks were hardworking homesteaders in their clean but plain clothing. Their rapt faces were lined and weathered, probably from years of outdoor labor and the harsh, dry climate.

Her eyes fell on the aisle across from her, where Luke sat with April. He looked very dashing in his dark suit and stiff white collar fastened at the neck with a black string tie. April's silky blonde hair fell down her back, and she wore a pale blue frock that matched her eyes, making her appear as fragile as a china doll. Crystal watched as April picked a piece of lint off Luke's sleeve. Crystal groaned inwardly. They made a striking couple.

But why should it matter to her? He was as stubborn as a mule, with a reputation that preceded him. Carmen had told her that half the girls in the territory were after him. But it appeared to Crystal that he had just one girl in mind.

Her wandering mind was brought back to the present. Bill talked about loving your neighbors as yourself and putting their needs above your own. Crystal thought he was so sincere and genuine, but from the way he looked at her, she was afraid he was starting to get ideas about her. He ended by reminding them of the church bazaar, whose proceeds would go for a much-needed organ.

Crystal followed Emily out to where her father was waiting in the wagon for Sara and Beth. Presently they loaded up, and with a wave to Kate and Rusty, Charles flicked the reins over the horse's rump. The horses set out in a trot across a field of wildflowers, and the ride was filled with laughter with Crystal's new friends.

Jube stood with his hat in his hands and stared after them. Luke led the horses by the reins but stopped short, noticing Jube's wistful look.

"Somethin' wrong?"

Jube's face flushed pink. "Naw . . . Emily's right purty, ain't she?"

Luke forced himself to keep from laughing, knowing how

sensitive Jube was. Now he was beginning to get the picture. Quiet Jube was sweet on shy Emily.

"She shore is. Does she know how you feel, Jube?"

"I kinda think she might. I'm not much with words . . ."

"Better let her know. You could lose her to that new preacher man."

"Aw, I don't think so. Besides, Bill has his eye on Crystal."

Luke's head swung around, eyebrows cocked, surprised at Jube's observation. "Well, he can shore enough have her. That little spitfire spells trouble. 'Course, I can't see her making a good preacher's wife—she's too mouthy."

Crystal tried not to act surprised when Charles stopped the wagon before a crude structure, which was partially in the ground and appeared to be made out of mud. As Charles helped the womenfolk down, he explained that their home was a sod house.

"Come on in. You'll find this is the coolest house in the valley," Sara commented with pride in her voice.

To her amazement, upon entering the homey interior, Crystal found it refreshing and cool. The inside of the soddy was plastered with pink clay.

"However in the world did you build this?" she asked as Beth took her hat and gloves.

"We got the clay from the banks of dry streambeds, and we cut the sod with a plow in long slabs for walls. It looks a little primitive, but it's cool in the summer and warm in the winter," Charles said in a heavy northern accent. He showed her into the kitchen, where Emily and Sara had already donned aprons and now proceeded to heat up their lunch, which had been prepared earlier that morning.

Crystal turned to where Sara was busy stirring gravy in a heavy iron skillet. "Can I help do something?"

"You are our guest. Just have a seat at the table, and we'll have dinner ready in no time," Sara said over her shoulder. "The preacher should be here any minute. He looked like he's in need of some home cooking." She laughed good-naturedly.

Beth set the table with rose-patterned dishes that were now well-worn and chipped. Crystal was sure the frayed linen napkins once graced a beautiful table back East. The entire scene touched a cord in Crystal's heart as she observed the family's humble home and their pride in farming in this wild territory.

Before too long, the rawboned preacher arrived and apologized that he had kept them waiting. Sara directed him to a chair next to Emily and said, "Emily has been keeping an eye out for you." Sara cast a meaningful look in Charles's direction, which the reverend ignored.

Emily stared down at her hands in her lap. Crystal was sure that Emily's thoughts had not been on Bill Alden.

Lunch consisted of steak and gravy, boiled potatoes, biscuits the size of a man's fist, and rhubarb pie for dessert. Throughout the meal, Emily quizzed Crystal about the South, and even Beth seemed to warm to Crystal's friendliness. Crystal told them of the special lushness of the trees and its many varieties of flowers, and Georgia's hazy mornings and high humidity.

"Must be the reason for your creamy complexion. I declare, this dry weather is so rough on skin," Sara commented.

Bill Alden hardly took his eyes off Crystal the entire meal, and later, over coffee, he told her he had promised Kate to bring her home on his way back. Crystal would have sooner walked but saw no tactful way to reject his offer.

She enjoyed her afternoon spent with the easygoing Johnsons, and the ride back to the ranch was not altogether unpleasant. Although eloquent when sermonizing, Bill was as nervous as a sinner on a church pew as he sat next to Crystal on the wagon. Crystal was naturally gregarious and took no notice when he stammered replies, which seemed to put him at ease. She could tell he was disappointed that their ride was not longer when he slowed down before he reached the porch. She thanked him for the ride home and watched as he headed back down the trail and away from the house.

Crystal turned to climb the porch steps. The lazy afternoon was so quiet that she almost didn't notice the figure leaning back in a chair at the end of the porch, boots propped up on the railing. It was Luke. She could tell that he was feigning sleep, his hat covering his face to keep the flies away. Suddenly he dropped his boots to the floor with a loud plop and stretched his long form upright. The noise startled Crystal, and she paused, looking down the long porch at him.

"He sure don't appear to be your type," he said.

She bristled. "And just what is my type?"

"Maybe one short enough to fit under that hat perched on your head in case of a summer rainstorm."

She flashed him a saucy smile. "I'll have you know, this hat is the height of fashion."

"Whose fashion?"

"You've been stuck out in this wild territory so long that you wouldn't know fashion if it hit you in the face."

Luke's laughter reverberated in the late afternoon stillness. "Out here, fashion won't put a roof over your head, feed you, or clothe you. All I need is a good meal, a warm bed, and a loyal horse."

"And likely that's all you'll ever get." She tore off her gloves and opened the door, slamming it behind her. Crystal heard a loud rip and realized too late that she had shut the door on her dress. She turned back and yanked her torn dress free, exasperated.

Luke settled back down in the big rocker and once again pulled his hat back over his face. *Ah, poor sweet thing! She tries hard to be tough.* In spite of her ridiculous hats, the hot sun had painted a pink tinge across her cheeks and the bridge of her nose, making her look even more appealing. She needed to find a man who could afford servants to attend to her. She was small and delicate, and ranch life would never suit her.

He sighed wearily and leaned back in the rocker, and he was soon dozing to the distant sound of a Steller's jay.

Blistering July heat settled onto the Yampa Valley, and by mid-afternoon, hazy vapors rose from the parched, cracked ground that had resulted from weeks without rain. Chores had been completed before the noonday meal. Men and women alike retired to the nearest shade tree or porch until late afternoon, when cooler air descended from the mountains. The rusty thermometer outside the bunkhouse registered 100 degrees in the shade. The drovers dragged their bedrolls outside the cramped bunkhouse to sleep under a blanket of stars in the cool, fresh air.

After four days of the miserable heat, and despite Rusty's warning that rain might follow, Kate and Crystal began their drive into Steamboat on a bright, cloudless day. They had promised Rusty that they would be back before dark, and now the creaking wagon rumbled away from the ranch house at first light in the morning, while it was still cool.

Crystal dressed in a light cotton dress, for once without her corset because of the heat, and Kate was in her usual garb of men's pants, sturdy boots, and a wide-brimmed hat. Crystal had become accustomed to getting up early and helping Carmen with morning chores. She found that she enjoyed rising once the rooster crowed. There was a special quietness about early morning that she had never known existed. She savored sharing her first cup of coffee with Carmen and Kate out on the back porch, before the crew stomped in for breakfast. Crystal was fast fitting into their way of life without even being conscious of it.

As the two approached the edge of town, shopkeepers, already busy with morning activities, propped open their doors to enjoy the morning breeze. In the distance, smoke curled lazily upward from the slanted roof of Flo's Café. Crystal guessed that Flo had been up for hours preparing today's menu. Smells of frying bacon wafted on the air, assaulting their nostrils and whetting Crystal's appetite. A piano tune sounded from the swinging doors of the Goldmine Saloon as Kate guided the horses down the main street of town, trying to avoid the larger ruts. She stopped in front of Franklin's Mercantile and called out to John Franklin, who was sweeping the steps that led to the landing. He waved and paused to wipe his hands on his white apron before extending assistance to Kate and Crystal.

"Mornin', Kate." He nodded at Crystal. "Been hot enough for ya?" He placed the broom against the wall, appearing grateful for an excuse to stop and visit.

"Boy howdy!" Kate replied, mopping her face with a handkerchief. "Never thought I'd say I'd be glad for cold weather, but this year's an exception."

John turned to Crystal. "Miss Clark, you never look wilted in this heat. Want to let us in on your secret?"

"Pshaw! If y'all think this is hot, you wouldn't be able to stand the humidity in the South. You'd think a wet dishrag had slapped you in the face." Her green eyes sparkled with playfulness. "Besides, Mr. Franklin, you don't seem to be any the worse for wear."

John flashed a warm smile at Crystal's teasing and Crystal felt instant approval from him. It was obvious that he and his wife were Kate's best friends, and this pleased her immensely.

"Come on in and let me holler for Mary. She's upstairs cleaning the breakfast dishes."

They entered the store, and a huge calico cat slipped from its perch on the wooden countertop and wound itself around Crystal's petticoats. She reached down to stroke the cat's fur and scratch the top of its head. "What's its name?"

"That's Bandit. But don't let the name fool you. She's fat and near to burstin' with a litter." John snorted.

"She's beautiful. I had a cat back in Georgia," she said.

Mary swept into the room with a ready smile, spectacles low on her nose. "I thought I heard voices. How's life treating you?"

"Fair to middlin', Mary. How 'bout you?" Kate answered, giving Mary a quick hug.

"Just fine, Kate. I'm making up a fresh pot of coffee and would love it if you two would stay and have some. Unless you'd rather have tea?"

"Sure, we could stay. Coffee would be fine, and we've got the whole day. Me and Crystal needed a change of scenery. Not much a body can do in this heat."

Mary led the way to the back and up a stairway into a sunny, spotless kitchen in the living quarters above the store.

"Indeed. Besides, I need to pick up my boots, and I'd like to look at some fabric for a new dress," Crystal said.

"Oh, you're making one for April's birthday party? I hear it's going to be the biggest party ever!"

"Well . . . no, I didn't know she was having a birthday. Maybe I'm not invited."

"Oh yes!" Mary bobbed her dark head up and down. "Just about everyone around for miles is invited. In fact, I placed your invitation in Kate's mailbox myself just yesterday. And you have another letter postmarked Georgia. Masculine handwriting, I'll wager."

Crystal's heart skipped a beat. *Drew. It has to be.* She was looking forward to a letter from home. It seemed so far away.

Mary prattled on as she placed her best china on a fine lace tablecloth amid a platter of warm muffins. "Kate, if you'll pour the coffee, I'll run and get your mail, and you can look it over if you want."

"It can wait," Kate said.

"Oh, it's no bother." With her high-buttoned shoes ringing out on the hardwood floor, Mary hurried out and returned breathless in a few moments. There were several pieces of mail for Kate, the invitation, and a letter from Drew for Crystal.

Kate and Mary watched as Crystal read the letter. When she laid it aside and bit into a muffin, both women said in unison, "Well?"

Crystal laughed. She now had two mothers. It would be hard to have privacy while she lived here.

"Oh, the usual. Hot and humid. He asked about my welfare, and he said he's getting married to Amy VanCleeve . . ." Her voice grew quiet, and she looked wistfully out the window. There was a sharp intake of breath from the two older ladies as they held their cups in midair.

"Dear me!" Mary said.

"My goodness! I thought he was waiting for your answer once you had time to consider," Kate said.

"Don't worry. I'm fine. I already told you, Aunt Kate, that I couldn't see myself married to him," Crystal replied with more confidence than she felt.

"Then why the long face?" Kate said.

"I guess I didn't want him to be with anyone else. Isn't that silly of me? I guess I always thought he would be there for me. We were fairly close. But I'm surprised I didn't figure out that Drew would marry someone else so soon. I've been away too long for him to wait, I guess." She tried to pretend that she wasn't hurt and absentmindedly smoothed the wrinkles in her dress. She laid the muffin back on her plate and sighed. "I'm not sure what I expected. Deep down I knew I didn't want to be a politician's wife. But it hurts to think he's forgotten me so quickly. I haven't been gone that long. I guess my pride is hurt more than anything."

"I'm sorry, Crystal." Kate reached out and patted her hand.

Mary popped to her feet. "Come. Let's find you the best piece of goods I have in stock for a dress worthy of a princess. I know I have just the thing for your dark hair and green eyes."

She dragged Crystal to her feet and pulled her in the direction of the store. Behind them, Kate waved at them to go ahead without her and said, "I've a personal errand to run."

The morning soon vanished as Crystal looked over the many bolts of material and patterns with Mary. The older woman had an eye for color and fashion that was surprising, and by the time she had settled on a cream silk, Crystal knew she had made a dear and wise friend. Mary told her how she had always wanted children, but God had not seen fit to allow her this pleasure.

"I'm indeed sorry, but I'll bet if you treat everyone as you have me, Mary, then you have many children." Crystal reached out to touch her hand and saw Mary's eyes shine.

Mary wrapped the fabric and the work boots and neatly tied a string around the two parcels, then set them aside until Kate returned. "I'm going to love getting to know you better."

Crystal warmed at her new friendship with the older lady. "Thank you." She glanced at the watch pinned to her blouse. "Please tell Aunt Kate that I'll meet her at Flo's for lunch at 12:30. That gives me just about a half hour to take a look around."

Crystal decided to peruse the rest of what the town had to offer. She stepped out onto the plank walk and opened her parasol against the sun. The town was rugged looking, but new businesses were beginning to spring up and flourish.

Entrepreneurs had hurried to open the new shops. According to Kate, some had hoped to get rich serving the community of miners, ranchers, and farmers. A weather-beaten sign boasted both doctor and dentist next to a bathhouse, where a bath and shave cost $1.50. Farther down the street was an attorney-at-law, but Crystal's eyes latched on to a shop across the street, whose gleaming window glass was painted with the words "Millinery."

She strode quickly across the street and stepped into the tiny shop. A bell tinkled softly above the door. The store clerk, a woman in her midthirties, paused in her paperwork behind the counter and greeted Crystal with a warm smile. When the clerk approached her, Crystal detected a slight limp in her walk.

"I'm Ruth Stibble, and you must be new to Steamboat."

"My name is Crystal. I'm Kate Morgan's niece. Nice to meet you, Ruth."

"Is there anything special that you'd like to see?"

"Maybe I could take a look at your hats."

Ruth invited her to take all the time she needed.

Crystal was bursting with excitement at the prospect of finding a new hat to match the cream dress she was going to make. But she must be frugal with the bit of money she had. She didn't have much money. Watching every penny was something that she had to learn after selling her family home.

After examining every single hat in the shop, Crystal noticed the lateness of the hour, so she settled on a beautiful ivory hat trimmed with tiny mauve roses and covered with a mantle of netting. *Drew would have loved this hat . . . and Luke will hate it.* She giggled.

Ruth told her she had made an excellent choice. As Crystal counted out the last of her bills, she wondered if she had made an overly impulsive purchase. Hatbox in one hand and parasol in the other, she left the shop and walked straight into Josh McBride.

"This is a pleasure." He steadied her elbow and took the hatbox from her. "Where are you going in such a hurry?" His brown eyes crinkled at the corners when he smiled at her. Under his warm gaze, so different from the brooding way Luke often looked at her, she felt small and pretty. Josh kept his hand on her elbow.

"I've tarried too long at the millinery's. I promised to be at Flo's Café ten minutes ago." She felt a little flustered by his firm hand.

"May I escort you?" Without waiting for her answer, he steered her in the direction of the café. As they walked, he talked about how much he had enjoyed dancing with her. "Later I tried to find you for another dance, but you were nowhere around."

"To be quite honest, I was beginning to have a headache and decided to sit the rest of the dancing out." She had indeed had a headache the next morning. Crystal did not want to tell him how his sister had hurt her feelings, or that she had been outside making a fool of herself with Luke.

"I'm so sorry." Then he added, "I hope you've received April's birthday invitation. I told her I wanted to escort you." He smiled at her again. He was so cheerful, and he had the warmest brown eyes that shone every time he smiled, Crystal noted. His sandy brown hair curled just under the edge of his fine Stetson hat.

So . . . it wasn't April who had invited her. Well, no matter, she was going. Let it be known that Crystal Clark never missed a party. No siree.

"I'd enjoy that very much, Josh." She smiled at him, thinking how much shorter he was than Luke. At least she didn't have to crane her neck up just to talk to him. "But I must go now and meet Aunt Kate."

They parted, and Josh stood watching her go. Crystal was anxious to show Kate her new hat.

Crystal and Kate lingered over their coffee longer than usual while talking with Flo, who rested with her feet propped up on a nearby chair. Most of her customers had eaten, and the café was almost deserted.

"I really like your new hat. It suits you." Kate admired her niece from across the table. "Guess we'd better be moseyin' on back, Crystal. I told Rusty we'd be back before dark."

"I'm so full, I don't know if I can even move," Crystal moaned. She stood, gathered her packages, and followed Kate out to the wagon. Kate looked up at the ominous sky, now a dark blue-gray that lay to the northwest.

"Is something wrong?"

Kate covered the parcels with a tarp in the back of the wagon. "I expect we might get the much-needed rain after all. I just want everything covered up in case," she said.

At some point on the ride back to the ranch, Crystal's head bobbed. The heat made her eyes heavy, and soon she was dozing. Abruptly she was awakened by the crack of the whip as Kate forced the horses into an all-out run.

Crystal hung on to the side of the buckboard. "Aunt Kate, what is it? What's wrong?"

"Baby, you see that dark cloud forming low to the ground?" Kate nodded to the northwest. "Looks like we may get ourselves a bad storm. We're not far from the ranch. I hope we can make it before it hits us, so hang on!"

Crystal had never seen the sky look the way it did now, and she'd never seen Kate look this anxious before. The horses were racing, yanking at their harness, ears laid back, eyes wide open with fear. Kate cracked the whip again, and her hair fell down around her shoulders in a tangle.

There was an uncanny stillness in the air. Large raindrops pelted them, and lightning flashed a jagged streak across the black sky.

Kate yelled to her niece above the noise of the rattling buggy to hang on tight. Thunder rumbled and crashed around them. The blinding lightning was the worse Crystal had ever witnessed. The low, dark cloud began to form a furiously twisting funnel. She could smell the dust as the cloud touched down to the earth.

Fear struck Crystal's heart, and she shouted, "Hurry!" The rain turned into hail, battering down on their unprotected heads and biting into their flesh with sharp stings. Kate struggled with every ounce of strength in her large frame to control the frightened horses from plunging into the ravine beside them. A sudden wind pulled at Crystal's hair and tore at her clothes. The tarp that covered their supplies ripped off the back of the wagon and flew past her.

The late afternoon had become pitch black, and what sounded like a train turned out to be the swirling wind funnel coming straight down the dirt road in front of them. Her heart pounded in her chest, and her legs felt like jelly as she watched entire trees being sucked into the whirling vortex. She heard the sound of splintering wood from the force of the wind snapping the trees and brush in its path.

Kate's screams rose above the din. Crystal tried frantically to reach her, but it was futile with the wagon bouncing. They were nearly flying down the trail into the path of the twister that was barreling down on them with incredible speed.

"Aunt Kate!" Crystal cried, but she couldn't hear what Kate said above the noise.

She watched in horror as the funnel cloud lifted the wagon with them in it off the ground, and then her sweet aunt flew through the air. "Oh, Lord, have mercy on us!" she screamed. "Help us, please!"

Crystal felt a sharp pain crease her brow, and then she was carried upward as a deep heaviness encompassed her like a warm shroud. For a period of time she was dreaming of her new ivory hat . . .

Luke pushed his hat off his forehead and wiped his face with his bandana. He looked in the direction of the town. He didn't usually worry about Kate because she was a strong and determined woman, but today he felt uneasy. He wasn't sure why, maybe it was just the eerie stillness that hung over the valley. For certain rain was on its way and would bring blessed relief from the heat. Maybe Kate and Crystal would get back from town before it started. He rode back to the barn, dismounted, then led his horse to a stall and proceeded to remove the saddle.

"Rusty, it looks like we're in for a storm."

Rusty's spurs jangled as he entered the barn. "Yep, I'd say so . . . I had Jube put the cows in the barn. It's starting to get purty dark northwest of here. I told Kurt and Curly to start tying things down." Rusty strode over to the barn's open doors and shut them tight. "Let's just hope all we get is a little wind and rain. That corn on my little toe is burning like a small fire. My ma always said that was a shore sign of rain. And we better see to the house. I thought Kate and Crystal would be back by now." His voice was a bit agitated.

Carmen was busy yanking the clothes off the clothesline in the backyard. The wind was beginning to kick up, and she struggled with the wash in her arms. Luke and Rusty closed the windows just as the cowhands gathered on the front porch to look at the sky that was growing blacker by the minute. Wind yanked at their hats while they scrambled to get the rocking chairs into the house. The dogs tucked their tails between their legs and retreated under the house.

After a glance at the ominous black cloud whirling across the meadow, Luke hollered, "Let's head for the cellar out back, guys. This here is no regular rainstorm. Looks like a twister is headed our way!" He grabbed Carmen's arm, spilling the wash from her basket. With Rusty and the boys right behind them, they raced to the cellar. Luke pushed Carmen ahead of him and waited until everyone was in before slamming the door down against the hail now battering the top of his head.

Carmen's black eyes were wide with fright. She huddled on the cellar floor. "Do you think Kate and Crystal will be okay?" She twisted the edge of her apron.

"Where are they?" Kurt asked.

"Drove into town early this morning. Let's hope that's where they still are," Rusty answered. But even as he said it, Luke knew they both thought the women were probably already on their way back.

"Maybe we'd better go after them," Curly said.

Luke leaned against the wall of the cellar and slid down into a sitting position. The wind was so loud he knew that the twister must have been passing within a few feet of them, if not directly overhead. "You can't go out yet, Curly. Don't you hear that racket?

Soon as it passes us, I'll head in the direction of town. Maybe they're holed up somewhere nearby, like at the Johnsons'. They'll be safe in their soddy." His firm jaw clenched as he spoke hopeful words, a painful contrast to the roar of the storm.

Luke observed how Kurt took his time to roll a cigarette between his slender fingers, unconcerned, and blew tiny smoke rings toward the ceiling. He had a deck of cards with him and with much savoir faire was trying to impress Carmen with a card trick. For a moment, the frown in her brow eased, and a reluctant smile tugged at the corners of her mouth.

Curly sat with his knees pulled up to his chest on the dirt floor of the cellar, his head bowed underneath his hat where no one could see. Luke wondered if he was praying silently for Kate and Crystal's protection.

Rusty leaned against the wall with deep concern on his ruddy face as he ran his hand through his now windblown red tangle of hair.

Strong wind rattled the storm door, and Jube's big eyes rolled toward its direction as though his staring would make it cease. He plucked imaginary lint from his ten gallon hat and ran his hand around its brim.

The hail sounded like marbles hitting the door, and the wind blew mightily overhead with a roaring, eerie sound. In a matter of moments it seemed the hail diminished with a random *ping* here and there. The raging wind stopped just as quickly as it had started, but in its wake a torrential downpour slammed against the cellar door.

"Reckon it's safe enough to go on out now," Luke concluded, pulling the latch on the door. "I'm going after Kate and Crystal."

"I'll ride with you." Rusty was right on his heels.

Five minutes later, they had saddled up and donned their slickers, leaving the others behind to assess the damage in the pouring rain.

Less than three miles into their ride, they slowed their horses where the bend in the road was visible. In the dusk and pouring rain, all they could see was the upturned wagon with its wheels still turning eerily, taking on a macabre form. The redhead yelled, "Dear God, no!"

With disbelief they spurred their horses the last hundred yards to where the wagon hung over the ravine and quickly dismounted. Rusty rushed ahead of Luke, unmindful of the rocks sliding under his boots. At one point he lost his footing and half walked, half slid to the front end of the wagon. Luke clamored behind, all but falling against Rusty. The horses had broken their harnesses and were standing fifty feet away, the reins tangled in the underbrush.

Several feet from the wagon Rusty found Kate's sprawled form, a grotesque twist to her neck. He fell on his knees, lifted her upper body to his chest, and clung to her as if trying to breathe his very life into her. Enormous tears spilled down his cheeks and into his beard as he rocked her back and forth, smoothing her wet hair from her face, while the rain continued its onslaught. Luke fought back his own tears. He didn't even need to ask if she was alive.

Luke had a sinking feeling in the pit of his stomach. He had to find Crystal.

After a quick search of the wagon, Luke found her sticking halfway out under its heavy weight. He placed two fingers to the side of her slender neck and felt for a pulse. He sighed with relief and turned to Rusty.

"Rusty," he said, touching his shoulder, "I'm so sorry." He felt tears stinging his eyes again. His curled hat brim formed a trough for the rain that splashed down the front of his slicker.

"Did you find Crystal? Is she all right?" Rusty's voice croaked between sobs. It pained Luke to see his friend hurting this way.

"I did. She's unconscious, and I need your help. She's pinned under the buckboard," Luke answered through the knot in the back of his throat.

Rusty placed Kate's head back on the rain-soaked ground with tenderness and reverently covered her with his slicker.

With the two of them, it was easy to turn the wagon upright. By chance the wheels were all still intact. Although one had a few broken spokes, Luke thought they might be able to make it the three miles to the ranch.

They worked side by side and said little as they righted the wagon and lifted Crystal's limp form to place her in the bed of the wagon. Crystal moaned, but her eyes remained closed. She was mercifully unaware that her beloved Kate, whom Luke and Rusty laid next to her, had seen her last Colorado sunset. Luke removed his slicker and tucked it around Crystal to keep her as warm as possible. Her face was a chalky white, and her beautiful hair, wet and matted with dirt, clung to her face and neck. Her small frame weighed no more than a sack of feed, and he was struck afresh by her delicateness.

They were soaked to their skin, but nothing mattered except their own private pain. Luke talked soothingly to the horses and, with Rusty's help, made a makeshift harness and hitched them to the buckboard.

After three attempts of slipping and sliding in the downpour to pull the wagon from the ravine, they managed to maneuver around the boulders and thickets and finally reached the road. Rusty tied his horse to the back of the wagon and took the reins. Luke mounted his horse, and with hearts heavy they slowly started home.

Carmen heard horses approaching and grabbed her lantern. She ran out of the house, holding her lantern high. Her hand flew to cover her mouth in horror when she saw the wagon approaching, and she tried to calm her thudding heart. The two men were soaking wet and muddy. Luke had a large scrape on his forearm that was bleeding, but he seemed to take no notice. Rusty's eyes were red rimmed.

"Hurry, Carmen, Crystal's hurt. We need to get her inside and warm," Luke barked.

"Kate?" Carmen pleaded, but one look at Rusty's face answered her. He said, "I'll send one of the boys to fetch Doc Gibbons."

Hot tears stung Carmen's eyes as she raced ahead to open the door and make way for Luke. Kurt had joined the small group on the front porch, and he gasped when he saw Crystal.

Luke scooped Crystal up, carried her down the hall to her bedroom, and placed her on the bed. He continued to stand around looking helpless, shifting his weight from one boot heel to the other.

"I'll take care of her and get those wet things off. You'd better do the same. There's hot coffee on the stove," Carmen said. "Go!" She tossed her head sideways, her big eyes now flooded with tears. Carmen loved Kate because she accepted her for who she was. What would she do without her?

99

Luke stepped into the kitchen, poured himself some coffee, and wearily sat down, then stretched out his long legs. It was still raining, and he watched the droplets slide down the wide kitchen windowpane. He remembered Kate's thrill when he and Rusty had ordered the glass window from Denver. It had provided her with a stunning view of the Rocky Mountains every morning.

Suddenly the full impact of Kate's death hit him, and he let the tears flow until his moustache was wet. She was the dearest person he'd ever known, and she'd raised him like her own. And poor Rusty. He knew that Rusty had been in love with her for a long time. Things would never be the same for either of them. A heavy knot formed in his chest, and he could hear his own heartbeat thudding in his ears.

"Boss," Jube whispered.

Luke hadn't heard Jube come into the room. He looked up over the rim of his coffee cup. The coffee's steam and heat were the only warmth he was feeling at the moment. He wiped his nose on the back of his shirt sleeve and noticed Jube's red-rimmed eyes. He was so consumed with his own grief that he hadn't thought about what the punchers must be feeling. After all, they had worked for a mighty long time at Aspengold.

"We placed Kate in her room. We figured Carmen will be needing some help, laying her out and all, so I sent Curly over to fetch Mary Franklin." Jube took out a large handkerchief from his hip pocket to wipe the tears that started to fall again.

"'Preciate it. How's Rusty?"

"He rode off somewhere. Should I go after him?"

"Naw, just leave him be. He'll be back. How bad is the damage around here?" It was hard to consider the damage in light of Kate's death, but Luke knew it must be done.

"Not too bad, considering everything else. We'll know tomorrow when it gets lighter if we lost any cattle. Well . . . I'll just be going." Jube backed up to the kitchen door.

Luke rose and took one last gulp of his coffee. "I gotta get out of these clothes before the doc gets here."

"Reckon you're officially in charge here now, Luke."

"Maybe. I expect Crystal will go back to Georgia if she recovers. Ranch life is new to her, and she won't know how to run one." That was the last thing he wanted to think about. A hard knot formed in the center of his chest.

Flowering dogwood and brilliant fuchsia-colored azaleas crowded the pathway, leading Crystal farther toward a bright light. Her father called out to her, and Kate whispered to her. Dressed in white, her beloved mother stood near the path, her delicate face smiling wistfully at her. On her head she wore Crystal's new cream hat with its trailing ribbons. Crystal reached out to her, feeling so happy and warm, but strong arms pulled her back. Drew guided her back away from the light and peacefulness surrounding it. She reluctantly followed, not wanting to leave her mother's beautiful, sweet face. The path widened, and the fragrant smell of honeysuckle surrounded her. Drew handed her a small bouquet, and Crystal drank in its sweet fragrance. Honeysuckle had always been a favorite of hers. Then the brightness began to fade away . . .

After a careful examination of Crystal, Doc Gibbons told Luke that she had a mild concussion and bruising, but fortunately no broken bones. Luke took Mary's place to let her have a little rest. She hadn't left Crystal's bedside in the last eight hours. A fire burned in the drafty fireplace, its logs crackling and popping in the quiet stillness. The candle sputtered and cast a soft glow on her pale skin and her thick lashes that lay against her high cheekbones.

Luke bolted up in his chair when Crystal stirred. He moved closer as she mumbled something. "Drew . . ."

He flinched. *Who is that?* He lifted one small hand, and her fingers curled around his as her eyelids fluttered open. "Kate?" she murmured.

"Crystal," he said quietly. "It's me, Luke. You've hit your head. Be still."

She struggled to sit up, but then she moaned and lay back against the pillow.

"Where's Aunt Kate? I want to see her." Crystal's voice was weak.

The bedroom door opened, and a sleepy-eyed Mary came to stand next to the bed, with Carmen close on her heels. Carmen and Mary both had red, swollen eyes from crying. Mary had lost her best friend in the world, and now this dear girl whom she had become fond of was lying there without her aunt.

"I heard her talking. Did you tell her?" Mary inquired with a quaking voice.

"No. I think you'd better do that. I'll be in the kitchen if you need anything."

Mary nudged him toward the door. "No, you go on to the

bunkhouse and get some sleep. Tomorrow we have to talk to the reverend and notify Kate's friends. I believe you were the only family besides Crystal that Kate had. I'll need you to be rested, Luke. Now off with you." She patted him on the arm. "She'll be all right. You can count on that."

Luke was too tired to fight her, so he left. He fell into his bunk and was asleep before he could take off his boots.

Three days later, as Crystal looked over the rolling valley, it was hard to tell that a storm had even occurred and touched lives with such havoc. Out of respect for Kate, Luke had hired someone from a neighboring ranch to continue patching the roof. The cowboys had the day off so they could attend the funeral. Already repairs were being made on the roof of the house and the barn. The ping of a hammer sounded, keeping time to the throbbing inside Crystal's head. She gazed out her bedroom window, her aunt's funeral so very fresh on her mind. Earlier that morning, Bill Alden had eulogized Kate as a beloved neighbor and friend to all whose lives she touched. Crystal couldn't bear to look at Rusty. His pain was written on every line in his rugged face.

The sharp pain in her chest had become a hard knot while a feeling of emptiness inside took over, and she couldn't eat a morsel of food. There was no word to describe how she was feeling. One more loss. How many more could she endure? She felt like an orphan with no family to speak of. It was just too much to bear.

Returning from the cemetery, Mary took charge, much to Crystal's relief. Kate's friends came by to pay their respects. Most of them Crystal didn't know. Many brought a covered dish of food or a dessert to be shared, but she had no appetite. She instead busied herself with making coffee for everyone.

Puffing on his cigar, Jim McBride approached Crystal and steered her away from the hot, stuffy room in the direction of the doorway. His huge frame commanded authority just in the way he stood, with the firm thrust of his chin and his thumbs hooked into the lapel of his expensive suit. Once he had offered his condolences, he immediately became the cattle baron and got right down to business.

"Miss Clark, I have a business proposition in which I would purchase Aspengold, allowing you to return to Georgia free of your aunt's debts." He chewed on his cigar.

"Mr. McBride, I do not think that now is the time to discuss business." Crystal could not believe his insensitive timing. With fury in her eyes, she started walking away, but he placed his hand on her arm.

"Perhaps not, my dear. But you see, I have to look out for my best interest, and since Kate was a little—how shall I put it?— strapped for cash, I was good enough to tide her over till the steers could be shipped to market. It would be best if you sold Aspengold lock, stock, and barrel and rid yourself of this problem. I am willing to pay top dollar since her property adjoins mine. And let's face it, you know nothing about ranching." His brown eyes pierced into Crystal's, and his smug face made her want to slap him. Then she was shocked that she had even had such a thought and that he had made her so angry. Now she understood Rusty's dislike of McBride.

"I don't need you to tell me how to set my aunt's affairs in order. Now, if you will excuse me, this little conference is over." She hadn't meant to raise her voice, and now she was aware of a dozen pair of eyes boring into her. Crystal removed McBride's hand from her arm.

Josh was now making his way to her side. Luke, who stood some distance away with April hovering near his side, made a step in her direction, but Josh was quicker.

"My apologies. We'll continue this conversation another time, very soon." McBride's level brown eyes were so like Josh's but lacked his warmth.

"Is there anything wrong?" Josh asked Crystal as his father bowed and walked away.

Crystal sobbed and pressed her hankie against her lips. "Nothing that I can't take care of," she answered with more bravado than she felt. "I'm a little tired. Perhaps I'll go lie down awhile."

"If you need anything, anything at all, you'll let me know?"

Looking into Josh's sincere face, Crystal knew he meant it. She knew she must look awful with puffy, swollen eyes. The pounding in her head was worsening, causing a splitting headache.

"I'll ride over in a few days to check on you, if that's all right."

Crystal mumbled, "All right, Josh." After speaking with Mary, she slid from the parlor and down the hall to her room. But she could not rest, and now, as she stood looking out toward the barn, she realized the hammering had stopped.

With a heavy heart, Crystal sat down in the rocker. She leaned her head back, closed her eyes, and let the tears flow. Once again her world was changing. Her dear aunt was gone. Her loving father, her mother, and Drew. Was she destined to have those dearest to her always leave? Part of what hurt so badly was that she had lived and Kate had died. The vision of her aunt being lifted by the twister flashed through her mind once again. How would she ever replace that memory?

After the funeral, even Carmen had to return to her family because she was needed desperately at home. Her mother had her hands full with seven children, and her sister was having a baby. Carmen hadn't wanted to leave right after the funeral, but she promised to return as soon as possible.

Crystal felt so weary, but now she was all cried out. She was tired of being strong. For once she wished someone would take care of her. There was no reason to return to Georgia, and she didn't know if she could stay in this rugged country. She did know that her aunt had loved the ranch and had worked hard to hold on to it.

Since Kate had borrowed from McBride, Crystal realized she had two choices. Sell and get out, or stall until the beef was shipped—something she knew little about, if anything.

Crystal pulled her wits about her. McBride would never own Aspengold! *Oh, Lord, please give me direction. I can't do this alone. Help me to know Your way and walk in it, and give me peace that can only come through You*, she prayed. Crystal knew that God would make a way for her.

Crystal decided that night to stay and fight. She had already lost one home. But this was the home she wanted to keep. Having made the decision, she felt some of the tension leave her shoulders. She felt a little peace and slipped into a dreamless sleep.

Mornings were getting cooler since the rain had stopped, and Crystal stood listening to the stillness. It was so quiet, and she was acutely aware of Kate's absence. How she missed her laughter and warm hugs. She felt like she was just going through the motions of living in order to have something to do.

With Carmen gone, she knew she must now cook for the boys, so she had risen early. After a strong cup of coffee to get her going, she had poked the cold ashes in the stove to start a fire to make biscuits. Now she stepped back into the kitchen to place sausages in the heavy cast-iron skillet on a low, simmering fire. She picked up the egg basket and made her way out to the chicken coop to gather eggs. She had meant to do that yesterday afternoon but had gotten busy and had forgotten. Rarely had she ever been near a chicken house, much less fried an egg, but it all looked rather simple. She remembered how Fanny, her cook in Georgia, gathered the eggs every day. Crystal's specialty had always been pies. That and biscuits were the cooking she had mastered. Well, she'd just have to start learning something new.

It was a fine, beautiful morning, and the sun just peeked over the dark purple ridges, bathing the valley with a golden hue. Crystal, an obstinate set to her straight shoulders, stepped up the pathway to the henhouse as a sharp breeze tugged at her skirts. With caution she entered the henhouse. She was glad she had on her sturdy brogans as she tried to sidestep the droppings on the floor. She thought how quiet the chickens were as thirty-six pair of beady eyes stared at her.

"Nice, sweet chickens . . ." Crystal tried to hide the tremor in her voice as she took a step farther, reached into the nest, and scooped up four eggs at once. Feeling more confident, she tried to be casual and reached inside the next nest, when she felt a sharp stab on her ankle and shrieked in surprise. Several chickens were pecking away at her new brogans and the stockings on her legs. She kicked at them and cried, "Shoo! Shoo!"

To her horror, a big white hen staring from her perch swooped down on her head and began pecking about her forehead as she helplessly flayed her arms to defend herself. The entire chicken coop was now in an uproar, with chickens flying about, squawking, and clucking, and Crystal yelling. Sure that they were out to peck her to death, Crystal frantically made her way to the door. In her haste, she tripped out the henhouse door on her untied laces. The egg basket went one way, and she went sliding on her knees onto the wet, squishy droppings. She groaned as she dragged herself up and looked at her once-clean apron, now covered with filth.

"Well, aren't you a sight for sore eyes!" Luke leaned on the fence post as Crystal wiped her hands on the soiled apron. She could feel her hair sticking out of its braid, and her chest heaved in and out under the housedress as she gasped to control her dignity.

"Just a mere altercation with a cantankerous old hen!" She could feel her face turning red. Angry that he saw her like this and made her feel foolish, she pushed her hair back from her brow with a shaking hand. That was the last time she'd set foot in that stinky chicken coop.

"What's the matter? They didn't like your perfume?" he joked as he plucked a chicken feather from her hair. She watched as he retrieved her basket, strolled through the henhouse, and gingerly picked up the eggs until he had a basketful.

She snatched the basket from his outstretched hand and glared up at him. Standing this close to him, Crystal felt very small. He smelled of shaving tonic, and she noticed the sharp angle of his nose just above the moustache twitching with amusement. Her heart was pounding, whether from the pecking chickens or what, she wasn't sure. She shook the dirt from her hem, averted her eyes from his, and smoothed the folds of her serviceable housedress. "I thought chickens were gentle creatures."

He thought she looked beautiful, even early in the morning with her green eyes clear and bright, snapping with anger. "As a rule they are, but there's always an ornery one in the bunch. Guess you found her." He chuckled. "Hey, a little dirt never hurt anyone."

"Breakfast will be ready in thirty minutes." She whirled and headed back to the kitchen, shoelaces trailing in the dust, and slammed the screen door behind her.

Luke watched her go and wondered why she always seemed irritated with him. Thank goodness all women weren't that way. He wondered if she had ever been kissed by that Drew fellow, the one she had mentioned when she had been unconscious. Well, Drew could have her. Couldn't even gather eggs. No doubt Drew would have servants to do such as that for her. A helpless female didn't fit into Luke's plan at all.

Since Kate had died, Crystal had said nothing about leaving, but he felt sure it would be forthcoming. He seemed to grate on her nerves, and she didn't exactly cotton to him either. Too bad he and Rusty couldn't buy the ranch. He sighed.

He missed Kate and her strength and exuberance for life. He

missed their daily routine on the ranch and her easygoing ways. But he didn't have time for daydreaming. There was plenty to do before breakfast.

The cowpokes shuffled into the kitchen. Crystal wondered if they expected termination of employment. Most of them had worked wrangling and punching cattle for Kate for several years. Unlike many cowpunchers who roamed from spread to spread, Kate kept most of them on through the winter.

"Mornin'." Crystal nodded to them as she placed fluffy biscuits in the center of the table alongside the almost-burnt, rock-hard sausages.

Curly, always the optimist, smiled back, took a biscuit, and started talking nonstop about how they'd lost almost fifty head of cattle. "If them steers hadn't sought shelter in a coulee during the storm, it would have been over for more of them."

Luke agreed. Crystal felt that Luke was keeping a watchful eye on her. She did have a lot on her mind.

Crystal served something that resembled runny scrambled eggs, trying not to notice their raised eyebrows when she plopped them on their plates.

Rusty was unusually quiet this morning. Without his normal banter among them, the cowhands kept a wide berth. Crystal reached for the coffeepot, filling their cups with the thick, black liquid.

Kurt took one big gulp and remarked, "Strong stuff, your Southern coffee." He winked at Crystal.

"Strong. You can't even cut it with a knife," Luke muttered

under his breath. But when he split open a biscuit, Crystal saw surprise register on his face.

Luke ignored the runny eggs and burned sausages and was on his third biscuit when Crystal broke the silence. She stood up and stretched her form to its full five foot two inches, hoping she had a look of authority. She leaned down and placed her palms on the table. Her face took on a serious look. "I've done a lot of thinking about what to do about the ranch, and I've come to a conclusion."

Forkfuls of food stopped midair as all eyes were riveted to the head of the table.

"Before Kate's unfortunate death . . ." Crystal took a deep breath to keep from getting emotional and continued, "She expressed her desire to hold on to Aspengold, despite the hardships of the last few years. For the time being, I will stay in order to ensure that we go ahead with the trail drive and ship the cattle to market. Your jobs are secure for now, but I can't tell what the future will hold for this ranch. I realize that I have much to learn, and I'd appreciate your assistance in any way that seems fit. We will have to be hopeful and try to secure the best possible price for our beef once it's shipped."

"Who's to be in charge here, Miss Crystal?" Jube asked.

Crystal looked in Luke's direction. "I'd like Luke to stay on as foreman but report directly to me."

Rusty stood up. "We're behind you, Miss Crystal, all the way. Kate was a mighty fine woman and trusted us like her equal. I think that's what Kate would want, huh, boys?" They nodded and voiced agreement. Luke said nothing. He pushed back his chair, a deep furrow between his brows.

"Oh, another thing," Crystal said. "I hope you've hired a cook for the roundup, Rusty, because I don't intend to cook for this outfit and ride too."

There was laughter all around, along with apparent relief.

"*You* intending on riding the trail drive?" Jube looked incredulously at Crystal.

"That is my intention." Crystal steeled herself for an argument, and when none was forthcoming she turned to Luke, who was muttering under his breath.

"Luke, may I have a word with you before you leave?" Crystal asked as they started to file out to their various duties.

"At your service, ma'am."

"Once I've gone over the books, I'll know better where we stand. I'd appreciate your willingness to work for me."

"Do I have a choice? Just what in thunder do you know about ranching? Maybe you'd be better off in Georgia."

"Are you questioning my capabilities?"

"Yes, I am, in fact."

"Please don't raise your voice at me, Mr. Weber. Save it for your saloon friends." The dishes made a loud clatter as Crystal began stacking them in the sink.

"I don't have any saloon friends. You don't know me at all. And there's a lot more to running a ranch than scrambling a few runny eggs."

She drew in a sharp breath and blushed. *Try to stay calm.* He must have been good at his job, or Kate never would have kept him. His blue eyes penetrated her green ones, and she couldn't help but notice an odd pull whenever she looked at him.

"I said I was willing to learn, and believe me, I catch on fast."

"Let's hope so, because winters here can be hard, not to mention lonely. There are dust storms so thick you can't breathe, and hail that can wipe out a crop as fast as lightning flashes. Taking care of livestock in the dead of winter can be a dreaded chore. Are you prepared for that? Only the tough survive."

"Meaning I need to be made of stronger stuff? I don't swoon at the first sight of trouble."

"What do you mean?"

"Oh . . . I was thinking of April. Let's see . . . she can brand cattle and have a hot meal simmering, all in a day's work."

He chuckled. "If I didn't know better, I'd say you're jealous." He took a step closer to her. "There's nothing wrong with a woman doing all those things and more."

Crystal took a step backward. "Don't flatter yourself. As to April, just because a cat has kittens in the oven, they're not necessarily biscuits!"

Luke roared with laughter, slammed his hat on his head, and strode through the door.

Crystal clattered and banged the pans and dishes into the sudsy water and attacked them with fresh fury. *Who does he think he is!* According to Emily Johnson, half the female population of Steamboat was after him. Let them fall for his charms; she wasn't about to. She would have to prove to Luke that she was a lot stronger than he thought.

She was more determined than ever to make this ranch pay for itself. She'd do it or die trying. *Dear Lord, please help me control my temper. He rattles me so . . . Help me figure out how to handle this situation with the ranch. Amen.*

Luke was glad of the cool, fresh air outside. Imagine her

warning him about April. Luke somehow felt he'd been put in his place when he lost his temper around her. What was it about her that made him shoot off his mouth like a cocked gun? She really didn't deserve being spoken to that way, he mused. Besides, she made the best biscuits this side of the Rockies.

Life at Aspengold was anything but routine in preparation for the anticipated trail drive. Everyone rose before daylight for meals and chores, and later in the evening congregated on the front porch. Sometimes Crystal would curl up in a chair by the fire to read her father's Bible. She fell into bed at night, exhausted but feeling like she had more purpose in her life.

Now it wasn't yet sundown, but Crystal felt a need to be outdoors after doing the supper dishes, away from the heat of the kitchen. She strolled in the early dusk, the air fragrant with the pungent smell of evergreen and pinion pines. Soon she found herself in the grove of aspens that ran alongside the back of the ranch.

Here the breeze stirred the aspen leaves, creating a quaking effect that suggested a season change was nearing in their green-gold color. Delicate cerulean columbine and mountain bluebells thrived in the thick undergrowth of the forest floor, a striking contrast to deceased conifers dotting the rocky terrain.

Crystal leaned back against a fat, white aspen trunk scarred with holes, understanding now why Kate had so named the ranch. She could almost feel her aunt's presence. A gurgling stream carved its way over flat, shiny boulders as it went farther down the mountainside. The entire alpine vista lent itself to a quiet peace and stillness that she was unable to describe but felt deeply. God had painted the azure blue sky as his backdrop for the majestic mountains. How could anyone doubt that there was a Creator? She was suddenly energized at the thought that God was so magnificent but still cared about what happened to her.

Yet she was lonely for Kate and felt an emptiness that she had never experienced before. More like a longing to belong to someone. She wasn't sure. She closed her eyes and thanked God for all that He had provided for her since her father's and Kate's untimely deaths. She prayed for guidance about her future. She ended her prayer by thanking Him for this splendid country and all that His hands had created.

She couldn't wait for Carmen to return. Not that anyone was demanding, but she was not used to cooking and cleaning and was worn to a frazzle. Now, looking at her hands that were once soft with ten perfect oval nails, she felt like crying again. Half of the nails were broken, and her hands chafed from being in water constantly. Then she giggled out loud when she thought how horrified Drew would be at her lack of sophistication if he were here with her now.

She bent over to untie her shoes and roll down her stockings, then discarded them both. She threw propriety to the wind, tucked her skirt into her waistband, and headed to the stream. With trepidation she stuck one toe in and then her foot. It was icy cold. Ah, but it felt good and refreshing, and she slowly placed the other foot in. She let her fingers trail the water and clutched her skirts with her other hand, then splashed the cold water on her face and neck. It cooled her skin, and she was just stepping up to the bank when she heard the piercing scream of a woman.

Fear gripped her heart, and it beat violently in her chest. She reached out with both hands to the bank but slid on the mossy rocks. She felt something pull at her skirt and turned to find that it was snagged on a rotting log. The scream sounded again, and she struggled frantically to loosen her skirt from the log. The material ripped, and she fell backward into the water and drenched herself thoroughly. The cold water shocked her senses.

Panic swept over her. Dragging her torn, wet skirt and petticoats, she was able to scramble up the bank—right into a pair of black, dusty boots. She looked up and saw Luke with an amused look on his face and his hat pushed back, lazily leaning against a huge boulder as if he had all the time in the world. She was gasping for breath, and he just stood there grinning down at her. She was acutely aware that in her sodden state, her clothes clung to her body.

"Did . . . didn't you hear that . . . woman screaming? Someone is hurt . . . or in trouble. Did you . . . see anyone?" She choked and sputtered on the water in her throat and blinked it out of her eyes.

"Well, Miss Crystal, what a harebrained thing to do! Go swimming with your clothes on. And you being a Southern lady and all." He could hardly drag his eyes off her wet, curvy form.

In the distance, the crack of a rifle rang out, causing Crystal to jump.

"Never mind that. What about the lady?" she said.

"That was no lady," he said. "That was a mountain lion. You shouldn't be roaming out here this far by yourself. The gunfire might've been Rusty trying to scare her away from the livestock."

Crystal was starting to shiver now and walked right past Luke to retrieve her stockings and shoes. He grabbed her by the arm, and she turned to look up at him. She was so close that he could feel her breath on his skin. The waning sunlight filtered through the trees, leaving just a trace of light, so it was hard to see her face.

"No need to get in a huff, Crystal. But don't come out here alone at night, understand? It might not be safe."

"I don't remember taking orders from you, Mr. Weber. And when I need your advice, I'll ask for it, thank you very much," Crystal snapped. "You had no right to follow me!"

Luke reacted like he'd been branded with a hot iron, bringing his hand back to his hip pocket. "I came up to the house to give you the list for the supplies we'll be needing for the trail drive. When no one answered the door, I decided I'd better go looking for you." He walked off and called over his shoulder, "Find your own way home, ma'am."

After stripping her wet things off, Crystal donned a warm flannel gown and prepared to retire. She had decided to stay in the small room, preferring it to her aunt's. Somehow she just couldn't bring herself to move in there. Not just yet. Her thoughts turned to Georgia. She shivered when she thought of the screams of the mountain lion sounding so much like a woman. Everything about this place was so different. Georgia—and civilization—seemed a million miles away. Would she be able to stick it out and keep her part of the bargain?

Even though her headaches finally went away, she was always thirsty, and her skin itched from the dryness. At this rate, her soft complexion would take on the appearance of the dried apricots she'd found in the pantry. Next time she was in town, she'd ask Mary at the mercantile store for some special cream for her hands and face.

She smiled, thinking how kind Rusty was. An hour before supper, he had walked in and said he was going to help her cook supper. She readily acquiesced, and he began to panfry slabs of beef while she peeled potatoes. Such a sweet man. He told her the story again of the blizzard in '87 when the drifts were as high as the roof of the barn. That year it was 46 degrees below up in Montana where his family lived. Many of the smaller ranches were about wiped out.

Crystal could only shake her head in disbelief at his stories. She noticed Rusty refrained from talking about Kate. She knew his loneliness was deep for Kate, though he never said anything, and her heart went out to him.

In a short time, supper was made, steaming hot and on the table before the rest of the crew staggered in. The meal vanished in a matter of minutes.

Crystal spent some time reading her father's Bible before going to bed. When she read Galatians, a verse in chapter 6 seemed written for her. It said not to lose heart in doing good and you would reap a reward. As always was the case, she found the strength and encouragement that she so needed. She knew that she wasn't alone.

Once she was snuggled under the quilt, she remembered April's party. She wearily got back out of bed, opened the wardrobe, and pulled out her lavender gown. Kurt had told her that anyone who was anyone would be there. She wished she had the material she had lost in the twister. Perhaps she could ask one of the cowboys to go looking for it.

Mindful of the talk about her dress at the last barn dance, Crystal decided to add more material to the décolletage. Not wanting to be the topic of conversation again, she would add a little lace with bits of ribbon here and there to reconfigure the neckline a bit. She dragged her rocker near the lamplight, opened the sewing kit, and began working until there was a nagging pain between her shoulder blades.

From where Luke stood at the bunkhouse, he could see a light still burning in Crystal's window. He hadn't been able to sleep. His thoughts had been consumed with running the ranch and wondering just how Kate had managed to keep up with everything. He sure missed her advice about horses and cattle alike, not to mention her presence.

He wondered what on earth Crystal was doing up so late. She sure was a feisty and outspoken little thing. In fact, he admired that streak in her, but he didn't want her to know it. He knew that once you told a woman she was pretty and took her to a church social in these parts, you were considered practically engaged. Yes sir, he'd better be real careful where this one was concerned.

11

Crystal had stayed up late the night before working on her dress. Although her sewing left something to be desired, it turned out better than she thought it would.

Once the breakfast dishes were put away and the kitchen was tidy, Crystal hurried through her morning laundry. She wanted to spend some time going over her aunt's ledgers, a task she had put off longer than she had intended to. She settled down in the high-back chair beneath the antique desk whose very existence showed its years by the many scars on its surface. *If only the desk could talk*, she thought. She lifted the rolltop and pulled several journals from their dusty cubbyholes. It seemed very peculiar to be going through someone else's possessions. She felt as though she was violating her aunt's privacy.

Soon she was involved in trying to make sense out of the entries. Month-to-month entries were almost nonexistent. In some places an entry of accounts received was recorded, but the thing that really gave her a blow was the outstanding debts tucked in the back of the journal. There were long-overdue bills to the mercantile store for feed, kerosene oil, and various tack and harness equipment, most of which Crystal had known nothing about. There was an outstanding bill to the blacksmith for repair of a wagon tongue.

But the most shocking of all was a sizable note signed by Kate Morgan naming Jim McBride as the lender to be repaid by the end of the year. Crystal was surprised not only by her aunt's poor bookkeeping but that, as far as she could tell, Kate had made no attempt to begin payments to McBride. Crystal had always seen Kate as someone in control and methodical. But in this case she was mistaken.

Maybe she could speak to McBride about the matter. If she had a chance tonight at April's party, she would. Yet McBride might decide to drive a hard bargain, and she might have to sell him the ranch.

She was thoroughly depressed now, something that was so out of character for her that she wasn't sure how to deal with it. Kate had commented on her sunny disposition and how her laughter made everyone feel good. What a joke. If Kate could see her now . . . She put her face in her hands and began to cry.

She felt frustration at the mess Aspengold was in, and then from acute homesickness. She longed to see her maid Lilly and even Drew. She wanted to be able to take a ride in her new, shiny buggy through the crowded streets of Atlanta and peruse the shops on Peachtree Street, have lunch with Mary Jo and Charlotte, and plan their next church bazaar. But the buggy, along with almost every possession, had been auctioned off that fateful day. A sharp longing for her family and home struck her, causing more tears to fall.

Lord, please help me. I don't know which way to turn. Crystal poured out her heart to God until her tears lessened.

As Luke crossed the yard on his way to the barn, he paused as his attention was directed to the clothesline that held Crystal's sheets fluttering in the breeze, alongside stiff white petticoats that seemed to be standing on their own. He reluctantly dragged his eyes away, feeling like he'd viewed something intimate and personal, and looked up at the puffy clouds the color of pink streaked with the pale blue sky. How he loved this country! There was nowhere else he'd rather be.

He was about to continue on his way when he thought he heard a whimpering sound. At first he thought it was one of the hounds, but as he walked closer, he realized the sound was coming from the house. He stepped lightly on the porch, tapped at the front door, and discreetly opened it a crack. Across the room, yellow shafts of sunlight filtered through the open doorway, placing golden highlights in Crystal's dark head on the desktop.

"Crystal?" he whispered. "Everything all right?" He moved to stand near the chair and reached out to touch her head lightly.

She jerked her head up and sniffed, wiping her tears with the back of her hand. Her face was swollen and tearstained, green eyes glittering, and her lashes were wet against dark circles under her eyelids. "Not really. I think I just had my first bout of real homesickness," she managed to croak between hiccups. She rose to stand and face him.

Crystal looked directly into Luke's blue eyes, unable to tear her eyes away. Her feet felt glued to the floor, and she was wedged between Luke and the desk with nowhere to go.

He placed a finger under her chin and tilted her head back to look deep into her glistening eyes, then leaned down and covered her quivering lips with his own. His thin lips were soft and caressing. Crystal felt an exquisite shock numb her very being. His hand touched the small of her back, gently pulling her to him until she felt his hard chest against hers. She felt safe here and wanted to stay in his arms. She leaned against him and closed her eyes.

When he released her, he said in a hoarse voice, "After you get things settled here, you can go back to the South. I can help you see to selling the ranch. I'd buy it myself if I had the money. If you like, you can leave next week. You don't have to stay till the trail drive. Me and Rusty can handle things for you." He took a big step away from her.

Crystal noticed his ragged breathing. She jerked herself back to reality, straightened her shoulders, and pressed her unruly hair back into its pins. So the kiss was to cheer her up. It hadn't meant anything to him. Why should she be surprised? Obviously, a kiss was something he handed out as easily as the peppermint candy he had given her.

He picked up the cold cup of coffee and said, "Goodness, this stuff is awful. Come on. I'm going to make up a decent pot of coffee for once." He headed toward the kitchen, and she walked stiffly behind him, not knowing what else to do.

"Now you just sit there and relax." He motioned for her to sit at the table.

"I'm not leaving, you know. Not yet. I never back down on my word," Crystal said. She watched his movements about the kitchen while he ground fresh coffee in the mill and proceeded to boil water.

He looked completely at ease in the kitchen and seemed familiar with the cupboards and their contents. He took out two cups and saucers and placed them on the table. He reached in the cupboard and removed a large tin that was hidden from view in the back. Inside were dubious-looking sugar cookies. Luke placed them on a plate between the two cups.

The smell of coffee permeated the small kitchen, and Crystal waited patiently with her hands folded in her lap. She watched him dart from one side of the kitchen to the other. His long legs moved with alacrity, and his spurs made a tinkling sound. He was small hipped, and his britches were well-worn and snug, and his shirtsleeves were rolled up past the elbow. He stood near the stove with his weight on one hip, making certain the coffee didn't boil over. He removed the pot from the stove and placed it alongside the milk and sugar on the table.

Outwardly he appeared calm, but inside, Luke's thoughts were running a mile a minute as he thought back to their brief kiss. It had felt so nice, so right. Why hadn't he felt that way when he kissed April? What was he thinking, doing that? He wasn't sure what it meant, but when he'd looked at the curve of Crystal's face tilted up and watching him, his heart had begun to thump hard against his ribs.

He poured the coffee and sat down to join her. He pushed his hat to the back of his head and crossed his outstretched legs in front of him. "See if you don't like my coffee, and if you do, I'll teach you how to make it." He winked at her. "This is the quietest you've ever been."

When she smiled back at him, he felt funny in his stomach. Probably the greasy breakfast. He was glad that he was sitting across from her, or he might be forced to kiss those quivering lips again. "Too bad we don't have one of those good pies Carmen makes. That would just be perfect."

She wasn't about to tell him that those had been her pies, not Carmen's. With his hat pushed back, she could get a better look at his face. His skin was richly tanned from the many hours in the saddle, and his wide forehead was low with two permanent wrinkles around his eyes from squinting in the sun. She liked the way his long fingers curled around the cup that he held in one hand. As he munched on a cookie, the crumbs caught in his moustache.

Realizing that she was staring, she sipped her coffee and took a bite of the cookie. "Very good, I must admit."

"I'm glad you like it. Made that batch of cookies up myself. I kinda have a sweet tooth. We gotta teach you to cook while you're here."

Crystal laughed. "I can cook a couple of things. Wait until you taste my skillet cornbread and red beans."

"You need to learn how to make sourdough biscuits."

"What's that?" She looked up into his blue eyes.

"Sourdough? Well, next to the Bible, sourdough is the most important possession on the frontier. You can make flapjacks and biscuits with it, patch a crack in the cabin, treat wounds, and even make brew."

Crystal wondered if that meant the Bible held some importance to him. "I've never heard of sourdough."

"Well, it was a popular item and a staple with the prospectors during the Yukon gold rush. They carried their starter dough buried in flour or in pots strapped to their backs."

"Why didn't you try mining? Maybe you'd have struck it rich and been able to have your own ranch."

"I did. Went to Leadville and Central City when I was just seventeen with dreams of getting rich, but all I wound up doing was working hard, spending every cent in gambling halls, and kicking up my heels. I was young and stupid. 'Bout the only strike I ever made was pyrite."

"And what, pray tell, is pyrite?" Crystal was enjoying this exchange of conversation.

"It's called fool's gold because it's usually mistaken for the real thing. Anyhow, a lot of people did become millionaires. Others squandered their money like it was water. Ever hear of Horace Tabor?"

She shook her head. He stood, reached for the coffee, and refilled their cups with the scalding liquid.

"He started out with a third of a grubstake and wound up almost instantly rich and purchased a dozen or so more mines. He was lieutenant governor back in 1878 for six years. He built the Tabor Grand Opera House in Denver. Yep, he was very rich." Luke paused in his story and reached for another cookie.

Crystal felt very content to be sitting here talking like friends instead of having their usual banter. This was an interesting new side to him that she wanted to know better. "Well," she nudged, wanting to hear the rest, "what happened to this rich Horace Tabor?"

"Let me see . . . He divorced his wife and fell in love with a woman called Baby Doe, who was also divorced. He met her on one of his trips to Leadville and lavished her with fine things. I heard tell from the stories that he gave her a $7,000 wedding dress and a huge diamond worth close to $100,000."

Crystal gasped. "Really?"

"They live in Denver now, and I hear his businesses and mines are all but petered out, except for the Matchless Mine. It seems he mortgaged all his real estate to develop new mines and has fallen on hard times."

Crystal sighed. "It sounds romantic but sad."

"Feeling better now? You have a party to go to tonight, and you don't want to go with a swollen face, now do you?"

"Are you and the boys going?"

"As sure as a snowstorm in February. Wouldn't want to miss it. We can all ride together."

"Actually, Josh will be coming to escort me." Crystal saw Luke's jaw tighten.

"Oh, I see . . ." He wanted to ask her about Drew. It had been nagging him ever since the night she was unconscious, but now wasn't the time.

"About the ranch . . . I meant what I said." He looked across the table, and their eyes locked for a long moment. He started to say something else, but decided against it and shifted in his chair, causing it to creak in protest. "You don't need to worry. Not after all that you've gone through." It was almost a carbon copy of what had happened to her in Georgia, and he was concerned for her.

"I'll be okay, don't worry. Once I get everything figured out. God has never let me go begging." Crystal sighed again, moving to place the dishes in the sink. "You've made me think about something other than my troubles for a little while."

Luke watched as Crystal assumed her dignified air, her back and shoulders set in their usual determined way. He had to admire her resilience.

Friday at six o'clock sharp, Josh came up the dusty drive in a shiny new buggy with a pair of high-stepping thoroughbreds. Crystal was just completing last-minute touches to her hair, but upon hearing the horses rattling to a halt out front, she picked up her white straw hat and hurried out to greet Josh. He was impeccably dressed in a tan suit with a brown silk cravat and his usual tan Stetson hat. Crystal noticed a red blotch where his stiff white collar rubbed his throat, and it continued to creep up his neck when his eyes fell upon her as she emerged from the house and waited on the top step of the porch. She wore a lavender silk dress and knew that it enhanced her creamy white shoulders. This time her bosom barely peeked from under the edging of ribbon circling the scooped neckline.

After setting the brake, he climbed down to where she stood waiting. He extended his large, squarish hand to hers and lifted her up to the shiny buggy.

"You are going to be the prettiest one at the party tonight." Josh's eyes twinkled.

"You're looking pretty dashing yourself," she said.

"Do you have a wrap, Crystal? It will be a little cooler when it gets late."

"Oh, could you just step inside the door? My woolen shawl is hanging on the rack."

He retrieved her shawl and settled her in the buggy before taking his seat beside her and clicking to the horses. She waved to Curly and Jube when they passed the bunkhouse and saw Luke and Rusty out of the corner of her eye as they walked up from the barn. They had all cleaned up and were fixing to saddle up to leave for the party. Curly whistled shrilly, and she turned around to blow a kiss at him. They guffawed and watched as the buggy faded over the hill and out of sight.

Dusk came quickly in the mountains and cast shadows against the backdrop of spruces and firs, adding velvet gentleness to the evening air. Josh and Crystal fell into an easy conversation on the ride to Rocking M Ranch. She found that he was easy to talk with, and she enjoyed his conversation.

"I should have been over sooner, but I wanted to give you some time to yourself after Kate's death," he said.

At the mention of Kate's name, Crystal's smile faded. "I miss her terribly. She was such a good person. More like a second mother to me. It's hard for me to understand why this had to happen. I miss her so."

"I'm sorry. I didn't mean to bring this up to make you feel sad. Let's change the subject. Do you think you'll stay or return to Georgia?"

"For the moment, I am going to stay, Josh. I just need to think about what I'm going to do. Even if I went back to Georgia, I'm not certain what I would do or where I could stay."

Crystal saw him swallow hard and his Adam's apple bob when she used his Christian name. He covered her hand with his and said, "I'll be right here if you have need of assistance, or if I can help you with the ranch in any way."

"Thanks so much." The feel of his hand on hers was warm and reassuring and not unwelcome, and she squeezed back. "Luke and I should be able to handle the ranch now."

Josh pulled back sharply at the mention of Luke's name. "I would be delighted to teach you the particulars of ranching."

Crystal smiled. "To tell you the truth, Rusty is going to teach me what I need to know, but thank you, Josh. It's sweet of you to offer."

By the time Crystal and Josh arrived, the party was already under way, and strains of a waltz floated on the cool night air. Crystal stared with incredulity at the enormity of the house at the Rocking M Ranch. It was a grand, two-story structure of Victorian architecture with porches delicately trimmed in gingerbread scroll and painted a bright yellow—at least as near as she could tell by the burning gaslights on the veranda. The front lawn was filled with beautiful shrubs and studded with statuary. Amidst the garden were heavy wrought-iron benches placed here and there, which lent a tactful balance to the landscaping. Bright lights beckoned from every window, extending warm greetings to the arriving guests.

"Josh, it's so magnificent! I had no idea your home was so beautiful," Crystal exclaimed.

"Thank you. It's large enough to house two families with ease," he said with obvious pride in his voice.

133

When they stopped in the circular drive, a groom took charge of the buggy while another assisted them down. Josh took Crystal's gloved hand and led her inside. April and her father greeted newcomers in the foyer, where exquisite imported tile covered the floor. Ornate mirrors and tall green ferns flanked either side of the massive doorway.

"Good evening, Miss Clark. I hope the ride wasn't too long or uncomfortable for you," Jim McBride said. Crystal eyed him coolly. After their conversation the day of the funeral, she wasn't sure what to make of him. She intended to take him one day at a time.

"It was a very pleasant ride, thank you," she murmured, allowing him to take her shawl. April was bedecked in a gown the color of moonlight. With her silvery blonde hair, the gown made her appear ethereal and angelic, and Crystal reminded herself that this was just an illusion. She wished her happy birthday and added, "Your gown is lovely, April."

"Daddy had it made especially for me the last time he was in Denver. Wasn't that sweet of him?" she gushed.

McBride puffed out his chest, and the buttons threatened to pop open his gray silk vest. "Nothing's too good for my baby's birthday." He beamed at April.

The two of them were making Crystal nauseated.

Josh touched her elbow. "Come along, Crystal. Let's get some refreshments, and I'll introduce you around." Crystal was glad for an excuse to escape.

Josh guided her toward a large room where the rugs had been removed to allow for dancing. Sounds of laughter filled the room, and couples swept across the gleaming hardwood floor to the latest tunes being played by a stringed orchestra. From across the room, Emily and Beth stood talking with Bill Alden, but when they saw Crystal and Josh enter the room, they hurried over to greet them.

"We've been waiting for you." Beth threw a friendly smile to Josh and Crystal.

"Did you come together?" Emily asked. She glanced around the room in obvious anticipation.

"Yes, we did. It's so good to see you both. I've been starved for some female companionship. Since Carmen left, I've been stuck way out there on the ranch with no one but cowboys, and I'm starting to talk to myself out loud." Crystal laughed.

"Well . . . some can be quite nice to talk to." Emily replied, a sharp edge to her voice.

Knowing she'd hit a nerve, Crystal considered Emily's comment. Who was she looking for? The proverbially charming Luke? Somehow he didn't seem to fit sweet, shy Emily's demeanor. She followed Emily's eyes to the entrance. Jube, Kurt, and Curly stood at the edge of the dancing and surveyed the room. *Ah . . . just as I thought. It's Jube she's sweet on.*

"I'll get us some punch," Josh said as he moved toward the huge silver bowl. "I'm a little thirsty after that ride."

"Such a large party. There must be close to a hundred people here," Crystal commented to no one in particular.

Emily nodded, her brown curls bobbing. "When McBride throws a party, he spares no expense."

"Especially when it comes to his precious April," Beth said after Josh was out of earshot.

"I thought y'all were good friends." Crystal arched one eyebrow in doubt.

"If you want to call it that. April won't let anyone get too close," Beth confided. "She likes to boss everyone around, including Luke."

"Shh . . . here comes Josh with our punch," Emily warned.

Soon Crystal was pulled onto the crowded dance floor and once again felt light on her feet. How she loved to dance. It made her forget all her troubles, and she was caught up in the thrill of the flirting, the music, and the laughter. This was like a dose of medicine for her spirit.

In one dance, every few minutes the music would stop, someone would call out "Change partners," and there would be a mad rush to grab a new partner. She met a rugged-looking sheepherder, a Colorado senator, and a wealthy miner up from Leadville. Each of them in turn reveled at her charm and friendliness. It wasn't long before she found herself in Bill Alden's arms. His angular body felt bony against her as he tried to hold her close.

"You look wonderful tonight, Miss Crystal." Bill's eyes swept over Crystal with obvious approval. But Crystal kept a space between them and was glad when the song ended.

"Excuse me, please," she said, extricating her hand from his. She headed to where Mary Franklin and Sara Johnson were sitting.

"Are you having a good time?" Mary asked.

"Oh, wonderful!" Crystal's eyes swept the dance floor until she saw Luke with April. She stiffened while she watched the two of them dancing. His head was bent down toward hers, almost reaching his shoulder. They made a fine-looking couple.

Hot jealousy flashed through her. She sat like a lump of corn-meal through two slow waltzes, refusing offers to dance and pretending that the two of them did not exist. When she could no longer sit and watch the way Luke held April, she decided to seek out Jim McBride. She found him talking with the senator and John Franklin.

"Pardon me for intruding, but could I speak with you privately, Mr. McBride?" she said. Her heart pounded.

He cleared his throat. "Certainly. Shall we go into the library?" He turned to the two men and said, "I won't be but a moment."

She followed him past the dining room and down a hall to an impressive room lined with books and paintings. He pointed to a stuffed chair and bade her to have a seat. He sat on the corner of his desk and, after a pregnant silence, said, "Well? You wish to discuss something?"

"Mr. McBride, I wasn't aware until today how much my aunt had borrowed from you. I found the note in her desk. Now I understand why you wanted to buy me out." She swallowed hard. Her mouth always turned dry when she became nervous. After all, what did she know about running a cattle ranch?

"Yes, sad to say, the blizzard of '87 was hard on us all. Many of the smaller ranchers went under. But since my property joined Kate's, I felt an obligation to at least help her out. I tried to buy Aspengold, but she adamantly refused and said she'd get the money somewhere. I loaned her the money with a promise that it would be paid off in December of this year. I was very generous, giving her five years to come up with the money."

Crystal wasn't taken in by his bragging tone. "I think you knew she wouldn't be able to come up with the money, and now you want the property that meant so much to my aunt and uncle, particularly since it adjoins yours near the Blue River."

"What do you propose to do with the debt that you've now inherited, Miss Clark?" He looked at her with his brown eyes glinting—or were they mocking? An extension of a loan couldn't make that much difference to one so wealthy, could it?

Crystal finally found her voice. "I need more time. I am going to see that the cattle get to market. I'll pay you back with interest."

"You seem mighty sure of yourself for someone who doesn't know one end of a steer from the other," he said.

"I'm a fast learner, Mr. McBride. Just sit back and watch me." She stood up to leave.

"Good luck. Just remember, end of December, Aspengold will belong to me if you don't play your cards right. I know Josh is already sweet on you, but that won't hold water with me. That you can count on!" He showed her the door. Her face flamed hotly under his gaze.

"I would never use Josh to keep Aspengold."

"Yes, he's kindhearted to a fault." Crystal could see the small muscle in his jaw flinch, indicating that he found this whole conversation irritating. She stormed down the hall, so angry that she ran straight into Rusty.

"Whoa there! Where you rushing to?" He steadied her arm.

"Rusty, walk with me outside a moment please." She looked around for the nearest door.

Rusty led the way to a bench away from the house. She told him of the loan and conversation that had just taken place with McBride.

"I don't trust him. I never have," Rusty said. "He has always

138

wanted Kate's land. Some people just never have enough money and wealth." His weathered eyes looked back at hers with concern. "We'll make it. This year will be a good one for us. Next week I'm gonna give you some quick training about all there is to know about ranching, little missy." He clasped her hand with his rough, callused one, and Crystal could feel his strength.

"I don't know what I'd do without you or Luke. I may have bit off more than I can chew this time." She sighed.

"Now don't you go worrying your pretty little head. Things will work themselves out. We should have a decent roundup this fall, and we'll wait until just the right time to get the cattle to market. Fatten those dogies up, and if we're lucky the price of beef will go up too." He sounded so convincing that Crystal could only hope he would be right.

"Besides, I'm not just doing this for you." His voice grew softer. "I'm doing it for Kate." Crystal squeezed his hand.

Luke's blue eyes scanned the room and fell on Josh and Crystal. She seemed to be having a good time, and Josh was making sure of it. His arm was possessively around her waist as the dance ended. Luke took his time walking over to where they stood talking with Emily and Jube. Throughout the evening he had entered into conversations with the senator and other respected community leaders, and they listened with interest to what he had to say. Women, married or single, twittered whenever he came near, and he responded in his usual charming fashion, knowing full well how he affected them. Now as he stopped at Crystal's side, he noted Josh's rapt attention to her.

Luke touched her elbow. "I wondered if you would give me the pleasure of the next dance." His eyes swept across her slender throat and shoulders, where curling tendrils touched, and then up again to look into her sparkling eyes.

"Well . . . I was going to sit this one out . . ." She stammered an excuse, but Josh nodded. "Go ahead, Crystal. Later we'll all be resting with our meal. The kitchen has been buzzing for hours in preparation."

Without waiting for an answer, Luke pulled her to the center of the room as the strains of a waltz began. The skin on her bare arms was as soft as a rose petal, and moisture dampened the curls at the nape of her neck. There was a sweet scent that clung to her, but Luke couldn't discern its origin. "That fragrance you're wearing, what is it?"

"It's gardenia, made from a beautiful white flower that grows in the South. Do you like it?"

He nodded. "Yes . . . it's very different. It suits you." She looked up at him as he swept them across the floor, weaving her between the other dancers with certain elegance. The span of her waist was barely wider than his open palm against her back. Luke enjoyed dancing with her, gliding in the glow of the soft gaslights, and holding her this way.

"You seem to be having a good time." He smiled down at her. The lights made her green eyes sparkle with brilliance. Luke was afraid to linger there too long, afraid that he could get lost in their depths.

"I am. You are quite a good dancer, Mr. Weber."

"Have to be. Have to keep the ladies happy."

"Yes, they are all lined up, just waiting their turn," she mocked.

He leaned his head down. "Except you," he whispered.

"What?"

"Uh . . . I was saying, I'm getting a little hungry. Be glad to have that midnight snack they promised us," he lied. What he really wanted was to bury his head in her sweet-smelling hair, which lay against beautiful shoulders encircled by the lavender silk gown. After his conversation earlier with McBride, he would have to keep his head about him. He wanted that land on the Blue River more than he wanted anything, and McBride had promised to give it to him as a wedding gift when he married his daughter. Soon Crystal would be returning to her homeland and to Drew anyway, who must be waiting for her. Then the ranch would go up for sale, if McBride didn't concoct a scheme to snatch it from her. So Luke decided to just enjoy the moment while he could.

"I think Jube and Emily are perfect for each other, don't you?" Crystal's eyes followed them as they danced, seemingly oblivious to everyone else in the room.

"He does seem taken with her, I'll admit."

"I think her mother has different plans for her, though."

"Is that right? Well, I'm no expert, but there's one thing a body can't do, and that's telling another where to put his heart—" He was interrupted with a tap on his shoulder from the reverend, but Luke caught the frown on Crystal's face when he released her hand.

It was not until the food was served that the orchestra stopped playing. Guests filled their plates with cold chicken, thick slices of roast beef, creamed peas, boiled potatoes, and fluffy rolls. Dessert was to be served last, along with a surprise.

Crystal sat with the Franklins and the Johnsons. The men stood about, allowing the ladies to sit and then balance their plates on their knees. Jim McBride stood in front of the punch bowl, now half empty, with April and Luke at his side.

"Ladies and gentlemen, would you give me your attention for a moment? I know that's hard to do when you men have worked up such an appetite . . ." Laughter reverberated from one end of the ballroom to the other. "As you know, we are here to celebrate my daughter's eighteenth birthday. It is also with great pleasure that I announce to you April's engagement to Luke Weber. Please join with me now in a toast to this happy couple and to April's birthday." He raised his glass to a smiling April. Her arm was linked to Luke's, whose face looked more somber than lighthearted for a man who had just become engaged.

Crystal's heart slammed hard against her chest, and she could only watch as others raised their glasses with loud cheers and laughter to the happy couple. She looked at Luke, but his face was turned away as friends came up to shake his hand and thump him on the back. The piece of chicken she chewed on stuck in her throat, threatening to choke her. *She's not right for you! Not April! Can't you see that?*

Her mind was playing tricks on her. How in the world could she be so drawn to Luke? *Because he likes to be in control and so do I.* Crystal took a deep breath, fighting with her emotions. *I don't even know if he believes in God.* All of these thoughts were swirling in her mind like bullets bouncing off tin cans at target practice.

He had just been flirting for the fun of it, she finally admitted to herself. She wished that she could talk to Kate.

Amid the din, a path was cleared as a servant wheeled a tea cart laden with an enormous birthday cake flaming with candles into the center of the room. The reverend started singing "Happy Birthday to You," and the rest of the crowd joined in. From across the room Crystal caught Rusty's eye, and she pretended indifference.

"Well, what do you know about that!" Sara said with a sharp intake of breath.

Mary Franklin, her mouth forming a tight line across her protruding teeth, snapped her disapproval. "Humph! She's been throwing herself at him for the last year."

Emily turned to look at Crystal and placed her hand on hers as if sensing her feelings, to let her know she understood. Crystal stared down at the rest of the food on her plate. The roll soaked up the juice from the creamed peas.

Josh appeared with two slices of cake, one of which he handed to Crystal. "Boy! What a surprise. I guess I didn't know they were that serious, but if that will make April happy, then I'm happy for her."

Crystal said nothing and looked at the cake. If it had been any other time, she would have enjoyed its light, fluffy texture and rich icing. Instead she picked at it.

"Is something wrong, Crystal? You've not touched the cake."

"Not at all. I've had a very nice evening." When she forced a smile, his face softened and his shoulders relaxed.

What about all those signals I got from Luke just this morning? Crystal thought. *He doesn't care about me at all.*

"I was thinking that I'd better go congratulate the happy pair." She put down the cake.

143

"I'll go with you." Emily followed Crystal across the room.

Luke stood motionless as Crystal approached him. She flashed him a strained smile and wished him well, then shook his hand with her trembling one and moved toward April.

Luke stared after her. Well, so much for worrying about her reaction. She seemed downright pleased as she sashayed on over to congratulate April. He watched them talking together and drew a sharp comparison between them. April, tall and slender, had a composed, hard look etched on her face as she coolly accepted Crystal's wishes. Crystal, petite and gently feminine, head tilted upward, gave her most gracious smile with decorum. He was unable to hear what was said because the cowhands chose that precise time to pound him on the back with congratulations.

"Guess your money problems are over now, boss," Curly said.

"Reckon you'll live in this mansion now. I hear they have six bedrooms. Take your pick." Kurt laughed.

"When's the wedding to be?" Jube asked.

"Nothing's been decided yet, boys. One thing at a time," Luke answered. All the while his mind was somewhere else, on the beauty in the lavender dress.

"Crystal, how kind of you to wish us well," April remarked tritely.

Crystal's smile faded. "It's the least I could do for my foreman."

"He won't be that much longer, I'm afraid." April's eyes fluttered back at Crystal.

"Don't be too sure. Luke's not a man to sit around and twiddle his thumbs, darling," Crystal drawled.

"I always get what I want, one way or another," April said, her blue eyes turning to liquid steel.

"Well, if what you want is a stubborn, thick-headed cowboy, I say good luck. I think you're going to need it." Crystal spun on her heels, leaving April sputtering words under her breath.

What Crystal wanted to do was cry. She was desperately trying to be kind and considerate; after all, Luke had never said anything to make her think he liked her in that way. She looked across the dance floor for Josh and made her way toward him with the best smile she could muster. He deserved a fine Christian woman.

April turned to Emily, feigning indifference. "Having a good time, Em?"

"I think the good time just came to an end. I wanted to tell you thanks for having us, but I think Papa is ready to leave now."

"Before you go, a word of advice." April's blue eyes narrowed. "I think you should stick to the reverend. You two would make a perfect couple. Besides, Daddy donated the pastor's home, and you'd have a small parcel of land to go along with it. Jube has nothing whatsoever."

"Strange, April, I thought you were marrying a cowboy, and I don't see that there's any difference at all." Emily walked past April without a backward glance.

13

Josh retrieved the carriage, then waited patiently while Crystal and Emily parted. Crystal promised Emily that she would attend the quilting circle the following Saturday. Lifting her at the waist, Josh swung her lightly up into the carriage. The fun of the party and the dancing had seemed to loosen his normal unobtrusive manner, and he was in high spirits.

While Josh talked, Crystal murmured the appropriate response, but her mind was trying to shut out the vision in her head of the handsome couple happily accepting congratulations. *Stop it!* she told herself. *You have a fine gentleman at your side who thinks you are wonderful and witty.* She turned her attention to Josh, and in spite of her thoughts, Crystal was soon laughing, especially when he described Widow Miller.

"She is as big as a watermelon about to burst. Widow Miller was lavishing all her attention on Reverend Alden and promising to fatten him up. He's so thin he could be used as a buggy whip," Josh said, and Crystal's laughter joined his.

With a slight pull at the reins, Josh abruptly stopped the horses in the middle of the road, and without any warning, he reached for Crystal, pulled her close, and kissed her soundly on the lips.

His lips were soft and full, just the opposite of Luke's thin but caressing ones. Now why was she comparing again? Crystal drew back, her hands pushing firmly against his thick chest. "Josh. Please. I barely know you." She could still feel the warmth of his lips and felt confused about her feelings.

"I'm sorry," he said. "It's just that I've wanted to do that all evening. I don't know what got into me." He picked up the reins and flicked them over the horses' rumps.

Crystal could see the red flush creeping from his neck upward to his face, but she chose to ignore it and merely adjusted the wrap about her shoulders. With her respectable Southern decorum, she brushed over his embarrassment by quickly changing the subject. As she adjusted her shawl, she noticed a lone rider, his hat slung low, quietly observing her and Josh through the lodgepole and spruce.

Luke wasted no time after breakfast but hurried to the tack room to get away from Crystal's cool regard and to finalize his list of provisions that would be needed for the trail drive. He didn't know why he was expecting a different reaction from Crystal at the announcement of his engagement, but in the back of his mind he halfheartedly hoped she'd object. Should've known better.

His eyes slammed shut when he thought of her in Josh's arms. He'd been on his way home from the party when he saw them kissing. He wondered if Josh knew about Drew. Probably not. No matter. April would make a good wife, and she was very knowledgeable about ranching since she had followed every step her father took since she was big enough to walk. He would have his spread on the Blue River. Besides, he was pushing thirty and was ready to settle down. He would grow to love April.

He jammed his list deep into his vest pocket, reached for his saddle, and carried it out to the corral. Buck pawed the dirt with his hoof at the sight of Luke. He lovingly stroked Buck's withers and adjusted the rigging rings, then reached down to tighten the cinch. He heard a noise and turned to see Crystal and Rusty approaching.

"Where ya off to?" Rusty said.

Luke turned and waved a greeting. "Going to ride out and see how Curly is doing with the herd. Maybe lend him a hand with the strays." He tipped his hat to Crystal and fished the list out of his vest. "Rusty, here's a list I came up with. If you need to add anything to it, go ahead."

"I'll take that." Crystal reached for the paper. "Rusty and I have things to discuss this morning, and I may have a few things for the list myself." Crystal conducted herself in a businesslike manner, not even looking at Luke. "I'd also like a list of the extra hands you've hired for the trail drive and what you've promised them in wages. I want to be certain that I'll be paying only for experienced hands since we can't afford too many losses on this trail."

Luke didn't like this new take-charge Crystal. What did she know about losses on a cattle drive? He was doing just fine on his own. When she said she'd stay on for a while, Luke assumed she had meant for him to take over running the spread for her. "I only hired the best hands," he answered, giving her an icy look.

148

"Fine. Rusty's been filling me in on the particulars of the roundup and trail drive, and I still intend to ride with y'all."

"Then you'll be about as welcome as a spot on a white Sunday shirt." He mounted Buck and glared down at her. "You'd better talk some sense into her, Rusty."

Rusty took the toothpick he was chewing on out of his mouth before calmly answering, "Well now, I tried that. Seems she's determined to learn firsthand."

"She'll only be in the way," Luke said through clenched teeth.

"Please do not talk as if I'm not even standing here." Crystal stood with her hands on her hips. Turning to Rusty, she said, "I'm ready for that shooting lesson now, Rusty."

Luke spurred Buck out of the yard, leaving the other two to choke on a cloud of dust.

Crystal's quick ability to learn and her keen sense of aim with the Colt in her hand made her feel more competent. She was pleased and felt that with a little more practice, she would do all right on the trail. By week's end, true to his word, Rusty had saturated her brain with as much information as he could. He showed her how to ride a cutting horse. He demonstrated the cutting horse's skill by using knee pressure alone to guide it, with little need for reins. The cowboys took a break to watch the lesson and perched on the top rail of the corral fence.

Crystal tried to emulate Rusty's adeptness with his horse while picking out a steer from the few he had placed in the corral. She hadn't anticipated the horse's sharp sidestep and quickly lost her seat. She fell on all fours into the dust and landed at the feet of a large steer, whose sides heaved and nostrils flared. It hadn't looked this big from the horse's back! "Nice steer," she said, backing away.

Kurt, Curly, and Jube roared with laughter, slapped their thighs, and poked one another at the sight of their proper boss covered with dust. But just as quickly they clamored down to assist her. She rubbed her backside but laughed right along with them and was ready to try again.

Crystal pulled herself back into the saddle just as Luke reined Buck in to watch the commotion. This time she was much better at it. When she had singled out the steer she wanted, Crystal urged it gently to the edge of the herd, and her mount rushed behind the steer, separating it out of the herd. When the steer found itself outside the herd, it tried to go back, but instantly the horse wheeled to the left and ran alongside it.

The steer tried to dodge the horse, but each time, the horse stopped and wheeled around again, keeping it outside the herd, until the steer gave up and ran out of the herd. All the while, Crystal managed to keep her seat. Rusty and the punchers cheered loudly for her, which was great for her pride, but she knew it was the alert and well-trained horse that actually did the work. It was the most fun she'd had in a long time, and through it all she knew she had earned the drovers' respect.

Luke said nothing, just sat with his arms across the pommel of the saddle, hat pulled low over his eyes. The past week, he'd been avoiding her like a bad case of the measles. Crystal pretended that it didn't matter, but in truth she couldn't understand why they couldn't still be friends, even though he was engaged.

Later in the afternoon, when Rusty and Crystal were in the barn putting away the lariats and bridles, Rusty blurted out, "Crystal, I've seen the way Luke looks at you and how the sparks always fly whenever you two are in the same place." He scratched his beard thoughtfully, which Crystal knew meant he was in a pensive mood. "Are you sure there's nothin' going on between you two? I'm not blind, you know."

"There is nothing between us, Rusty, believe me," Crystal answered a bit too quickly. "I don't usually flirt with engaged men, so put your mind at ease." She shook her head. "Thanks for the horse-handling instructions, Rusty. I need to go get cleaned up and rustle up supper." She hurried out of the barn to avoid any further questions, but she knew she hadn't fooled Rusty one bit.

"Have something for you." Luke held a bundle out toward Crystal as she approached the porch.

"What is this?" She drew her breath in sharply. "Oh, you found it." With shaking hands she unfolded the bundle. There, wrapped with the crumpled cream material, lay her ivory hat. Luke thought it looked more like a wrinkled mushroom than the beautiful hat. She held it to her chest as tears began to well up, spilling over her sunburned cheeks and onto the bundle she caressed.

"I rode down the ravine where . . . well, anyhow, I came across it and thought you might still like to have it. I didn't mean to upset you and make you cry." He resisted the urge to wipe away her tears and shifted his weight from one boot heel to the other, spurs jingling.

Crystal sniffed and wiped her eyes on the back of her hand.

151

"It's okay, Luke. The material and hat made me think about Aunt Kate. I miss her so much sometimes that it hurts. God bless her sweet soul." She moved past him, and a sob caught in her throat as she opened the front door. "Thank you, Luke. I'll try to get the stains out. Maybe someday I'll make it into a dress for a special occasion."

Feeling responsible for Crystal's tears, Luke floundered for something to say. "Uh . . . I didn't mean to yell at you the other day. I am really sorry about Kate. I loved her like a mother. But I don't think you should be going on the trail drive. This is definitely a man's job. It's too dangerous, and you could get hurt. Stay here and make your dress or something . . ."

Crystal stiffened. "Indeed." She gazed at him coolly through misty eyes. "We shall see. This is my ranch, and I will run it firsthand. That is what I intend to do, with or without your blessing."

He watched her go, and the door slammed behind her. Luke just shook his head. Foolish woman. He'd be glad when the beef was shipped and done with. Maybe she would go back to Georgia then, and he wouldn't have to see her every day. But he sure would miss those green eyes.

14

Crystal bounced along in the buckboard, urging Bess over the rugged trail toward the Johnsons' soddy and humming a tune on this cloudless day. Her sanguine nature kept her from feeling down for long. The only visible motion in the bright azure sky was two blue jays showing off their wings in the brilliant sunshine. Though the misty mornings in the South took several hours to burn off, Crystal never failed to marvel that in the Rockies, every morning dawned bright and clear.

She was grateful for this ride alone, for it gave her time to think and delight in every new plant and flower she came upon. Bear grass, or—as Rusty said some called it—squaw grass, was blooming. What appeared to be conical, white clusters from a distance in the meadow were striking white flowers atop their slender stems. Amazing to her was the fact that they bloomed every five to seven years. How lucky she felt to be able to behold their cream finery. Rusty had told her the leaves were used by Indians to weave fine baskets, and whenever the squaw grass was flowering, the young mountain bluebirds were fledging. What a sweet thought.

Consider the lilies of the field, how they grow; they neither toil nor spin . . . That verse had been a comfort to her since Kate's death. Crystal realized again that she need not worry. Her future was in the hands of the very One who had ordained all of her days.

Rusty had adopted her, taken her under his wing, and she couldn't have been more grateful. The tough cowpuncher was taciturn and doggedly independent. He embodied a keen wisdom that living on the land had afforded him. Yes, he was becoming very dear to her.

Once she had asked him why he hadn't married Kate. He'd said she was still in love with the memory of her dead husband, but sometimes he felt like she was beginning to return his feelings. Besides, he'd been working the Aspengold outfit for twelve years. He didn't have much to offer her. Crystal had been stunned to think it had kept him from marrying her all those years. So tragic. Amazing how men thought.

Crystal believed that true love was hard to come by. Which made her stop and examine her own feelings. What was she truly feeling about Luke? Jealousy? Why in the world was she drawn to a loud, flirtatious, pigheaded cowpoke? Well, he'd made his decision to marry April, and though it left a dull ache in her chest, she wasn't certain that it was love.

She supposed April would be at the quilting circle today as well. They had been working on a quilt for the reverend, and today they would be discussing the upcoming church bazaar.

The outlying buildings of the Johnson farm came into view, and Crystal flicked the reins across Bess's back. She guided the buggy to a stop alongside a sharp black surrey with red velvet cushions that she recognized right away as April's.

The front door of the soddy was propped open, and Crystal

walked inside. Emily sat her cup and saucer down and greeted her warmly.

"Crystal. Come in. We were just getting started." Emily guided her to the kitchen table where coffee and warm muffins were laid out, and poured a cup for her.

The ladies sat in a semicircle at the one side of the large room that served as Sara's parlor. The other side served as the kitchen. Chattering dwindled as Sara exchanged pleasantries with Crystal and pulled her toward the group. Beth drew up another chair for Crystal, seating her next to Flo. "I believe you know everyone here, am I right?"

Crystal glanced around the circle of familiar faces and nodded. Alice smiled in her direction, and April's lips curved upward in a smile, although her eyes remained cold.

Mary, in her no-nonsense fashion, took control of the meeting. "As I was saying, this year's bazaar is to be the biggest and best. We will be trying to raise money for a new organ." She shoved her sliding spectacles up the bridge of her nose.

"We'll also need to buy new hymnals this year. The ones we have now are breaking apart at the binding," Sara added.

April tossed her silvery-blonde hair across her back and leaned on the edge of her chair. "Mrs. Franklin, maybe my father could donate most of the money for church. Don't you think so, Mother?"

Alice flashed her daughter a dumbfounded look. "Well, I . . . couldn't speak for your father . . ." Her answer dangled in the pregnant silence of the room.

"But that would take all the joy and purpose out of having our yearly church bazaar in the first place, April." Mary voiced her disapproval, puffing up her stout bosom.

155

"She's right, April. The community looks forward to the bazaar every year." Alice seemed to have found her voice again.

April's face colored pink, and she sat back in her chair.

"As I was saying, there's much to do in preparation. I'll need someone to head up a committee of able-bodied men to see that the booths are erected. Do I have any volunteers?" Mary scanned the room.

"I can see to that," Sara said. "Charles is very handy with a hammer, and I'm sure we can recruit other members to help out when they hear that there's food involved." She laughed heartily, and others joined in.

Mary flashed Sara a grateful smile. "Wonderful. Ladies, it's not too soon to decide what you can contribute to help out. Any needlework, such as quilts, aprons, etc., will be needed, and of course, any fruit preserves and jellies are always a bestseller. And I hear that Crystal makes a delectable apple pie."

"Who told you that?" Crystal grinned with modesty.

"I did." Everyone turned to look at Flo, whose ample frame draped over the edge of her chair. Her dress sagged like a swing between her spread legs. "Carmen told me herself." She fanned her flushed face with her apron. "Told me she just might garner my blue ribbon."

"That's not likely. We all know Flo's Café has the best pie in these parts," April blurted out.

"And just what is your specialty, April?" Crystal asked, sipping her coffee.

April gave her a smug look. "Oh, I'm accomplished at a good many things." April's mother shifted nervously in her chair.

Emily stood and began collecting coffee cups, apparently trying to divert the growing tension. "Ladies, we'd better get on with the job at hand. We should be able to get this quilt top pieced and then break for lunch, which Flo has graciously provided for us today from her café."

The morning flew by, and the group of women chattered, laughed, and traded stories while their fingers rendered perfect tiny stitches on a basket pattern quilt. Crystal enjoyed this new feeling of friendship, of women working with a single purpose that derived pleasure at the same time. But at times throughout the day, she caught April watching her.

While Emily and Beth spread blankets over the grass for their guests, Flo passed a large box of fried chicken around, and the women had their lunch under a large cottonwood tree. The subject of a bridal shower for April came up, and a cloud descended over Crystal's otherwise bright day.

"I would like to give April a shower soon, and you're all invited," Mary remarked.

April's head shot up. "Oh, how thoughtful. Thank you."

"You're welcome."

Flo leaned over and whispered in Crystal's ear, "The reason Mary even considered it at all was for her dear friend Alice. Certainly not for her snooty-nosed daughter, who has everything in the first place."

Crystal didn't respond. Gossip was not ladylike, and while she didn't care for April, she didn't want to talk about her either.

"The store will be a little cramped for space, though," Mary continued.

Crystal wanted April to know that it didn't make any difference who she married, so she offered her ranch to have the shower at. Emily and Beth exchanged quick looks but said nothing.

"Are you sure?" Mary asked.

"Quite. In fact, I insist. Just let me know what week you decide." Crystal looked over at April and said, "Has a date been set for the wedding?"

"No, but I'm sure it'll be soon. You'll be the first to know." April continued picking at the chicken leg on her plate.

Flo licked her fingertips and wiped her mouth, then shot Crystal a quizzical look. "Reckon that'll be after the roundup then. Luke said you're going on the trail drive, Crystal."

An audible gasp sounded from April. "What? Why would you want to go on a cattle drive?"

Did he tell Flo *everything*? "I want to learn ranching from the ground up," Crystal replied.

"A trail drive can be very dangerous, dear." Sara clicked her tongue against the roof of her mouth.

"I intend to be careful. Luke and Rusty know what they're doing. I'm already learning how to handle the horses and the cattle—enough to have a lot of respect for them."

The somewhat mollified Sara pursed her lip into a tight, thin line. "Do be careful. A stampede can get mighty out of hand. Men are sometimes gored by frightened steers."

"I'm sure she'll be looked after. And she'll be in the company of some mighty fine-looking men," Beth declared.

Mary and Emily laughed, but April obviously didn't see the humor at all. "Still, you really don't have any business out on a cattle drive alone with a group of men." It was obvious that she meant Luke.

"I promise to mind my p's and q's, April," Crystal teased.

Flo chuckled. "Yours are not the ones she's worried about."

April stood, brushing the crumbs from her skirt with her long, thin fingers. "Ma, we'd better get a move on. Luke promised to ride over tonight for dinner."

"Dear, you didn't tell me he was coming." Alice's brow furrowed.

April appeared flustered and started gathering her things. "Well, perhaps I forgot to mention it. But now you know," she snapped at Alice.

Crystal felt a sudden pang for the delicate Alice. Maybe it was the way April spoke to her with that dictating voice. She would never have talked to her mother the way April did. As if Alice couldn't think for herself. She was beginning to dislike April more every minute. In her heart Crystal knew that she should be at peace as much as possible with all people, but it was not going to be easy with April.

The sunny afternoon came to a close with Alice and April's departure, and soon afterward, Mary and Flo, who had ridden in together, followed suit. Crystal helped the Johnson girls pick up the remains of their picnic, then prepared to leave.

"I enjoyed the day, Mrs. Johnson," Crystal said, giving her a quick hug.

"Call me Sara, that way I don't feel so old."

"In that case, I shall. I hate for the day to end."

"Me too." Emily sighed. "I was hoping to get a chance to talk with you."

An idea quickly formed in Crystal's head, and she suggested that Emily ride back with her and spend the night. "That is, if you can spare her, Sara."

"Oh, please, Mama, could I?" Emily pleaded.

"Well . . . I suppose we can do without you for one day. What do you think, Beth?"

"Let her go, Ma. I'll tend to her chores. Besides, I think there's someone at Aspengold she wants to see." Beth rolled her eyes upward with a knowing look.

"Beth!" Emily looked horrified, and her face flamed paintbrush red.

Sara ignored the comment. She waved her hands toward the door. "Go on, get your things. Crystal doesn't have all day to stand here lollygagging."

Luke and the boys were sprawled across the front porch, some in rockers, others on the steps, when the wagon turned down the drive to the house. Luke sat on the porch rail, leaned against the stout post, and chewed on a toothpick, hat pulled down across his eyes. Seeing Emily in the wagon, he shot a look in Jube's direction to observe his reaction. Jube stiffened momentarily but removed his dusty hat and smoothed his unruly hair. Crystal's bubbling laughter drifted ahead of her. She appeared to be in a much better mood today than usual. He wished he knew why it was that when women got together, they always found something to laugh about.

Springing down from the wagon, Crystal surveyed the group. "Looks like you boys are waiting for the cook. I brought home a guest, so supper will be a little late tonight."

Jube hurried forward and helped Emily with her carpetbag.

"What a nice surprise." He took the bag from Emily, and she

160

gave him a shy smile when he took her elbow. "This is worth waiting for supper any day."

Crystal stripped off her leather gloves and turned to Curly. "Please see to the buggy while we get supper going." Turning to Luke, she advised, "Better get a move on, Luke. I believe April is expecting you for dinner tonight, and I don't believe she likes to be kept waiting."

Luke swung his long legs over the porch rail and pushed back his hat. His eyes narrowed. "Tonight? I don't remember telling her that."

"It's perfectly all right to forget things when one is in love," Crystal said.

"Thanks for the reminder," he said sarcastically, and moved in the direction of the barn.

He was tired and didn't feel like riding over to the Rocking M tonight. But he supposed he must in order to stay in good graces with McBride. At least he would get a good meal.

Sometimes April irritated him with her clinging. He wasn't about to vanish into a vapor. Luke didn't like it when women clung, and he didn't want to feel owned. When he was with her, he sometimes felt like he had no breathing room.

Funny, somewhere along the line his feelings for her had taken a different turn. He had always admired her way with horses, and she was accurate with a gun. She wasn't afraid of anything, always figuring she could do anything as good as or better than most men could.

Maybe that was it. He decided that April was a bit arrogant and high-strung. Luke blamed McBride for giving in to her every whim. Then his thoughts strayed to Crystal, whose silvery laughter came from the kitchen as he made his way to the barn for Buck. *All soft and feminine. Very feminine.* She exuded charisma, and her laughter was infectious, making people want to be around her. *Stop it, Weber. You've made a bargain, and you're going to keep it.*

Luke always enjoyed Josh's company, and conversation was never lacking between them. April hovered close by after dinner. They had coffee in the parlor, and he felt himself relax as he listened to Alice playing the piano with a faraway look in her eyes. Josh excused himself shortly after they'd had coffee.

McBride smiled at his beautiful daughter and asked, "Have you young people decided on a date for the wedding?"

"Oh, Daddy . . . we haven't had much time to talk about it, have we, Luke?" She placed her hand on his arm.

"Maybe we should take a stroll and discuss it. How does that sound, April?" Luke took her hand.

McBride answered for her. "Yes, you two run along. Enjoy this fine weather while it lasts. Alice, I'm about ready to turn in." He gave Alice a decided look, signaling the close of the evening. Closing her music, she rose and bade Luke good evening, then obediently followed McBride up the stairs.

Luke and April strolled toward the garden in the cool evening shadows. Linking her arm through Luke's, April leaned close enough that he could smell her perfume. Her long, slender fingers stroked his forearm.

"Luke, don't you find me attractive?" She stopped walking and turned to face him with a pouting look.

"Well . . ." He hesitated. "Sure I do." The moonlight had turned her blonde hair into golden streaks the color of ripened wheat, and he reached up and stroked her hair.

"Then why don't you kiss me? You haven't in a very long time." Her tall frame swayed against his.

His strong arms pulled her to him, and he bent to press his lips hard against her slightly parted ones. Her lips responded to his, and she pressed harder against his long frame, encircling his neck with her arms. A small groan escaped her lips, and at once he withdrew her arms and pushed her away from him. He hadn't felt even a flicker of desire. What was the matter with him?

"I'm sorry. I didn't mean to do that." Luke swayed, and his mouth felt dry. His head was spinning with too many thoughts.

"Was I complaining?" she asked flirtatiously. "It's very normal between engaged couples to express themselves so." Luke realized she probably had taken his abruptness as a sign to quell his mounting desire. "I don't want you to stop," she murmured.

"Your father would skin me alive, and I have no wish to become one of his trophies mounted above his fireplace." With a firm grip he took her elbow and guided her along the garden path back to the porch. "Besides, I'd better leave. It's getting late. Some of us have to work."

"Well, you won't have to for long. I'll see to that. Our days and nights will be of our choosing. You'll have all the free time you want."

"April, I think you'd better understand something here and now." He stopped and turned her to face him. "I like to choose what I do and when I do it. No one is going to tell me how I spend my time."

"Shh . . . you don't have to yell, Luke. We'll work it out."

"There's nothing to work out. I–I have to be going." He untied his horse's reins from the porch railing and in one fluid motion was on Buck's back. He tipped his hat and looked down at her. "Be seeing you."

On the ride back home, Luke tried to clear his head of churning thoughts of April. He realized they had never gotten around to setting a date, and he was somewhat relieved. What had he gotten himself into? He was nuts to think he would feel passion in their kiss, but he'd had to prove it to himself. The problem was he knew she felt desire for him. He thought he could make it work, but now he just didn't know. *April's too scrawny. Crystal's curvaceous. April's a tomboy. Crystal's feminine. April's cool and calculating. Crystal's friendly and vivacious. April's rich. Crystal's poor.* Ah, and there it was, he admitted to himself. Marrying April meant he'd get the land he'd always wanted, and land had to be worth more than any woman . . . or was it?

Good grief, man. Stop this. You can't have everything. Besides, Crystal had Drew waiting for her—and then there was Josh. But Luke knew there was something different in Crystal that he couldn't put his finger on. He rubbed his brow and sighed. He was tired of thinking.

Since Kate's death there had not been a lot of laughter around the ranch, but tonight there had been gaiety and foolishness as the cowboys tried to impress both Crystal and Emily. After supper they played checkers with much cheating and uproarious hilarity, until Kurt was declared the undefeated champion. Now they had retired to the front porch, and it was growing late and chilly. Jube pulled up a rocker close to Emily's side, making it perfectly clear to the others that he wanted no interference from them.

"Miss Crystal." Curly cleared his throat. "Remember you promised to play your Autoharp for us?"

"Oh, please, Crystal," Emily implored.

"Well, I guess now is as good a time as any." Crystal was gone a moment, then returned with her case.

The talking ceased as she began to play soft and low. She sang a lover's tale with a clear, lyrical voice, and her audience watched and listened with rapt attention. Curly looked as if he'd died and gone to heaven as he watched her face in the moonlight. Rusty leaned back in his chair and puffed on his pipe with a faraway look in his eyes.

"Bravo!" Kurt exclaimed when she had finished, and the group applauded. "What a lovely voice you have. Please, do us the honor of another song."

Luke figured everyone had retired since it was so late, but instead he was greeted with the most enchanting sound he'd ever heard and realized that someone was singing. As he drew closer to the house, he could faintly make out Crystal's shape on the porch, her Autoharp on her knees. What a beautiful silhouette she made with the moonlight touching her hair. The faint glow of the drovers' cigarettes lent just enough light to illuminate her

166

face as her small hands strummed the instrument. He felt a lurch in his chest.

Crystal finished the song and was glad it was dark so no one could see her blush from their obvious pleasure. Her breath quickened as Luke's spurs jangled loudly on the porch steps.

"Don't stop on my account."

"I wasn't," Crystal said. She proceeded to open her case and place the instrument inside, hoping she looked composed. "It's very late, y'all." She smiled at the boys. "Emily and I are turning in."

Jube cast a quick look at Emily. "Aw, we were just starting to have fun," he teased.

All the cowhands shuffled off in the direction of the bunkhouse, with the exception of Jube and Luke.

Emily touched Crystal on her sleeve. "Crystal, I'll be back in a little bit. I told Jube I'd go for a short walk with him, if that's okay." Emily couldn't contain the smile on her face, and Crystal shooed them on their way.

After they were out of earshot, Luke turned to Crystal. "You have a pretty voice. I'm sorry I missed the performance."

"Well, Mr. Weber, the hour appears to be very late for a visit now, so if you don't mind . . ." She started for the door, but he stepped in front of her. She could smell April's perfume still clinging to his clothes, and her throat felt dry. She didn't want to think about April in his arms.

Luke reached up and stroked her cheek. "Crystal," he murmured in a husky voice. He took a step closer as if to pull her to him. Crystal wavered between taking a step toward him and running into the house, but she only stood there. She could faintly make out his face in the darkness.

"Don't, Luke." Crystal pulled back. "I can smell April's perfume still on you."

Luke took another step forward, with his hand holding her elbow. "I only wanted to kiss the lips of such a beautiful voice."

Crystal wished that he would wipe that stupid grin off his face. "Do you even remember that you are betrothed to another? Have you so quickly forgotten that you will soon pledge to honor, trust, and love only April forever?"

His face sobered. "Who made you chief? Of course I care about April. You just looked so sweet standing there on the porch in the moonlight that I guess I lost my head."

So she had guessed right. He really did love April. Her spirits were dashed. With a sinking feeling she yanked her arm free, turned sharply on her heel, and carried her case through the door, closing it with a bang. She was shaking as she leaned with her back against the door. She hated the way she was feeling now. Part of her wanted to smooth the lock of dark hair away from his forehead and touch his thick moustache, while part of her wanted to rail against him and everything he stood for. She didn't understand him at all. One minute he acted as if he really liked her, and another minute he berated her capabilities or the way she dressed and cooked. Yet she continued to feel painfully aware of his charm and rugged good looks. And she had almost let him kiss her. Again.

Chiding herself for even being attracted to such a man, she decided to turn down Emily's covers and get ready for bed herself.

168

The cool night air did little to clear Luke's head as he lay in his bed staring up at the knotholes in the pine beams. He couldn't get Crystal's dark hair out of his mind. He wondered what it would be like to snuggle with her on a cold Colorado night, with her long hair unpinned and spread out on the pillow next to him. He mentally shook himself. She'd made it pretty clear that he was nothing more to her than any other cowpoke that had only a horse and a bedroll to call his own. She, on the other hand, was educated and had previously led a genteel way of life. Yep, all manners and charm. And yet there was something about her that made him want to be better, to prove he was basically a good person. Maybe it was because he knew she had a deep faith. Luke believed in God, but with Crystal it went beyond that.

He tried to let his thoughts drift off to April, but try as he could, he could not imagine her asleep in the curve of his arm. All he could think about was Crystal's sweet singing.

After staying up half the night talking, the girls rose slowly and began preparing the morning's breakfast before church. If Crystal had doubts before of Emily's affections for Jube, they were soon dispelled. Emily had told him he could come courting, and now she asked Crystal if he could have the morning off to drive her home. Crystal readily agreed and teased Emily about the reverend tripping up over Jube's boot heels.

"He's all yours now," Emily said. Crystal shook her head, and suddenly they both burst into giggles. Last night they had vowed to push Reverend Alden in the direction of Widow Miller. They might make a perfect match.

The men trooped in for breakfast. Crystal was quiet when Luke entered and took his place at the table with barely a glance her way. Crystal returned the favor, talking amicably with Rusty and the others but ignoring Luke.

But this morning it didn't matter, for Luke had decided this weekend they would move the cattle out. He was planning to put as much distance between himself and April as quickly as possible. He needed some time, and there was a lot to be done before Friday. He only wished that Crystal would not insist on tagging along. Not only would she be in the way, but she would be a constant reminder of who was in charge and owner of the ranch. Rusty had assured him that she was well informed of the dangers, and he had personally taught her to rope and stay astride a cutting horse.

Luke grunted and poked at his food. At least she'd finally learned how to fry a decent egg and make a strong pot of coffee. He glanced up to find her brilliant green eyes boring into his for a moment before looking away.

16

Luke's boot heels pounded loudly as he took the steps to the bunkhouse two at a time the following morning. He barked orders to anyone in earshot that today they would start moving the cattle up from summer pasture. It would probably take a few days to round up the cattle for the trail drive to Denver.

Fiercely yanking his rope off the wall hook, Luke startled Jube, who was already packing his bedroll. Luke was riled, so the punchers had better give him a wide berth today.

Kurt appeared with Curly right on his heels to get specific orders. "Rusty's waiting out by the corral with the horses. Miss Crystal is packing us some grub," Luke said, reaching above his bed for his coat.

Without another word, Luke headed back outside, and the drovers followed him to where the horses were saddled and waiting. Rusty and Crystal were talking, and she handed Rusty a muslin sack that he strapped on the side of his horse.

"I'll be fine, Rusty. It'll give me time to get squared away here before the drive," Crystal was saying. "There are the cows to milk, the chickens to feed, and the wash to keep me busy."

At the very thought of her going along on the trail drive, Luke clenched his jaw but said very little and did not acknowledge her presence. He strode over to where Buck was hitched and in one fluid movement was astride his broad back. With a sideways glance he saw her slight frame standing rather forlornly as she halfheartedly raised her hand in farewell to the boys as they disappeared in a cloud of dust.

Crystal watched him until his red shirt became a dot in the distance, then swallowed the lump in her throat and turned back to the house to do her morning chores.

Managing to keep busy all day was not a problem. She was certainly learning that running a ranch and all that it entailed was no small feat. It was a never-ending job, but she relished the challenge, rarely finding herself idle for too long.

Crystal had plans to spruce up the much-neglected cabin with new curtains for the kitchen. She had been spending a lot of time in the kitchen lately and was in sore need of work space and a few more cupboards. She would ask Rusty about who would be skilled enough to build something suitable. While her aunt had the bare necessities, Kate had not been one to decorate for the pure pleasure of it. This would give Crystal something to do during the winter months, since everyone around her had stressed just how cold and confining they would become. She intended to have a flower garden planted by the time spring rolled around. These thoughts occupied her mind as she washed the laundry on the rubboard and carried it out to the clothesline.

The wind had kicked up, making it difficult to pin the sheets on the clothesline, and they whipped back into her face. The air was a bit cooler today even though the sun was out. The laundry would be dry in no time. *Good*, she thought. Tomorrow she would write up a list of things needed for her first trail drive. Rusty had already told her to pack only what was necessary and could be carried on horseback.

Her hands were numb from the cold and wet clothes. She quickly hung the clothes and scurried back inside to heat up the coffee to chase the chill away. She had just finished cleaning the kitchen when she heard the dogs start to yap. Walking to the front porch, Crystal saw Josh approaching the walk with his usual grin, and he swept his hat off in greeting when he saw her.

"Afternoon, Miss Crystal," he said as he gazed up at her.

As the wind blew softly against her calico dress, her thick hair escaped its pins. Crystal reached up to smooth her hair back and wiped her hands on her apron. Gads! She must look a fright. She had hardly been expecting anyone. "Josh, do come in."

"No thanks," he said, propping a boot heel up on the top step. "I'm on my way over to the Johnsons, but I wanted to stop by here first to ask if you'd like to ride with me to town. We could have an early dinner at the hotel, and I'd have you back before it got too late. What do you say?" His smile split his face with such warmth that Crystal couldn't think of any reason to refuse.

"All right. I'm alone tonight anyway, and I was probably going to heat up leftovers. It beats sitting here alone tonight." As soon as she said it, she regretted it. A frown replaced his smile. "I'm sorry, Josh, I didn't mean that the way it sounded."

He shrugged and placed his hat back on his thick hair. "I understand. I'll be back for you in a couple of hours. Till then." He tipped his hat, mounted his horse, and spurred it into a brisk trot down the drive.

Crystal stood watching him leave. She knew that she should be tickled that he invited her out. At least she would be getting away from this lonely place for a while, but she was not sure she wanted to encourage him in that way. He was a kind and attractive person, and somehow she knew that despite the fact he was April's brother, he was a man to be trusted, the salt of the earth. *Well, it's only dinner,* she thought. It would be nice to be treated as someone special, and Josh had a way of doing that. Good thing she had pressed her blue serge and white blouse. The jacket would be just the thing for this evening's chill.

Crystal sat across the table from Josh and laughed about his latest escape from the family's prized bull. She could hardly believe that she had had doubts about this evening.

The hotel boasted the finest accommodations that Steamboat had to offer, and the management spared no expense in its decor to make it so. Heavy rich brocade drapes of hunter green covered the windows that ran from floor to ceiling, and the tables were covered in white linen, lending a perfect complement to the scene.

As Josh reached to refill her water glass, Crystal noticed the wide expanse of his hand, tanned a golden brown. He had changed to a dark suit with a black string bow tie and a stiff white shirt that looked like it could stand on its own. As she lifted her glass, Josh's fingers brushed the back of her hand. Looking up, she saw his warm brown eyes smiling into hers. She felt her face turn pink, and she quickly looked away—right into the face of April, who was walking toward them with her parents right behind her.

Crystal blotted her mouth delicately with her linen napkin and shifted in her chair. She managed to say, "Hello, April."

"Hello, Josh." April ignored Crystal's greeting and leaned over to give his neck a squeeze. "Thought you'd be here feeding your face, but you should have told us. We would have waited for you." She shook a finger at him.

Josh smiled back at his sister and chuckled. "You know me, Sis. I love to dine with a beautiful and interesting woman. I'm just lucky to have the pleasure of Crystal's company tonight."

Crystal felt her face flush again. Alice and Jim McBride paused at their table to exchange greetings.

Alice smiled warmly at Crystal. "Crystal, you must come by some afternoon for a visit."

"That would be nice," Crystal agreed, recognizing the sincerity of the offer.

Jim stood by and puffed on his cigar. "By all means. Crystal and I may have some business to discuss," he said with a shrewd look.

"If you mean the ranch, Mr. McBride, I've already told you that I plan on keeping Aunt Kate's ranch for now. The selling of Aspengold is not up for discussion." Crystal's voice was steady and firm as she held McBride's eyes.

Alice sniffed. Her eyes darted around the room, and she looked uncomfortable.

"Humph. You may have little choice in the matter," McBride said. "But we'll leave that discussion for a later time, perhaps?" He bowed slightly and steered Alice in the direction of their table. Alice cast a feeble smile over her shoulder in Crystal's direction.

April finally turned to look at Crystal. "Well, you'll not be able to tangle with Daddy. Maybe you'd be better off giving in. The sooner you do, the quicker you can go back to Georgia, before you lose that famous peaches-and-cream complexion. Looks to me like the sun has already taken its toll."

"April, I'd like to salvage what's left of our meal, if you don't mind," Josh interrupted with clenched teeth. April seemed to know she wasn't welcome, which made her all the more contrary.

"I won't be going back," Crystal said calmly, but her heart was hammering against her chest. Why did April make her feel this way? "At least not for a while. I'm beginning to like it here. It's such a challenge for me, and I have made some good friends in such a short time."

"Excuse me," April said abruptly. "They're waiting for me." She threw Crystal a sharp look, tossed her golden curls, and sashayed in the direction of her table.

Crystal gave a sigh of relief, and Josh apologized for his family's interruption.

"Crystal, you have more manners in your little finger than April has in her entire frame." Josh's voice held obvious pride.

His comment warmed her heart. "Shall we have some coffee?" she asked. She wanted to forget the encounter, but inside she was boiling. *How dare she talk to me like that? If she thinks I'm some simpleton, she has rocks where her brains should be.*

Crystal needed to work on her temper where April was concerned. *Lord, please control my mind and tongue. I've already forgotten my promise to You.* Her hands shook as she placed the cup before Josh, but if he noticed, he said nothing.

Later that evening after Josh left, Crystal changed into her nightgown and dragged her rocker close to the fire, watching the flames dance around its burning logs. The fire, along with a cup of coffee to warm her after the ride back from town, was just what she needed on a chilly night. She was beginning to enjoy this ritual that she had started shortly after Kate's death.

After the day's chores were completed, she loved to curl up with a good book or her father's Bible, but today her mind was swirling with the confrontation with April. She read the same passage of Matthew three times before giving up. Gripping the coffee cup tightly, Crystal wondered if she was mad because April was just a disagreeable human being or because she belonged to Luke. It wouldn't be long before April would be his wife, in his embrace, and—oh, it was too unbearable to think about . . .

Since Luke was the trail boss, he had positioned Crystal with Curly on flank. Their job was to keep control of the moving cattle and chase back any strays. Kurt and Rusty were placed on drag, the worst position to hold because of the dust and the lamed or orphaned yearlings. Jube rode point with another hired cowboy to open the trail for the cattle. Luke scouted ahead for pasture and water. A young man named Slim was the wrangler. His job was to drive the remuda and have fresh mounts available to the drovers on night guard.

By the end of the first day of the trail drive, every bone and muscle screamed out for relief in Crystal's small body. Rusty told her that he calculated that they had covered ten miles across the valley today. She was too tired to stand up when Sourdough, the cookie, heaped beans and biscuits onto her tin plate. With his toothless grin, Sourdough urged her to sit down and brought her a cup of hot coffee. Gratefully she did as she was told. She found a clump of rocks and steadied her plate on her knees and watched the cookie at work.

Rusty had told her when they hired him that Sourdough

had gotten his nickname years ago because he made the best sourdough biscuits on the trail. He was always the first man to rise in the morning. Not only did he drive and pack his chuck wagon, he cooked three hot meals a day and doctored cuts and sometimes stitched a tear in a drover's shirt. His last chore of the evening was to point the chuck wagon in the direction of the North Star in order to let the trail boss know the direction for the morning.

Sourdough had been surprised that a beautiful young girl would even consider a trail drive, much less know how to drive the dogies and ride from sunup to sundown alongside the other cowboys with nary a complaint. Crystal knew that the cowboys admired her for her determination. If he expected her to comment on his cooking, though, he would be disappointed. She was too tired to eat and picked at her food.

Kurt sat down cross-legged next to her. "You doin' all right, Miss Crystal?"

He pushed his hat back off his forehead so he could look at her. She noticed Luke watching from his place in the grub line.

"I don't know if I have ever been this tired in my life," she answered. She choked down a forkful of beans. "But a hot bath would be a dream come true."

"Know what you mean. Maybe when we make it to Denver you can have one and sleep in a real bed."

Curly strode over with his plate and squatted down on one leg. Between bites he told her that he was right proud of how she handled her horse. "You really kept right up there with us." His face shone with approval.

"I had a very good teacher." Crystal smiled at Rusty. She knew

Rusty felt proud that she had done as well as she had the first day. He tipped his hat to her in thanks.

"Better get Sourdough to give you something for that sunburned face," Luke commented. "Or else you'll be hurting tomorrow."

Crystal looked over at him in surprise. That was about the first time he'd said anything to her the entire day. Since he was riding lead with the chuck wagon, she had not seen much of him. When they stopped for lunch he had avoided her, but she felt his eyes on her. No matter. She was too tired to even think about him at all.

One of the new hired hands started collecting plates for the cook and reached to take hers. She murmured her thanks. Sourdough was always the last to take a plate, making sure everyone else was served first.

The red ball of fire was fast slipping behind the majestic mountains, and the now-crackling fire was a warm welcome. One of the cowpokes pulled out his harmonica and began to play. Some sat around talking in low voices, and others began to pull out bedrolls. Kurt struck up a conversation with a drover from Texas who sat rolling a cigarette. Others, like Crystal, slumped in sheer exhaustion. Luke assigned three of the boys to take the first watch, three more at midnight, then three others after that.

"Miss Crystal, looks like you'd better turn in for the night. I'll get your bedroll and a quilt," Curly said.

"I appreciate your help, Curly. But without a pocket watch, how will the boys know when to relieve the first watch?"

"Well now, they just look up at the Big Dipper, and it'll tell them exactly what time it is." He pulled her to the edge of the camp, pointed to the sky, and told her to look for the North Star. "The Big Dipper rotates around the North Star, so when the North Star is right below the Big Dipper, we know that it's ten p.m. When it gets right above the dipper, it's midnight, and just a little above the ladle part, it's two a.m., and so on." They gazed up into the magnificent expanse of black sky dotted with twinkling stars.

"Yessiree, God had it all figured out, even for a fool." Curly continued to stare at the stars. In the western sky, clouds were moving in.

"I never knew all that . . . but it's so very simple isn't it? Simple, just like the truth of God." Her voice was reverent and hushed. "Guess I'll turn in now. Dawn will seem just a blink away."

"Yes, ma'am. It shore will."

Luke loved sleeping out under the stars. The sky was incredibly beautiful dotted with twinkling stars. He had overheard Crystal's comments about God, but he wasn't certain what she meant. He was a little curious. He knew in his heart there was a God out there somewhere like those stars high above, maybe watching. But that was as far as it went. Something about her made him feel like he was not good enough for her. What was it? Her education? He couldn't put his finger on it. She certainly never made him feel inferior. Except the night that he had come from the McBrides'. Crystal's disapproval had been very evident. He had let his feelings for her take over and wanted to kiss her. What an oaf . . . and him an engaged man. No wonder she was disgusted with him. She had more respect for April than he did.

It was strange lying here just a few feet away from Crystal and thinking about her, when he was about to be married to April. He knew that night when April insisted on kissing in the garden that there was nothing deep between them. McBride had made it apparent that he would help Luke acquire his property, but Luke was surprised that he would even let a mere foreman court his daughter, however strong willed she was. He struck Luke as a man looking out for himself, and Luke wondered what he hoped to gain.

He was getting a headache just thinking about all of it. *Time to get some sleep.* He had second watch. He pulled his hat over his eyes to shut out the light of the campfire, lay back against his saddle, and crossed his arms. The familiar yet pleasant sounds of the night were vaguely comforting. There was a gentle breeze carrying the smell of Kurt's cigar. Soon he was lulled to sleep by Kurt's distant song:

> "Last night as I lay on the prairie,
> and gazed at the stars in the sky,
> I wondered if ever a cowboy
> would drift to that sweet by and by.
> Roll on, roll on,
> Roll on little doggies, roll on, roll on.
> Roll on, roll on,
> Roll on little doggies, roll on."

Crystal thought she was dreaming but groggily realized shouting had awakened her.

"Miss Crystal! Here, put this slicker on. It looks like a hailstorm may be heading our way!" Jube shouted above the wind. "We're gonna have to ride. Slim is saddling our mounts."

Crystal struggled to a sitting position. "What's going on?"

"The cattle got spooked with the lightning."

She snatched the slicker from his hands and felt the cold, pelting rain. She was wide awake now. She slammed her hat on her head and flattened the brim to keep the rain off.

The campsite was bustling with activity, as all the cowboys, including the cook, staggered to their mounts. A jagged bolt of lightning lit up the dark sky. Slim hurried over with Crystal's horse, Rebel.

Slim swore under his breath. "The remuda has stampeded with 'em! I barely managed to hold some back!" he hollered.

Rebel reared and stomped his front hoofs, but she managed to drag herself onto him and followed Jube's lead toward the now-stampeding cattle.

"Crystal, stay left, on the outside flank, and out of harm's way!" she heard Luke yell as he spurred his mount into action to catch up with the leader of the herd.

Now hail as large as goose eggs pelted down with a vengeance. Crystal cried out in protest. She raised one hand for protection and held on to her saddle horn with the other. She winced as she felt the hail bite into her flesh. Thankfully she was astride Rebel, one of the best cutting horses from the remuda. She managed to ride faster than she had ever ridden in her life along the outside edge, keeping in check any yearling that had lost its mama, urging it and pressing it back with the gentle pressure of her knees against Rebel's flanks. She was exhilarated with the excitement in spite of the danger.

Kurt and the others were also riding flank, ignoring the slashing rain and hail and trying desperately to keep up with the bawling cattle to gain control. Cowboys whooped and yelled, "Yee ha!"

They began waving their arms while pressing in on the right side of the stampeding cattle. Luke and Rusty, along with the other hired hands riding point, managed to turn the cattle back until they slowed and were forced into a circle.

Almost as suddenly as it started, the hail stopped, but the rain continued to beat down.

Given out and beaten down now after riding herd all day, the drovers slumped in the saddle, breathing a sigh of relief. It had been a long day, made worse with little sleep.

Crystal could barely manage to make out Luke against the dark, rain-soaked sky. Curly rode up near her. "You okay?"

"Yes." She was not about to say she had multiple cuts on her arms. Together they slowed their pace and met up with Kurt and the other hands.

Rusty barked orders. "Reckon I'll meet up with Luke. Crystal, pull your bedroll up under the supply wagon outta the rain. We'll assess the damage in the morning. I'm sure we've lost some. Curly, you go back with Crystal. The rest of you come with me."

The rain was letting up now, which Crystal was grateful for. Now that the stampede was over, fatigue overcame her. She was sore everywhere, not to mention the cuts from the hail on her forearms and hands. There hadn't been time to don her gloves.

What a long day. She was starting to wonder if she should have even come on this trail drive.

She managed to remove the slicker and crawl under the wagon with a dry blanket. Right before she fell asleep, she heard Curly slip away to join the others.

Carefully easing into the saddle the next morning, Crystal was acutely aware of how sore and stiff she was. Her chambray shirt was torn in several places from the pelting hail in spite of the slicker she'd worn last night. She had tried to get the tangles out of her hair and had smoothed it as best as she could to create a long braid that she could tuck under her hat.

Breakfast had been a quiet affair with some of the cowboys still sleeping after being up most of the night. Others were wolfing down hot coffee and hardtack in a hurry to get back to the herd before they lost any more strays.

Crystal watched Luke as he made his way toward her, slapping the dust off his gloves on his thigh as he walked. "Crystal, we lost about ten head last night that either were trampled or strayed away from the herd. Thought you would want to know."

She searched his clear blue eyes for clues as to how she measured up, but he just continued to look into hers.

"Is that bad? Or is that a low number?"

"Considering the stampede and that we got control pretty quick, I'd say that it's a low number. At least Slim was able to round up all the remuda. We should be able to cross the Yampa River today if we make good time and don't run into any trouble. From there we'll pick up the trail once we cross the Colorado near Wolcott, through Bear Valley, and make our way on into Denver."

"Are you expecting any? Trouble, I mean?"

"Ma'am, you have to be prepared for just about anything. But don't you worry your pretty little head about it." He tipped his hat to her and headed back to the open range.

Crystal felt like a child who had just been dismissed. She wondered if more trouble had to do with wild animals. Of that she was very afraid. She rose from the tree stump that served as a seat and thrust her head back with a determined look. No matter, she would face every day trusting the Lord to guide her. He would meet whatever need she encountered.

The day proved to be uneventful with the now-docile longhorns following the lead bull. By lunchtime they had covered a lot of miles, and Sourdough promised them a good stew and biscuits for supper. With mouths watering, the cowboys looked forward to supper time.

The afternoon warmed up considerably. Crystal decided that she loved the low humidity and drank big gulps from her canteen as she looked out across the valley. It literally took her breath away each time she saw the Rockies. They looked invincible. Nothing in any book she'd ever read prepared her for their formidable beauty.

With a sharp pang in her heart, she wished Kate were here with her. Crystal was beginning to love the ranch, and she certainly was not planning on selling it. She hoped that with the sale of the cattle she would be able to pay the drovers, Jim McBride, and Franklin's Mercantile for the supplies that were purchased on credit. Then she would keep just the most needed cowboys.

Curly trotted up to her, interrupting her reverie. "Miss Crystal, we are nearin' the Yampa River. You need to play it safe just in case the dogies decide to make a run for the water. They won't let anything get in their way once they smell it. Make sure you're near the back of the herd, you hear? Sourdough and the chuck wagon will cross over first with Luke so cookie can get set up."

She nodded her understanding and watched him turn his horse around and trot off toward the flank side. Quickly she reined her horse around, cantered to the back, and rode drag with Kurt and Rusty.

"This crossing can be tricky, but I'm sure that Luke has searched out the best spot to cross over," Rusty said as Crystal reined in alongside him. They rode in companionable silence until Kurt slowed.

"They must smell the Yampa River," Kurt said. "They're starting to turn toward the east."

"Keep your ropes handy, folks, just in case one of 'em gets stuck in the rush to the other side." Rusty wiped his brow with his bandana.

Crystal looked ahead, and sure enough, the cattle picked up speed and turned east just as Kurt had said. Even on the valley floor, dust rolled up and formed a thick cloud, forcing them to pull their bandanas over their noses and mouths in order to breathe. Bawling and bellowing, the steers were in a race to see who could get to the river first. Unfortunately, the chuck wagon's back wheels were stuck halfway in the riverbed, and Sourdough scrambled out into waist-deep water to try to lighten the load. He struggled to calm the now-exhausted horses, all the while keeping an eye on the cattle moving furiously toward the river.

On the spur of the moment, Curly and his mount splashed into the fast-moving river to lend a hand. He reached down and hauled Sourdough to safety onto the river's edge just as Luke scrambled to release the horses from their harnesses and slapped them on their haunches. They ran up the riverbank to safety.

The longhorns entered the river with tremendous speed. In

their haste, some trampled over others. The noise was deafening. Luke swung his lariat deftly overhead, looping it around the tongue of the chuck wagon. He urged his horse backward to pull the wagon out of the river, but it seemed immobile, stuck on the thick mud of the Yampa.

Curly swung off his horse and ran to the back of the wagon, pushing with his upper body to aid in Luke's efforts. Just as the wheels rose up out of the murky water, Curly tried to move out of the way of the oncoming cattle.

Crystal, Kurt, and Rusty had just come upon the chaotic scene, and they watched in horror as the steer snagged Curly and pulled him under the water as other cows thundered into the river. Slim and other cowhands ran toward the edge of the river but could only stand by helplessly, some swearing, others mute with stricken faces.

Crystal's heart squeezed hard in her chest, and momentarily she held her breath. Tears left a trail as they spilled down her dusty cheeks. How had this happened? How could her sweet friend be snatched from her so quickly? *Dear Lord*, she prayed, but no other words would come.

Late that same afternoon, sunlight dappled the leaves, creating an intricate pattern on the hastily dug mound that held Curly's body. The cowboys chose a hill not far from a cottonwood tree and, with hats in hand, paid their last respects to Curly. He had lived his short nineteen years in the truest sense of the word to the Code of the West. Those who knew him for his easygoing, cheerful nature had thought of him with much affection.

Rusty began, "Curly was kindhearted. The kinda guy that took everything in stride. Always had a good word for you and always lent a helping hand, even when he had completed his own chores. He worked at the Bar Q up in Montana when he was barely fifteen before he came to work for us." Rusty choked on his words and paused to clear his throat. He twisted his hat in his hands and continued, "He fit in well with our bunch, and we are really gonna miss him. Good-bye, my young friend." With a shaking hand, Rusty wiped the tears from his eyes.

The other cowboys were a solemn bunch. Crystal wondered if each one was thinking it could have just as easily been one of them. Some had tears in their eyes, others held back their real feelings.

"Could I say something?" Crystal asked.

Luke looked up with surprise on his face and nodded yes.

"Curly and I were talking about the stars and how God had everything planned out perfectly. In light of my conversation with him, I'd like to read from the Bible, in his honor, if that's okay."

When they had dragged Curly out of the river, Crystal had been so shaken that she'd had to pull away from the group to keep from caving in. While they dug his grave, she remembered her father's worn Bible that she had packed in her saddlebags.

"Go ahead." Luke shifted from one boot to the other.

Crystal opened her Bible and began to read from Psalm 8. " 'When I consider thy heavens, the work of thy fingers, the moon and the stars, which thou hast ordained; what is man, that thou art mindful of him? and the son of man, that thou visitest him? For thou hast made him a little lower than the angels, and hast crowned him with glory and honour. Thou madest him to have dominion over the works of thy hands; thou hast put all things under his feet: all sheep and oxen, yea, and the beasts of the field; the fowl of the air, and the fish of the sea, and whatsoever passeth through the paths of the seas. O LORD our Lord, how excellent is thy name in all the earth!' "

Crystal looked up. "Curly became a good friend to me in a very short time and treated me with such respect these past couple of months. As the Scripture that I just read says, God cares for us more than all of creation. I know his soul is resting in heaven, though his body is here. I will miss him . . ." She bent down to place a handful of wild asters on the raw mound.

"All I can add to that is, amen." Rusty placed his hat on his head, signifying that the little ceremony was over.

The cowboys began to head toward the direction of camp, talking in low voices. There would be no more work today, just night watch to maintain order of the now-docile herd.

"Crystal, that was mighty thoughtful of you." Rusty guided her by the elbow toward camp.

"Oh, Rusty. What a terrible tragedy. Life can be so cruel." Crystal wiped her nose with her soggy hankie.

"Yes, it can. I'm glad Kate didn't have to see that tragedy. She treated all the boys like her sons and hated to let any of them go during the winter months. Many times she had no choice."

"Well, one thing is certain. It makes us appreciate every day that we are given, doesn't it?"

Sourdough and the others had been able to retrieve most of what had been thrown from the wagon at the crossing in order to lighten the load. As Crystal neared the chuck wagon, she saw that Sourdough was already lighting the fires for supper. He was very subdued compared to his normal cheerful self.

"Curly lost his life while saving mine." Sourdough sighed.

"Don't blame yourself, Sourdough," Crystal said softly. "You would have done the same for him."

"I'll see to it that the men are fed and the fire is warm tonight. I owe that much to Curly."

Crystal reached out and patted the cookie's shoulder. They were all hurting.

There was an evening chill after the sun slid behind the majestic peaks that evening. Crystal drew her legs up close to her body and pulled the quilt up to her chin. She gazed into the glowing embers of the campfire and once again doubted whether she should even be here in the first place. Thinking of Curly's death just naturally brought to mind Aunt Kate and her parents.

Tears began to spill out of the corners of her eyes and slid down her cheeks. She knew God cared that her heart was hurting, but she felt the need of human contact. Someone who cared about the pain she was feeling. She was plagued with so many doubts. Doubts about her own future. Was she listening to God? Or was she doing things Crystal's way? Maybe she should sell the ranch to McBride and be done with it. But then what was she to do? If she left now, she would be admitting defeat.

"Cris . . . are you warm enough?" Luke whispered. He tenderly reached down and tucked the quilt tighter around Crystal's shoulders. The use of a nickname was endearing to Crystal and made her heart lurch.

"Sometimes the nights can get pretty cold, no matter what the daytime temperature is," he said. She knew he must have heard her crying and was just trying to think of something to say to comfort her.

Crystal sniffed and wiped her eyes on the back of her hand. "I'm colder inside right now than outside."

"Know how you feel." Luke eased his body down and sat on the ground next to Crystal.

"How could you? I've just lost my aunt and not long ago my dear father," Crystal blurted out, but she regretted saying it at once. *That wasn't nice, and you know it.*

Luke ignored her outburst and continued, his brow deeply furrowed. "Well, I lost my parents when I was young, but I still remember the feeling, and Kate was always like a mother to me. I loved her as if she *was* my mother. And now Curly. He was my friend too. But that happens sometimes on the trail. It just couldn't be helped. He was in the wrong place at the wrong time. Maybe I'm partly to blame. I should've watched out better for him."

"I'm sorry. I shouldn't have said that," she said. She leaned back and propped herself up on one elbow to stare into his eyes. "You can't blame yourself. It was an awful accident. I guess you knew him a lot longer and better than I did."

"Yes, I did, and he had a way of getting under your skin. Once Curly and me were out hunting up strays, before the winter set in and we were holed up in a line shack. It was one of those early snowstorms that can come on you without much warning out here. We spent several evenings cozying up to a nice fire, with strong coffee and yarns for entertainment." He paused, giving her a thoughtful look. "Aw . . . I'm boring you."

"No, please tell me more." She snuggled further under the quilt.

"Well," he continued, "Curly told me about the time he was out searching for strays, and when he reached the top of a ridge, he looked down into the creek. He saw a beautiful young woman bathing." Luke paused for impact. "He acted real quiet-like, so as not to let on he was watching. He was afraid to take his eyes off her because she was so beautiful. He wondered why she was in these parts so far away from anywhere, 'cause he didn't ever remember seeing her before. He had made up his mind that as soon as she finished her bathing, he'd wait till she got dressed.

Then he'd make himself known and go down to the stream to introduce himself."

Luke turned to see if Crystal was still with him. "What happened? What in the world was she doing there alone?" she asked.

"Well now, that's when the story gets good. The beautiful woman dove into the deepest part of the stream. Curly waited with bated breath for her to come up, which seemed a couple of minutes. Thinking she was in trouble, Curly started removing his boots and started running down the ridge when all of a sudden she came up for air. She slung her long hair around and dove in again. The last thing he saw was a beautiful pair of fins where her feet should have been."

Crystal laughed long and hard. "Oh, my sides hurt now."

"Had you goin', didn't I?" Luke was laughing too. It made his heart feel lighter to hear her laugh.

Crystal wiped the tears of laughter from her face with the edge of her shirtsleeve. "You did. A mermaid? Luke, honestly, did you make that up?"

"Heck no. That was Curly's story. When you spend a lot of time riding line camp, a cowboy can envision almost anything." He paused and looked into the campfire. "He was the best of this bunch."

When Luke looked back at her, Crystal's eyes were big and luminous from her tears, sparkling like jewels. He felt a pull in the center of his chest. Once again he found himself wanting to kiss the tears away, but instead he touched her on the arm.

"Try to get some sleep. Tomorrow's a new day. Things always look better in the daylight." He started to stand up, but she reached out her hand to touch his sleeve.

"Please . . . could you just sit here with me a bit . . . till I get sleepy? Unless you have first watch?" she pleaded.

He paused, then sat back down a little closer to her. "Sure . . . I have the second watch."

Crystal looked over at him out of the corner of her eye. He sat with his arms on his knees and rubbed his callused hands together absentmindedly. Large but gentle hands. Long fingers with nails in need of attention from days of grime and dirt. His jeans so worn that they looked soft. His boots dusty, the heels worn down, in bad need of replacing. *Maybe I can do that for him. He is my foreman, after all.* Then she reminded herself that he belonged to someone else. Still, she was lonely.

Maybe it was his manner and the softness of his calm and reassuring voice, or his big hands pulling the quilt about her, but she somehow felt momentarily at peace. Soon her eyes were heavy. The wind skimmed the tops of the cottonwoods, touched her face, and lulled her with its sighs into that space between consciousness and sleep.

Luke was content to be near Crystal until it was almost time for his watch. He lay back, propped himself up on his elbows, and watched Crystal until her breathing was slow and even. He wanted to hold her close like a little kitten.

He knew he should be sleeping instead of watching Crystal sleep. She lay on her side with her hands tucked under her face in sweet repose, while the wind lifted strands of her dark hair across the soft curve of her cheek. What was he going to do? He was drawn to her in a way that was new to him. Most of the time, all they did was argue. But today was different. Maybe it was because of Curly's death, but they had come together in their grief.

Luke had been quiet that evening. He hated losing Curly more than he cared to admit. He hoped Crystal was right about him being in heaven. She seemed awful sure about that.

Luke gazed at the stars twinkling in the spacious Colorado sky. Never again would he be able to look at the stars without thinking of Curly.

19

The sun was high in the crystal-blue sky as the outfitters traveled the trail carved years before by other brave souls seeking the gold of this magnificent mountain range. The view of the valley that lay behind was so splendid with conifers as the backdrop.

Now the cowboys concentrated on the task ahead. The creek beds were not deep at this juncture but were brisk and cold, something that both the cows and cowboys alike enjoyed amid the summer heat.

Crystal dismounted along with the rest of the cowboys, rolled her sleeves back, and splashed the icy creek water on her face and neck. She didn't know that a person could get so dry and dusty. Now her hands, forearms, and face glowed with a rich tan from the outdoors.

"Nothin' like cold water to refresh and cool you off on a day like today," Rusty said. He unknotted his bandana and wiped his face and beard.

"It's so invigorating," Crystal agreed. Even though this didn't compare to a real bath, it would have to do until they reached

Denver. She intended to have a long soak in a real tub once they arrived.

Luke left the grazing cattle in the meadow, reined Buck in next to where Rebel was drinking from the creek, and dismounted. Exposing his now-flattened black hair, he hung his hat on the pommel of the saddle. He scooped cold water onto his suntanned face and ignored the fact that it soaked his chambray shirt, which stuck to his chest. Once he was refreshed, he turned to his compadres.

"Rusty, I figure after we cross the river, we can push on into Bear Valley tomorrow and then into Denver. Grazing should be good there." Luke scratched his head before donning his hat.

"Whatcha figure? Two days? Three maybe?" Rusty picked up the reins of his horse, preparing to mount.

"No more, unless we run into trouble." Luke reached into his vest pocket, pulled out a stick of peppermint, and handed it to Crystal. "This'll help your dry throat."

Crystal took the stick of candy, broke it in three pieces, and popped a piece into her mouth, then offered some to Rusty. She reserved a small piece in her shirt pocket. "Mmm . . . I hope this is not going to be lunch," she joked. Impulsively she bent over to splash water on her companions, bubbling with laughter at their surprise.

Luke splashed back at her while the drovers slapped their thighs and poked one another with enjoyment, causing more fracases that led to a few being thrown into the creek, all in good-natured fun.

"All right, stop the lollygagging, and let's git them dogies 'cross the creek by noon." Rusty shook his head. "Just like a bunch of young 'uns."

Crystal smiled sheepishly at Luke, who shrugged his shoulders with resignation.

"He's right. Men, let's git them dogies movin'. We'll stop just the other side where Sourdough is already set up and have our lunch." He threw a sweet smile toward Crystal, who smiled back, her sunburned face even pinker now.

The cowboys followed the Yampa River, then veered east across the valley, pushing the steers. Here they would pick up the Colorado River. And what a sight it was. Today was a sparkling, fresh morning, the kind that gives one joy at being alive. The jagged walls of the red-rock canyon rose up from the Colorado River, towering high above the riverbed, while the cowboys were careful to pick their way over rocks and bunchgrass along the river's edge.

Once they were between the canyon walls, darkness belied the sun, though it was mid-morning. Luke had scouted ahead, knowing exactly where they would cross downstream after the whitewater rapids mellowed out. White water could make crossing the river a nightmare, something they could all do without. He did not want a repeat of Curly's unfortunate incident. He knew that once they crossed the river, a lush meadow lay on the opposite side not too far ahead. That's where they would stop for their noon meal. Looking at his surroundings now, he knew they were in the best place for crossing and motioned with a circle of his arms for the crew to split into even numbers on each side of the herd.

Luke reined Buck in, tilting his hat back to watch the small band of cowboys urging the cows on either side to ford the river. He had to admit to himself that Crystal was carrying her weight on this drive, and he was secretly proud of her. She rode her mount in one fluid motion like one bred to horseback, never minding the splashing water and danger of a steer's horn. Watching her was a stunning thing. She yelled and waved her hat along with the others, encouraging the cattle into the river's edge.

She had become an asset to the trail drive, and her skills amazed him. Would April be as adept? April was an excellent horsewoman, but if she was working with steers, the dust, and the danger of being on the trail, she probably would not have held up as well as Crystal.

He enjoyed the fun they'd had earlier. He liked that about Crystal. She had a playfulness about her that was sweet and innocent. Now he was poignantly wishing he had met up with her before he'd met April.

Well, it was a done deal now, no matter what his feelings were. He and Jim McBride had made a deal. Luke would get the property he wanted on the Blue River. Luke would miss Crystal once she went back to Georgia, but that fellow Drew would probably be waiting for her. Besides, he figured that it didn't matter what he thought. Better that he keep his mind on the chore at hand.

Though it took a full hour, it couldn't have been a smoother crossing than if Luke had drawn it out on paper. The cattle, now tired and thirsty, entered the cold river. It wasn't long before the tail end of the herd crossed to the other side without a hitch, fanning out now in the meadow to graze in a comfortable fashion.

The remuda was a little less inclined to cross, but Slim was skilled in horse handling. He used gentle pressure from the lead reins to coax the horses to swim and then led them to the other side.

Lunch was a quick affair of beans and biscuits, but Sourdough promised them a cherry pie for dessert, which gave the drovers something to look forward to. Weary and bedraggled, the men got fresh mounts again, eager to get on the trail to finish out the day.

The sun beat down on Crystal, scorching her back and shoulders through her shirt. Up ahead, she saw Luke reclining on a huge boulder, taking a break, and she decided to do the same. Dismounting Rebel, she started toward Luke but stopped dead in her tracks. There on the boulder right behind him slithered a copperhead snake, obviously enjoying the warmth of the rock. While Luke wiped his face, he watched his men off in the distance dutifully pushing the cows and rounding up any strays.

Crystal looked around. There was not another cowboy in shouting distance. Crystal knew she would have to take matters into her own hands. Could she make a clear shot from this far off? She would have to try. She took a deep breath.

Shaking now, Crystal pulled her pistol from her saddle and stepped closer with as much ease as she could muster without making a sound.

"Luke," she whispered, "don't move a muscle." She pulled the trigger back and prayed that she would hit her mark, then fired at the coiled snake now poised to strike. Her mark was dead center.

Luke jumped three feet at the sound. He sprang off the boulder just in time to see the snake flail, momentarily spring up as if hit by lightning, and fall back down onto the rock. It slid lifelessly to the ground. "Jumping jackrabbits!" He stared down into the grass. "Lucky for you that was a good shot. You could have killed me, Crystal."

Crystal was rooted to the spot, amazed at her own skill. "It was nothing," she joked, a nervous giggle bubbling up. She leaned over to make sure the snake was dead. "I hope he was a poisonous snake. I've never shot one." Crystal laughed again. "Other than at practice, I've never shot anything."

"He was poisonous, all right. I'm glad you came up when you did just now, or I'd be pushing daisies instead of enjoying that cherry pie Sourdough promised. I reckon he liked sunbathing on that warm boulder."

"Yes, well, this sun is just about to bake my brains right through my hat."

"Crystal, thanks. I guess Rusty taught you well. I owe you."

Crystal blushed under the deep glow of her tan and replaced her gun. "You don't owe me a thing. Glad I was able to save your skinny hide."

"Aw . . . I didn't know you cared." He patted his hand over his heart. Turning aside, he kicked the limp snake with the toe of his boot. "He was a big one."

"I can't afford to lose my foreman now, can I? Not this close to the end of the trail. There's the ranch at stake here." Crystal allowed him to assist her back up into the saddle. Everything about him sent warning bells off in her head with his nearness. His shoulder briefly touched her leg once she was in her seat.

"What was that shootin' about?" Rusty came rushing over at a fast clip, reining in his mount to spin around in a semicircle.

"Crystal just saved my hide, that's what."

Rusty shook his head. "That could have been a deadly situation. Atta girl, Crystal. I told you she was a quick learner." He glanced at Luke.

"Guess I've earned my piece of pie tonight, huh?" The mere prospect of such a rare delicacy on the trail made Crystal smack her lips. She hoped it would meet her standards of pie making.

"All right, enough yakkin' about it. Let's hit the trail so we can wind this afternoon up before dark. I'm bone tired." Luke mounted Buck, signaling the conversation was over.

True to his word, Sourdough had pies cooling off to one side of the chuck wagon as the cowboys hurried through their usual meal of stew and johnnycakes. Later, Crystal enjoyed assisting Sourdough in cutting and serving generous slices of pie along with strong cups of coffee.

Each night the air was colder, but the campfire was a welcome spot as they sat around licking the last specks off their forks. The conversation naturally turned to the day's events, with the incident of the snake being the hot topic.

"I hear tell that was mighty fine shootin' out there, Miss Crystal," Kurt said.

Crystal was a bit uncomfortable with all the attention she was receiving, but she sensed they all had come to respect her endurance after grueling days in the saddle. Holding on to the ranch was her driving force, and without it she didn't know if she would have been able to complete the trail drive.

"I would have done it for any one of you," she said. She collected plates and placed them in sudsy water, then tried to change the subject. "Sourdough, that was almost the best pie I've eaten in a long time."

Sourdough shuffled over to the washtub, beaming as he cleaned up. "Almost? Do I take that as a compliment, missy?" But the cowboys continued their teasing, and Crystal didn't have a chance to respond about the pie.

"Did you feel that bullet whiz behind you, Luke?" Slim teased.

"Matter of fact, I did. I wasn't sure if she was shooting at me or something else." That brought a round of laughter from the men.

"I always said it's good to have a woman at your side," Jube added to their comments. "I think you should show your thanks to Crystal by putting her up in the best hotel in town when we get to Denver, instead of that tiny Evening Shade, where we always stay."

Crystal raised her eyebrow with interest at the talk of accommodations.

Rusty added, "That would be the Oxford, across the street from Union Station. I heard they have fine dining too." He winked at Crystal.

"That's true. They opened up last October. It's a grand building." Kurt threw a glance in Luke's direction.

"How about it, Luke?" Crystal's aching body cried out for the softness of a real bed, but she thought it would be selfish to have a bed when the other cowboys didn't.

Luke seemed to know when he was beaten. "Okay, I owe you . . . but just one night. If you want to stay longer, you're on your own."

"Ooh . . . I can hardly wait." Crystal pulled her arms overhead to stretch her back muscles. "But tonight I'll just settle for going to bed early." She turned to retrieve her bedroll, then laid it out neatly not far from the fire. Night temperatures dipped in spite of the warm days.

Jube pulled out his harmonica and played haunting tunes while the rest agreed on who would have certain watch times. They divided up carrying out various nightly duties. Crystal's eyes became heavy as she snuggled down into her quilt, thinking pleasantly of the bustling streets of Denver.

Two days later the group, tired but looking forward to some excitement and a taste of Denver, picked their way along the last leg of trail. The sand and dust was thick, the air dry. They had followed Clear Creek and later the Platte River alongside the sprawling cow towns nestled in the valley. To the south of them lay Pikes Peak, and though its imposing sight looked close, it was still sixty miles away. To the northwest lay Longs Peak, its sharp outline visibly imposing against the clear sky.

After a brief respite following the cattle crossing of the Platte River, they saw low brick buildings begin to crop up in the outlying areas. By late afternoon they would be at the rail station, where Luke and Rusty would wrangle a deal to sell the beef as quickly as possible.

"That was about the fastest deal I ever made, Miss Crystal." Rusty clapped his gloves against his thigh with obvious enthusiasm.

"*Who* made the deal?" Crystal poked her finger into Rusty's chest.

"Well . . . Mr. Hunter was taken with you, Miss Crystal, and you drove a hard bargain. Although how he could tell you were a woman under all that dirt and grime, beats me." Luke chuckled.

Crystal pursed her lips coquettishly and fluttered her eyelids, not at all embarrassed at the way she had handled the sale. In fact, she would now be able to pay her punchers and her debts.

"I'll go pay the boys. Luke, you walk Miss Crystal over to the Oxford like you promised. We'll see to the horses. I'll meet up with you later," Rusty said.

"Shall we?" Luke offered his arm to Crystal as he picked up her carpetbag. "It's about a few short blocks to the hotel."

Placing her hand under his arm, she felt an unexpected tangle of emotions. If April were here, she would be clawing Crystal's eyes out, but since she wasn't, Crystal was going to enjoy the moment.

The Oxford Hotel, though five stories tall, did not impress Crystal very much from the outside. But once inside, Crystal clapped her mouth shut and stifled her outright delight so as not to seem lacking in manners. The beautiful, rich oak furnishings and marbled floors were gleaming. A crackling fire beckoned warmth to patrons from its ornate oak fireplace, which was flanked by overstuffed tapestry chairs. A Victorian settee in rich gold brocade sat facing the fire, inviting guests to converse. Velvet drapery with deep swags adorned the windows overlooking the burgeoning metropolis that had started out as a mining town.

Crystal was elated as they strode straight up to the clerk at the front desk, who peered over his spectacles at them with an inquiring look. Crystal felt his gaze, knowing full well that she must appear a little the worse for wear with her worn chambray shirt, pants tucked into her boot tops, and hair trailing down her back. *Not a proper lady!* his look said.

"Yes?" He removed his glasses and waited.

"We'd like a room, please." Luke seemed to ignore the clerk's stare.

The clerk cleared his throat. "Of course. You must pay in advance, er, Mr. and Mrs. . . ."

"Oh, no." Luke waved his hand. "Just one person. One night."

Embarrassed, Crystal spoke up. "I'm Crystal Clark. I'd like a hot bath sent up as soon as possible to wash away the trail grime."

The clerk cocked one bushy eyebrow but said, "No problem, ma'am. Will you be dining with us as well?"

"That sounds heavenly." Crystal turned to Luke. "Would you and Rusty care to join me at seven?"

Luke hesitated, so she added, "I'm paying."

"If you insist." He started counting out the money for the night's stay.

"Excellent. I'll meet both of you at seven o'clock sharp," Crystal said. A bellman appeared at her side and guided her up the carved oak staircase as Luke arranged for dinner.

Crystal was delighted with her exquisite room on the fourth

floor. She waited for the maid to prepare a hot bath and stood looking out her own private window.

What a wonderful change from sleeping on a bedroll under the stars. She was thrilled that she had her own water closet and electricity provided by the hotel's own power system. She would enjoy this night, she was sure.

There was a wonderful view of the bustling activity of 17th Street below with vendors, streetcars, horses, and buggies. A stroll after dinner would be a pleasant outing, if she could stay awake. The gaslights were already casting a soft glow against the backdrop of the mountains that lay west of Denver in the twilight. Crystal could just imagine how beautiful it would look at Christmastime with a blanket of snow.

"Ma'am, your bath is ready now. Would you like assistance?" The maid stood near the bathroom with her hands clasped and awaited further instructions. It was apparent from her disapproving looks that she did not consider Crystal a lady.

After a slight hesitation, Crystal shook her head, excused the young girl, and started peeling off her grimy clothes. A few months ago she would have expected and accepted assistance, but that seemed long ago now.

"Ahh . . ." Crystal groaned out loud when she stuck her feet in the tub and then scooted down as far as she could until the soap suds were up to her neck. *Now this is close to heaven!* This would ease the sore muscles and make her feel like a woman once again. She had packed her blue serge dress and hoped it would be appropriate for the dining room. Her mouth was watering at the thought of dining out instead of by the campfire. She lay back and closed her eyes while the hot water did its magic, and she was soon fast asleep.

Pounding on her door awakened her one hour later. The bath water had long ago become cold. "Yes? Who is it?" she called out.

"Rusty, Miss Crystal. I'm here to fetch you for dinner as ordered by Luke. Is everything okay?"

Crystal was mortified. She must have slept a very long time. She reached for her towel, almost slipping down in the process, and leaned against the door. "I'm so sorry. I guess I fell asleep. Give me twenty minutes, and I'll be right down."

"He's runnin' late too. I'll be waitin' in the parlor."

"I'll hurry."

Luke snapped open his pocket watch and checked the time. He had half an hour before he was to meet Rusty and Crystal for dinner at the Oxford. He had bathed and shaved, then donned a clean shirt and new waist overalls before strapping on his thick black belt with its huge silver buckle. Then he tied a thin black necktie in a neat knot around his throat and threw on his black leather vest and hat.

He looked down at his boots. He had tried to polish them up a bit, but they had seen too much wear and tear. As an afterthought, he decided to wear his duster. Once the sun slipped below the mountains, it would be much colder. He hoped they could get back to Aspengold before snow closed the passes.

Well, who are you trying to impress, anyway? he reminded himself. He argued in his mind that it was because he'd been without a real bath in a long time.

He had to hurry or he wouldn't have time to meet with Mr. McCarthy. He wondered what an attorney could possibly want with him.

Luke made his way down the boardwalk to the attorney's office, his spurs making a faint jingling sound.

A bell jangled above the door as it swung open when Luke entered the small, stuffy, book-lined office that smelled of cigars. Stacks of papers and books surrounded an older man with round spectacles that threatened to slide down his large, pink nose. When he saw Luke, he struggled to his feet.

"You Luke Weber?" McCarthy asked in a rich Scottish brogue. He lost no time in needless talk. Luke knew he had been expecting him and had stayed open until he arrived in Denver, as Luke had requested.

"That's right." He extended his hand to shake McCarthy's in a firm grasp. "I'm sorry that I was unable to get here until now, but we've been pushing cattle down from the Yampa Valley. I appreciate you staying open late. I must confess when I got your telegram, I wasn't sure what you wanted with me, but it sounded urgent."

"Well, matter of fact, it is. Katherine Morgan and I go way back. Have a seat." He gestured toward the chair in front of the desk. "I offer my condolences. I was very shocked to learn of her unfortunate death."

"Is this about Kate?" Luke took the proffered seat, his long legs half under the wooden desk.

"It is indeed," McCarthy said. He shuffled through the enormous stack of papers and found the one he wanted, then paused to push his glasses up. He cleared his throat. "It appears that Kate made you the sole heir of Aspengold." McCarthy looked at Luke over the top of his spectacles.

Luke jerked up in the chair and gripped the wooden armrest, his knuckles turning white. "What . . . did you say?"

"Are you hard of hearing, boy? I said you are now the owner of Aspengold. With a few stipulations, of course, but I'm sure you won't have a problem with that."

"I can't believe it. What about Crystal, Kate's niece?" Luke's mouth was dry.

"This will was written last year. It provides a Crystal Clark with a Columbine pin and the proceeds from the sale of the cattle, but that is all. A said Rusty Wendell is to have the right to live on said ranch for as long as he lives, but the five hundred acres of the land adjacent to the Blue River and its livestock belong to you now. You will, of course, have to pay taxes on the property in the spring." McCarthy clasped his hands behind his head and leaned back in his chair. "I take it that this is a surprise by your reaction."

"You could say that. I had no idea. I assumed Crystal was the rightful owner." Luke was flabbergasted.

"When we drew this up, Kate told me that you were like the son she never had. She wasn't expecting anything to happen, of course, but she did want to make certain that you were provided for. I have the necessary papers here that you will need to sign."

"I had no idea. None." Luke sat with tears in his eyes. He stared down at the worn floor, grateful that Kate would do such a thing but feeling terrible for Crystal.

"I'm sure that you will make her proud, son. Now, if you don't mind, I'd like to get your signature on this before you go, stating that I gave you a copy of the will and deed and that I discussed all this with you." He held a pen out to Luke.

With hesitation, Luke scrawled his name.

"Is Crystal Clark still at Aspengold?" McCarthy asked.

"Actually, she drove the trail drive with us, and she's in town right now."

"Is that a fact? Boy howdy. Never heard of a female going on a trail drive."

"You don't know Crystal Clark," Luke said, his voice softening.

"Do I detect a hint of interest there?" Not waiting for an answer, he continued, "Well, you'll have to tell her about the will. I'm sure she will understand. After all, Kate raised you and not her. Anyway, as Kate's attorney, I respect her decision."

Luke cleared his throat. "Actually, I'm engaged to marry April McBride. Perhaps you've heard of Jim McBride?"

"Matter of fact, I have done business with him. Quite a wealthy cattleman. Congratulations."

Luke rose and took his deed. McCarthy rose as well and shook his hand.

"Good luck to you in the future. That's beautiful land. You could always sell it to Crystal, if she was inclined to buy."

"Nope. I'll never sell Aspengold. You can count on that." Conviction was firm in Luke's voice. He bid Mr. McCarthy good day and made his way out onto the busy streets of Denver, shoving the deed deep into his vest pocket.

Darkness had settled in over the sprawling cow town as the gas streetlights began to glow. Crystal waited with Rusty at the Oxford, her toe tapping against the wooden floor. She glanced through the crowd and anxiously searched for Luke. When she spotted him, she rose to meet him. He looked dashing in his long black duster, and she thought the thin necktie added a nice touch. "Well, it's about time!"

"I'm sorry, I didn't mean to keep you waiting. I had some business to tend to that couldn't wait."

"I figured that. We've been waiting awhile, Luke Weber, and we were just about to go ahead without you. As usual, your manners are sorely lacking." Crystal's comment seemed to create immediate tension between them.

"I said I was sorry . . ." Luke sounded lame.

Rusty rose and picked up his hat. He looked at Crystal and then back to Luke.

"Now that we got all of that out of the way, let's go eat." Rusty took Crystal's arm, and she walked past Luke toward the dining room.

Crystal knew she was being silly because she had been late herself, and if the truth be known, she would still be asleep if Rusty hadn't awakened her. She couldn't help herself, though. Part of her just wanted to act indifferent to him since he became engaged, and part of her wanted him to put his arms around her and hold her fast to his broad chest. *I'm acting like a sullen child.*

Now that the cattle were sold, maybe the best thing she could do was just pay off her aunt's debts, go back to Georgia, and try to pick up her life there. Then she wouldn't have to see Luke every day. Not that he would stay at the ranch anyway once he married April.

The truth was that Crystal had come to love this wide-open land, its mountains, and its people. She had accomplished something—saving Aspengold—and felt useful. Crystal knew that God had given her this peace and sense of belonging here because nothing happened to her without God's involvement. She vowed in her heart to spend some time alone praying about her dilemma.

"Ma'am?" The waiter bowed as he pulled out her chair.

Crystal's wandering mind was pulled back to the present moment. "Thank you," she murmured and took her seat.

Rusty sat next to her and Luke across from her. The table was gleaming with fine Haviland china bearing the hotel's name. Finely cut glass adorned the table, along with engraved silverware lying against damask linens. A silver vase held one single red rose, and a candle's glow in the center created a soft patina over the entire setting.

Crystal felt like she was being treated like royalty the entire evening and decided not to think about anything but the two men in attendance and the delicious food. They talked about the trail drive, how pleased they were now that it was over, and the tidy sum they had made.

"Crystal, are you spending another night? This place is incredible. I saw where they have their own Western Union, barber shop, library, and pharmacy. You never even have to step foot outside and get your skirts dirty." Rusty's smile showed his approval.

"I reckon not. I don't want to be extravagant. One night will be sufficient."

Luke seemed more than a little restless as the night wore on.

Crystal thought that he was distracted. Maybe he couldn't wait to get back to April and begin planning their wedding.

"I think it's best if you and Rusty take the train as far as Central City and then the stage on back to the ranch. Jube, Slim, and I can bring our horses with the remuda." Luke's voice took on a serious tone.

"It beats riding horseback for two weeks," Crystal agreed. "But what's the hurry?"

Rusty answered, "For one thing, we will be workin' against time. It's August. The mountain passes sometimes get snow early on. Then you'd be stuck." He continued to eat every morsel on his plate, then wiped his mouth. "Time for some coffee and dessert, huh?"

Luke couldn't keep his eyes off Crystal. The candlelight made her face softer, and she looked even younger tonight. Her green eyes sparkled even as the evening wore on and her lids started drooping with fatigue. She held the fragile china cup and sipped her coffee, her every movement expressing her femininity. Her delicate lace blouse peaked from beneath her blue serge waistcoat and drew his eye to her small waist. Her skirt fell in soft folds.

What would she think if she knew Luke owned Aspengold? He couldn't ask her to leave. Where would he go when he was about to marry April? This would change everything. How could he leave the only place that he ever knew as home?

A myriad of thoughts about April were beginning to gnaw at him. Luke admitted that he'd led April on. He *had* liked her in the beginning. But now he wasn't sure he could follow through with the wedding. Now he realized why McBride would give him a big parcel of land near the Blue River—because he thought he would eventually own Aspengold. Try as he might, Luke could not see April living there.

Now the tables were turned. Somehow he couldn't bring himself to tell Crystal about the deed to the ranch. Maybe because he didn't want her to leave. Crystal was like a magnet pulling him in. Then again, Luke didn't think he could live up to her standards. He hadn't always made the right choices. Just look what he had done with April. He should have told April when his feelings started changing.

But when had his feelings changed? If he was honest with himself, it was when he had helped Crystal down from the buckboard the day she had arrived, fresh as a Columbine flower and such a greenhorn. But over the last month he had changed his mind on that note when he saw how capable she could be.

While he was excited and honored that Kate had left the ranch to him, he felt bad for Crystal. Well, she more than likely would go back to Georgia. He would have to get used to the idea. He would tell her once they got back to the ranch.

Crystal's low-throated laugh caused Luke's heart to skip a beat, and he tried to refocus on the conversation. The evening was coming to a close, and Rusty and Crystal stood up to leave.

"Okay, y'all. I'll be ready to leave first thing in the morning," Crystal promised. "I'll go straight to bed, and I promise to be ready this time."

Rusty and Crystal laughed, and Luke wondered if he was missing something as he followed them into the lobby.

Luke took his time walking back to his hotel while Rusty saw

Crystal back to her floor. He wanted to get some fresh air. He walked toward Union Station to see what time the train left in the morning. With his thoughts in turmoil, Luke paused at the end of 17th Street to gaze up at the stars twinkling with brilliance in the cold night air. He thought of Curly and felt genuinely saddened. What had she said? *God knows every one of us by name like the stars in the heavens.* Maybe it was time for him to have a heartfelt talk with the man upstairs . . .

The outlying cottonwoods and aspens were ablaze with fall color when Crystal returned to Aspengold. In her absence the Johnsons had split and stacked firewood as high as the rooftop. Luke, Jube, and Kurt would be returning in a few days on horseback with the remuda in tow. She was glad that Rusty insisted she travel back with him on the train to Central City and later the stagecoach the rest of the way home. Crystal was happy to be back at the huge log house, and even more so to see Carmen, who bustled with excitement in the kitchen at her return.

"You look different, señorita." Carmen surveyed her friend's tanned skin and leaner form. "You've lost a few pounds."

"Have I?"

"Don't worry, it makes you look taller."

"Good. I always wanted to be a bit taller." Crystal giggled. "Pour us a cup of coffee and tell me what's been happening in my absence. When did you come back?" Crystal pulled up a chair while Carmen retrieved the cups from the cupboard and filled them.

"I came back two days ago. My sister had a healthy baby, and my mother is feeling better."

Crystal loved the way Carmen rolled her r's. "I'm happy to hear that. I've missed you. I feel like I've been gone for months."

"Tell me . . . what was it like on the trail?"

Crystal blew on the steaming coffee and noticed her broken nails curled around her cup. "It was the hardest thing I have ever done in my life. But at the same time, it was an experience I will never forget. I learned a lot, Carmen, about the cowboys and about myself." Crystal sighed.

"I heard about Curly. So sad . . . he was so special." A tear slid down Carmen's face, and she looked down at her hands in her lap with a deep sigh.

"Carmen, did you have feelings for Curly?" Crystal wondered how in the world she had missed that. She chided herself for being too busy trying to run a ranch to notice their budding romance.

"Sí, señorita. I think he may have felt the same toward me. He was very kind to me, and I thought he was such a good man. We were going to go to the church bazaar together."

Crystal leaned toward Carmen, covered her hand with her own, and looked into Carmen's luminous brown eyes. "I'm sorry, Carmen. When I first came to Aspengold, I thought it was Luke you had your heart set on. I guess that's what I get for assuming without asking. I truly am sorry. Curly will be so missed by all the other hands. I considered him my friend."

Carmen's eyes flooded with tears. Biting her lower lip, she took a deep breath. "Thank you. I liked Luke, but there never was any romance between us. Curly stole my heart. I have had some time to think about it. My mother told me that God must have someone else in mind for me someday." Her lip quivered.

"Your mother is a wise woman, Carmen. God does care about your future, and one thing I know for sure, Curly believed in God too." Crystal patted Carmen's hand. "You will be all right, I know."

"You are so kind, Miss Crystal. You seem changed . . . more settled. Tell me, what is different?"

"I do? Well . . . I've decided to stay here in Colorado. I have a purpose now. Saving the ranch. I feel comfortable here."

"Yes, I understand what you mean. When my family left Mexico to live here, I immediately loved this beautiful country and its mountains. It's as though God has touched the very landscape with his hand."

"That's so true. Now then, tell me about the bazaar. Did they set a date? I've promised to bake a pie for the auction to help raise money for an organ." Crystal was already thinking about what kind of pie she would make.

"It is this Saturday. It always brings all the ranchers together. And with your pie, you will bring the highest bidder." Carmen chuckled.

"Don't sell yourself short. Your pies are delicious too. We have lots to do, but first I must pay a visit to the Rocking M."

"Can you still afford to have me stay on? I know Kate was having a hard time making ends meet. I will understand if you need to let me go." Carmen looked crestfallen.

"Of course you will stay. Besides, I need the help around here. I can't do this alone. Trying to take care of everything was very hard for me when you were gone. I quickly found out that it takes a lot of energy to run this place. I don't know what I would do without Rusty . . . or Luke, for that matter." The way she said

Luke's name spoke volumes. Crystal rose and placed her cup and saucer in the sink.

"Miss Crystal . . . are *you* falling for Luke?"

"Please, we are friends. Call me Crystal." She tried to avoid answering but felt her face flush. "It doesn't matter what I think or feel. He is engaged to April."

"You are not answering the question," Carmen pressed.

Crystal turned around to lean against the sink. "I'll admit I am attracted to him, but I would never come between him and April. That just wouldn't be right, so don't go getting any ideas."

She knew Carmen wasn't fooled, but Carmen simply commented, "As you wish, Crystal."

True to her word, a few days later, Crystal harnessed the buckboard to ride over to the Rocking M ranch with the money she owed McBride safely tucked into her handbag. She also planned to make a stop to see Reverend Alden. It was colder today, and she pulled her coat tighter. Crystal's breath hung in the cold morning air that indicated winter was on its way. She had never seen snow and was excited at the prospect.

Crystal rapped on the massive door with an ornate door knocker until a stout maid dressed in a crisp uniform answered. "I'm here to see Mr. McBride." The maid nodded and suggested Crystal follow her into the parlor.

Sitting on either side of the fireplace were April and Alice. Alice rose as soon as she saw Crystal enter the room.

"My dear Crystal. What brings you out so soon this morning? Here, warm your hands." Alice pushed her to the fireplace.

Crystal removed her gloves and hat, and the maid took them. "I came to see your husband, Alice. I've sold my herd and want to pay off what Aunt Kate owed him."

April snorted. "It's about time."

"April. That is not necessary." Alice looked embarrassed by her daughter's outburst. "Tilly, please ask Mr. McBride to come to the parlor. I believe he is in his study."

"Yes, ma'am." The maid turned with haste and left the room.

"How are the wedding plans coming along?" Crystal asked.

"They are coming along just fine." Alice nodded to her daughter. "We have compiled the wedding list."

"April, don't forget that I will be having your shower at my place, although Sara Johnson is in charge. I've never given one before." Crystal plastered on the sweetest smile she could muster. Her heart thudded under her shirtwaist.

"I am not about to forget something like that, Crystal. It must be *hard* for you to give a shower instead of having your own. Kate let it slip that you were engaged to a certain gentleman back in Georgia for a time." Her words were hard and calculated.

"April, really. It's not nice to gossip," Alice reprimanded her daughter.

Crystal got the distinct feeling that April wanted to humiliate her. *Well, I won't sink to her level. How in the world could a nice woman like Alice have such a despicable daughter?*

Crystal measured her words carefully. "Oh, you mean Drew? It was mutual, and we decided to break it off when I left Georgia. He offered me a life of ease, to be sure, but I was seeking more adventure than the wife of a politician had to offer. Now that I have experienced the West and the trail drive, I can't imagine anywhere else I'd rather be, except running Aspengold."

"Good for you, Crystal." Alice smiled, then glared at April.

"Humph!" April fidgeted in her chair.

"Please have a seat, Crystal." Alice gestured toward the settee. "I don't know where my manners are."

Crystal moved toward the settee as the door flung open and Jim McBride's large body filled the room. "To what do we owe this morning pleasure?" he boomed.

"I am here to settle the debts my aunt had with you." Crystal continued to stand.

"Miss Clark, come with me so we can talk privately." McBride started toward the door, then turned to Alice and April. "Excuse us."

"Mr. McBride," Crystal interrupted, "there's nothing to discuss. I have the promissory note and the money with me. That will pay you everything that Aunt Kate owed you."

"Now, my dear, don't be too hasty. You may be in need this winter if you pay the entire note." He seemed to be stalling for time. "However, I would still like to extend an offer to you to buy Aspengold. Then you could return to your homeland and pick up right where you left off before your unfortunate problems, and still have money to spare." McBride slowly poured himself a cup of coffee without looking at Crystal.

McBride thinks he has it all figured out, she thought. The smug look on his face made Crystal angry. "I'm not leaving, Mr. McBride, and I will not sell the ranch. I intend to stay. At any rate, it's no concern of yours now." Crystal reached into her bag for the note and the money. "Please count it. You will find the entire amount is there."

Quickly McBride counted the money. "My, my . . . I guess you made out fine on the price per head." He seemed surprised, and he studied Crystal's face. But if he was waiting for information, she was not inclined to talk about it, especially to him.

Crystal took the promissory note, unfolded it, and handed it to him. "Now if you will just sign the note that I have paid you, I'll be on my way."

McBride gave the note a quick glance, scrawled his name with "paid in full" across the note, and handed it back to Crystal. "I admire how you handled yourself in a financial situation. If I can ever be of assistance again, or you find yourself longing to go back to Georgia, just let me know. I'll be more than happy to work with you."

"I appreciate the help you gave my aunt, and I pray that I won't need assistance in the future," she said as she retrieved the note from his hand and stuffed it into her bag.

"Good day to you, Mrs. McBride—and April." Crystal turned to leave.

"Why don't you stay and have lunch, dear?" Alice asked.

"I appreciate the invitation, but I must go. I have been gone a few weeks and have much to attend to. April, when you're ready, we'll set a date for the shower."

April rose from her chair. "I'll show you out."

As Crystal walked to the foyer, she couldn't help but compare herself to the beautiful April. She moved as lithely as a doe in the woods with a light step. Crystal was aware of how much shorter she was. She followed April to the door, conscious of her own deeply tanned face and callused hands. She felt dowdy today, and a quick stab pierced her heart. Luke and April would make a very handsome couple at their wedding ceremony.

As they reached the foyer, April tossed her long silky hair and reached for the door. "Crystal, I wanted to ask you why you really went on that trail drive."

"I went because I wanted to see if I could make a difference and hold this ranch together. The best way I could do that is not to ask more of the cowboys than I was willing to give." Crystal could tell by April's face that she was doubtful.

"Is that so? I thought maybe you were looking for a husband, you being the only female surrounded by all those men." April's thin lips pursed together in a smirk.

Crystal continued walking out into the fresh morning air with April following close behind. "Believe it or not, April, marriage is not on my mind. I have a ranch to run, and I want to learn it firsthand. What better way than to go on the trail drive? Now I have a better respect for all the hard work and long hours the cowboys put in every day."

"Have it your way. I thought that was what a foreman was for. Luke won't be your foreman much longer once we are married."

"What do you mean?"

"Oh, we'll live here. There's room for all of us until we build our own place."

"Well, in that case . . . I guess I need to find a replacement for him . . . that is, if he has agreed to this." Crystal's brain was whirling. She knew what April was trying to do, and she was not going to be pushed into an argument.

"Don't tell me you thought Luke and I would live in the bunkhouse at Aspengold." April laughed. "That's too funny."

Crystal's face flamed red. "I hadn't thought about where you would be living." She climbed onto the buckboard.

April chuckled again. "Luke and I will build a home on the Blue River. My father owns the land, and we will start on it as soon as we are married."

Crystal picked up the reins and tried her best to smile down at April. "If you and Luke have selected a wedding date, we need to go ahead with your shower, don't you think?"

"I'll bring my list to church on Sunday." April turned and went back inside.

Crystal made a clicking sound to the horses and flicked the reins across their rumps. She wished now that she had never volunteered her place for the shower. What was she thinking? April set her teeth on edge every time they talked. Maybe that was because the topic always revolved around Luke. She exhaled deeply. Might as well get used to it. Soon April and Luke would be married.

Bill Alden lived next door to the community church in a small house provided by the generosity of Jim McBride. Though nothing fancy, it was adequate. Crystal slowed the horses to a walk before entering the churchyard. She noticed another horse and buggy standing outside the gate. Then she spied Beth, basket in hand, standing by the well and looking up at the skinny pastor. The thought struck her that they made a fetching picture, with the sunlight glinting off Beth's deep auburn hair, her bonnet trailing down her back, and the preacher smiling down at her. Crystal watched as he lifted a blue napkin from the basket and took a deep breath. "Ahh . . ." When he lifted his head, he saw Crystal approaching.

226

"Well, hello there, Crystal." His face flushed as she observed their interchange. Beth spun around.

"Reverend . . . Beth." Crystal nodded to them. "I hope I'm not interrupting . . ."

"No, no . . ." Beth's face blotched red. "I just brought over some fresh homemade bread to the reverend. I was just leaving."

"Don't do that on my account. I just wanted to give you this." She climbed down from the wagon and handed him an envelope. Crystal was chuckling inwardly. *So . . . there's been some real sparking going on during my time on the trail drive.*

"What's this?" Bill reached out a bony hand to take the envelope.

Crystal cleared her throat, and her eyes rolled upward. He nodded as if he got the message. He tucked the envelope into his hip pocket. "How about I make us some coffee to go with this delicious-smelling bread?"

"Not for me, thanks." Crystal held up her gloved hand. "I want to get back to the ranch . . . lots to do." She picked up her skirts to climb back into the buckboard.

"Will we be seeing you at the bazaar this coming weekend?" Beth asked.

"I wouldn't miss it for anything." Crystal waved over her shoulder and left the two of them alone.

Feeling deeply satisfied that she had paid off the debt and made her tithe, she was lost in thought on the dusty road back to the ranch. In the distance, she saw a horse and rider appear on the road. She knew at once that it was Luke by the way he carried his shoulders and held his reins. She was excited that he had made it back from Denver.

227

"Whoa." Luke pulled his horse up and called out to her. He tipped his hat back, leaned forward, and rested his arms on the saddle horn. "You're up and about early."

Crystal slowed to a stop. "Good morning. I was just taking care of business. And yourself? Paying a morning call to April?"

"I was. Did you just come from there?"

"In a roundabout way. The ranch is clear of debt, at least for now. When did you get back?" Crystal swallowed hard. So he was going to be with April. No doubt to make plans on building their home on the Blue River.

"Late last night." Luke straightened in his saddle to leave. "See you back at the ranch, Crystal." He tipped his hat at her and dug his heels into the horse's flanks.

Crystal loved the way he said her name. His voice was deep and husky. *I hope April will be good to him. She is such a little snippet!* Immediately she chided herself for having such thoughts. They didn't reflect a very Christian attitude. She'd just try harder where April was concerned.

The day of the bazaar was a spectacular and pristine one. There was not a cloud in the sky, and an Indian summer breeze dropped in just in time for the merriment, food, and fellowship for the little white church. The steeple was visible on the hilltop in resplendent autumn color offered by surrounding aspen trees. Carmen and Crystal, their buggy laden with their pies and jams, were one of the last ones to arrive in the churchyard.

Things were in full swing with booths set up for displays of quilts, homemade jams, and leather ware. Rusty was playing his

228

fiddle while couples danced on the lawn adjacent to the booths. Children played in groups, and older boys were trying to outdo one another with kick balls.

The women placed their pies on a side table along with pies of different varieties that were to be auctioned off to raise funds for an organ. Sara Johnson wrote their names on the bottoms of the pie plates.

"That's some mighty fine-looking pies you made," Sara said.

"Thank you, Sara." Carmen pointed to the big basket of preserves she carried and said, "I'll take these over to Mary Franklin and get them tagged. I can't wait to look through the pottery that I spied."

Crystal was glad to hear the cheerfulness in Carmen's voice. She knew Curly's death had hit her hard.

Kurt made his way over to her side to offer his assistance, and to Crystal's surprise, Carmen took his arm.

Flo arranged their pies along with other desserts on the plank tables that were draped with pretty checkered tablecloths from her café. "I'm so glad to see you're back, Crystal. That was a pretty brave thing you did, going on that trail drive."

"It was an eye-opener. I feel a little rough around the edges now, considering my tanned skin and broken nails." Crystal laughed good-naturedly.

"I think you look gorgeous, Crystal. Don't you agree, Sara?"

Sara paused in her task long enough to give Crystal a quick glance. "Indeed I do. Now you fit in just like the rest of us women of the West. Tough and determined."

Crystal felt a warm glow. "I'll take that as a compliment, Sara."

"It was meant as one." Sara smiled as she looked at Crystal. Crystal knew that they accepted her as one of them now.

"You be sure to sample some of my fried chicken, and let me know if it tastes as good as the Southern way." Flo led Crystal to the main food table holding every variety of good eats.

"Looks delicious, Flo."

"Now, you get some of this in you, and it'll put a little meat back on you after the trail drive." Flo snapped her fingers, "Oh, excuse me, Crystal. I left some roastin' ears on the pit I've got to see to."

Flo lumbered off, and Crystal wandered around to look at all of the booths. The quilts showed exquisite needlework, but she paused at the booth of leather wares.

The smithy, Lars, greeted her. "See anything you might be interested in?"

Crystal fingered a beautiful tooled-leather belt. "What's your asking price for this belt?"

"That one would be $5.00." He picked it up and handed it to her. "Nice one too."

"Would you take $4.50?" Crystal thought this would be a good Christmas present for someone in the future.

"Best I can do is $4.75. Take it or leave it."

Crystal handed him the money, and he rolled the belt, then placed it into a small sack for her. Later she found a beautiful shawl and purchased it for Carmen. This was the most fun she'd had in a long time, and it felt wonderful to be under the canopy of a clear blue sky and watch the townsfolk enjoy themselves after a week of hard work of harvesting their fields or rounding up cattle. Crystal was glad that the trail drive was finally behind her, and she had a certain lightness in her heart this fine day.

Emily and Beth called out to her and fell into step beside her. "We are so glad you're back!" Emily said. "You'll have to sit with us for lunch and tell us all about the trail drive. What was it like?"

"Did you sleep out under the stars too? Did you have to cook?" Beth joined in with her own questions.

"Whoa, one at a time. I'd loved to sit with you and tell you all about it." Crystal linked arms with Emily and Beth. "But I'm famished. Shall we eat?"

They sat at a long plank table surrounded by laughter and conversation. Luke and April joined them, then Kurt and Carmen. Jube hurried over with his plate and sat next to Emily with a look of pure adoration on his face. It wasn't long before Reverend Alden showed up to squeeze in next to Beth, who blushed a becoming pink.

Crystal felt like the odd one out. Everyone was paired with a sweetheart, and it pierced her heart. There was much talking, laughing, and flirting. Fighting back her tears, she folded her napkin and tried to appear interested in their conversation. She wished Josh were here, but she had not seen him among the crowds today.

Flo yelled out to the crowd that it was time for the pie auction. "Now, you men, we need to fetch a good price for these pies. You all know it's to raise money for the church's new organ. So all you gather around near the pie table, and we'll start the bidding."

Flo moved over to the pie table. Folks satiated from the fried chicken made their way toward the auction.

"Remember, if you are outbid, sit down. If your bid is accepted, you must take your dessert and claim the maker of the pie to share it with her. Okay? Let's get started."

Sara picked up the first pie and held it up high for all to see. The bidding started and ended before Crystal could catch her breath. The first pie was none other than Beth's, and the folks enjoyed watching as the young preacher played a bidding war with a couple of cowboys until he won. He walked up front to receive his pie.

"Name's on the bottom, Reverend, so all is fair," Flo told him as he lifted the beautiful pie up to read Beth's name on its bottom. "So, whose pie is it?" Sara teased.

"It's Beth Johnson's. Beth, would you do me the honor of sharing this pie?" His Adam's apple bobbed up and down when he talked, and he smiled at Beth. Beth stepped out to meet him, and they made their way through the crowd to a shady spot under a cottonwood tree.

The bidding continued with fun and frivolity as the men tried to guess whose pie they were bidding for. Crystal waited and wondered who would pick her pie, if anyone. No sooner than she had the thought, her apple pie was lifted off the dessert table by Sara to start the bidding.

"I'll bid $1.50." Josh raised his hand. Crystal hadn't seen him earlier, but she was quite pleased that he was there after all and bidding on her pie.

"I'll make that $2.00." Crystal heard a familiar voice behind her. Without turning around, she knew it was Luke.

"$2.50," Josh said quickly.

"$3.00." Luke spoke again without looking at Josh.

"I'll give you $3.50."

"Make it $4.00."

The crowd was into it now and egging them on.

"Don't give in, Josh," April said loudly enough to be heard above the crowd.

"$4.25," Josh said.

"$5.00."

"$5.50. And that's my final."

"$6.00!"

"$6.00," Flo said. "Going once . . . going twice . . . sold for $6.00 to Luke. Step right up and get your pie." Flo handed the pie to Luke, and when he was close enough, Crystal heard her say, "Wise choice, my friend."

Luke lifted the pie to read the name and called out, "Crystal Clark!" His voice held surprise. "Would you care to share your pie with me?"

Crystal, embarrassed that anyone would spend that much on her pie, made her way forward. "I accept your invitation."

Crystal stole a look at April, whose face was like stone. April stood with her arms crossed, and Crystal realized she was probably agitated with Luke for not bidding on her pie. Crystal's heart skipped a beat, and her mouth went dry as she followed the tall cowboy past the cheering crowd. She smiled weakly at Josh, but he stared back at her with a wounded look in his eyes.

"Hope that pie was worth spending $6.00 on." April spoke through clenched teeth.

"Would you care to join us, April?" Luke asked.

"Yes, please do, April," Crystal said.

"No thanks, I'm sure my pie will fetch a fair price when the bidding starts. Too bad you will miss out, Luke." April's tone was bitter.

April tossed her long silky locks and sucked in a deep breath, then whirled around to listen to the next bidding. Her sad-looking pie, frothy meringue now melting under the heat, was the next one up. As Crystal watched from the back of the crowd before leaving with Luke, she noticed that no one was bidding. April's father made a halfhearted attempt to get the bidding going but wound up with the dubious-looking dessert in his possession. April's face clearly showed her embarrassment, but she followed Jim McBride out of the spotlight.

In the rush for preparations before the bazaar, Luke had barely seen Crystal, and he had been relieved—as long as he didn't see her, it was easier to put off telling her about Kate's will. But now here he was with her pie and his hand on her elbow. He hadn't figured on that at all.

Luke steered Crystal near the creek bed and placed the pie on a big boulder. Taking out his pocketknife, he proceeded to cut large slices of the delectable-looking apple pie. He had been shocked when he discovered the pie belonged to Crystal and not Carmen. If it tasted half as good as it looked, then the money was well spent.

"Crystal, I had no idea you could bake a pie. You surprise me all the time," he said. He handed her a slice after she held out her napkin. Luke licked the sticky apple off his fingers. "This is excellent, and the crust is so light. Who taught you this?"

Crystal beamed at his compliment. "My cook in Georgia did. It's the one thing I like to do in the kitchen."

"Why didn't you tell me a long time ago when you and Carmen were baking?"

"Seems you had your mind made up that I couldn't do anything ... so I didn't care if you knew or not."

Luke sank his teeth into the last bite and swallowed hard. "I'm sorry if I hurt your feelings that day. I just assumed the pies were Carmen's and you were just there cleaning up." His legs felt weak every time he looked into her large green eyes. *Why does she do this to me?* He'd better hurry back to the churchyard, or April would be looking for him. He'd seen how upset she was that he picked Crystal's pie and not hers. It was an honest mistake, but then, he had asked April to join them.

Crystal continued to look into his eyes, and he felt unnerved somehow about keeping the truth about the ranch from her. Since the trail drive, there had been an unspoken truce between them. Luke genuinely enjoyed being around her with her infectious charm and sweet Southern voice.

"Don't worry about it," Crystal said. "Maybe April cooks a good pie too. For your sake, I hope so, since you'll be married." Luke sensed that Crystal felt as uncomfortable being alone with him as he did with her. "Speaking of April, here she comes." *Oh boy, April's not happy about this*, he thought as she headed their way.

"Luke, are you through devouring that pie? We need to return to the bazaar. There will be a sack race, if you're interested. I will be your partner." Luke noticed that she seemed to ignore Crystal standing there. April placed her arm on his possessively.

"Sounds like fun, April. Care to find a partner for the sack race, Crystal?" Luke watched her face.

"Don't worry about me, I'll go look for Josh," she answered in a sweet voice, and then left.

When Crystal was out of earshot, April turned on him. "Did

you have to make a fool of yourself with that ridiculous bid for Crystal's pie?" April spat.

Luke knew that April was jealous and answered firmly, "I had no idea the pie belonged to her. It just looked delicious. Matter of fact, it is. Would you like a slice?" he taunted her.

"I wouldn't eat it if it were the last piece on earth! You should have been bidding on *my* pie! Now everyone's talking about it." April stamped her foot and folded her arms.

"You are acting just like a spoiled brat! I'm engaged to you, not Crystal."

"That's my point," April fumed. "Maybe you wanted to be alone with her. I've seen how you look at her when you think no one is looking. I will *not* play second fiddle to anyone, Luke!"

Now she was treading on thin ice. Luke did not like this irritable and jealous side of April. It was not becoming, especially since Crystal didn't have anything to do with it. But it was true, he did steal glances at Crystal. Ever since the trail drive, he had a new respect for Crystal. She was so much tougher than he thought.

"How was I to know it wasn't your pie? And I won't have you telling me what to do!" he slung back at her. He watched as her face crumpled. With pouting lips she came close, fingering the button on the top of his shirt. "Sometimes I get the feeling you don't want to be married to me, Luke. You never touch me or kiss me."

"I must admit, I have been having second thoughts, April," Luke said. As soon as the words tumbled out of his mouth, he regretted his timing.

Looking stunned, April took a step back and let her arms drop to her sides. "What do you mean? Are you seeing Crystal behind my back?" she sputtered.

"No, nothing like that, April. I'm just not sure we're right for each other. We always end up fighting, and it's usually about your jealousy and temper." Luke studied her eyes for clues to her reaction.

"No, you're lying. Ever since you got back from that blasted trail drive, you've been different. Did something happen out there?"

"Nothing. Honest. Just a lot of thinking on my part. I had a lot of time to do that," Luke admitted. He could see the hurt in her eyes. But he had to be truthful.

"Well . . . I reckon I'm not good enough for you. Who would've thought it? A lowly cowboy without one red cent to his name, rejecting a cattle baron's daughter. Well, I won't hang around to be humiliated, Luke. You can consider this engagement off!" April's eyes flooded with tears, and she ran toward her family carriage hitched outside the churchyard. She climbed aboard and turned the horses out, and with a sharp snap of the whip across the horses' backsides, she flew past the bazaar like the devil himself was chasing her. Luke saw her mother call out to her, but her voice was lost in the wind.

Luke stood rooted to the spot. He hadn't meant to pick a fight. But now he was glad this farce was over. He admitted in his heart that he didn't love April. She was just his ticket to the property on the Blue River, nothing more. While he was ashamed to admit it, if he were honest with himself, breaking things off was the right thing to do. He felt disgusted for letting things go on as long as they did. She deserved better than that.

The rest of the festivities passed in a blur. Luke knew people were talking about April's hasty departure. Even when Rusty tried to ask him about it, he brushed him aside. Rusty picked up his fiddle and called a dance, probably trying to lift the mood of the cowboy. Yet Luke couldn't help but notice Josh leading Crystal by the arm in the dance.

Luke took his time in getting back to the ranch after the bazaar. He listened to the night sounds of the mountains along the trail and paused along the ridge overlooking the ranch. An owl hooted from its perch, his enormous eyes glowing in the thick darkness. Wind was stirring the spruces around, and their pungent fragrance filled the night air. He saw the lights at the ranch softly glowing in the distance and smoke curling from the fireplace. Crystal was probably getting ready for bed.

As he thought of her, his heart lurched in his chest. He was relieved that he had admitted to himself that he cared for Crystal. Maybe he loved her. She had managed somehow to creep into his thoughts most of the time. He thought back over the trail drive, how she had worked as hard as the next cowboy. How she didn't give up and gave it all she had. He was drawn to her, and he thought she felt it too.

He knew she was strong in her faith, although not blatant about it. He knew she prayed, and more than once she had said she relied on God. Luke wished he could do that. He wanted that confidence she had. Assurance that someone other than himself was in control and cared about him. Luke had never thought God was interested in him. Why would God care about him? He was just somewhere above the stars.

Luke remembered the night that Curly and Crystal talked about how God had created the stars. Luke looked up into the cold, dark night at the beautiful full moon. Someone had to have created this vast universe. He was awed when he saw the billions of twinkling stars sprinkled across the sky and the moon illuminating the valley.

Maybe it was just a matter of trust.

"God, if You can hear me . . . Crystal has something special. I need to know if You are there. The preacher said once that You sent Your Son to die for us. I want to believe that and ask You to forgive me. Bill said we are all sinners. I know I can never be good enough, and I have messed up where April is concerned. Crystal said that You care about everything in our lives. Gosh, even Curly believed. I don't know how to handle this thing about the ranch or how to tell Crystal. I need someone smarter than me to point me in the right direction. Maybe You are just the One to help me.

"To be honest, I've never thought about dying until Kate died, then Curly . . . I need to get things right with You. Maybe You have a purpose for me since I didn't die from typhoid when my parents did. Just show me what to do, and thanks for what you did. Amen."

Luke felt a heavy load lift from his shoulders. "I think I just talked to the God of the universe, Buck," he said softly, nudging his horse down the steep slope toward the bunkhouse. Buck tossed his mane, and Luke laughed out loud.

21

Indian summer was swept away with a blast of sudden north-east winds that brought heavy frost. The aspen leaves that once shimmered brilliant gold and red were fading to a dull brown, whispering that winter wasn't far behind. Crystal had settled into a comfortable routine since the trail drive, and now work around the ranch was slowing down a bit. Luke would go over the small details that needed tending with her and then delegate one of the drovers to do the tasks at hand. But for the most part, Crystal and Carmen took care of the cooking and laundry. Rusty was always there to lend a hand, whether it was mending fences or going to town for supplies when needed.

Crystal was happy to see Carmen and Kurt becoming closer than just friends. Carmen talked less about Curly now, and the sadness was slowly fading from her eyes like the fall colors of the leaves. Now her eyes lit up whenever Kurt was around.

Crystal hadn't seen much of April since the bazaar. April had been absent from church that next morning, so Crystal didn't get the guest list for the shower. She would have to ask Mrs. McBride about it or perhaps send Rusty over to the Rocking M for it.

Crystal lifted her coat off the peg by the front door and stepped out to the porch, carrying her cup of coffee. She loved the mornings here. They were almost always clear and bright, unlike Atlanta with its morning haze from either humidity or fog, depending on the time of year.

Carmen had draped blankets across the rockers, and now Crystal placed one across her lap to ward off the morning chill. The heat from the coffee warmed her hands, and she blew on the steaming liquid. She saw Luke come out of the barn and watched as he went about his morning chores with Jube. They had pulled the barn doors wide open while caring for the livestock and worked in companionable silence. Crystal was getting used to the fact that most cowboys worked in a quiet fashion and communicated with a mere word or two.

She sensed something different about Luke. He seemed quieter than normal, but she couldn't be sure. Maybe he was thinking about his marriage to April. Had they set a date? Life would be easier once Luke no longer worked for her and moved to the Rocking M. Then she wouldn't be reminded that he belonged to another. She wondered if they could handle everything without him.

While she followed Luke with her eyes, he paused and tipped his hat to her. Crystal's heart gave a small flip-flop, and she lifted her hand in greeting. She watched as he crossed the wide yard with long, fluid movements. She liked the way his boots caused his hips to swing slightly. *I shouldn't be having thoughts like this.*

Luke reached the porch, placed one dusty boot on the step, and propped an arm across his leg. He tilted his hat back in order to see her better and smiled. "The mornings are gettin' cold, but it always warms up by lunchtime."

"Yes, but I love starting my day on the porch while it's still quiet." Crystal thought back to her father's veranda, of the many times her family had exchanged pleasantries or ended their day together at dusk on a sultry Southern night.

"Better enjoy the mild weather while you can. This time of year it can change faster than a bronco can buck you off its back."

"I guess we need to be prepared for it. Do we have enough firewood cut?" Crystal watched his blue eyes, searching them to see if she was the only one having confusing emotions whenever they were together.

"Nope. But that's one thing we'll take care of today." Luke gazed at the western sky. "I have a feeling the bitter cold is almost on us. Check out those low-hanging clouds."

Crystal noted the clouds to the west. Would she soon be seeing her first snowfall?

"I reckon you and April will be starting your own ranch pretty soon?" She hadn't meant to be so blunt. But she wanted to know if they had set their wedding date without too much prying, lest she appear too concerned about it. "Guess I'll have to ask Rusty to be my foreman to run things around here after you're married."

Luke stepped back from the porch and straightened his hat. "We'll see . . ." His voice trailed off, and he changed the subject. "I'll go get Jube started on the firewood. You can't ever have enough wood." He headed back in the direction of the barn, motioning to Jube.

Crystal leaned back in her chair and finished her coffee. He had been very vague, but then it was not her business to be asking personal questions.

She was happy for Jube and Emily. She remembered their small but happy ceremony right after the trail drive. Emily had looked lovely in her mother's wedding dress, an antique white lace gown. With trailing ribbons in her hair, which had been braided to encircle her head, she'd made a striking vision and seemed to float down the aisle of the country church to join her beloved Jube at the altar. Crystal smiled, remembering their spoken vows and the tenderness in Jube's eyes.

A big gust of wind whipped up again, sending the fallen leaves scattering across the yard. Sometimes she felt like those leaves, with no idea where she was going to end up. She knew she loved this place, but was it a good idea to stay without a partner to care about? Without someone who came home every night to spend the long winter evenings with her? Longing for someone to love pierced her heart. *I know, God, that You have Your own timetable, but is there someone out there for me?*

Crystal and Carmen had just cleaned the kitchen after lunch when there was a sharp knock at the door. "I'll get it, Crystal." Carmen threw open the door and there, with the wind whipping around her skirts, was Emily.

"Come in, Emily." Carmen pulled her through the door, closed it against the wind, and led Emily into the parlor. Crystal was right behind Carmen.

"You look marvelous, Emily," Carmen said as Emily removed her coat.

Emily's face was pink from the wind. She pulled off her gloves, laid them aside, and said, "I just couldn't wait another minute to tell you, Crystal." Emily's eyes flashed with excitement.

"I'll leave you two alone." Carmen started toward the kitchen, but Emily stopped her.

"No, Carmen. I want you to stay." Emily patted the settee and motioned them to take a seat.

"My goodness. Hurry, tell us," Crystal said.

Emily sat between them and took a deep breath. "Jube and I are going to have a baby!"

"Oh my! How exciting!" Crystal reached over and hugged Emily. "I'm so happy for you two."

"We weren't expecting to have a baby quite this soon, but . . . we're so happy. Although I have to admit I am a little nervous." Emily looked down at her hands, rubbing them together for warmth.

Carmen's eyes were wide with happiness, and she patted Emily's hand. "This is wonderful. I too am happy for you. I helped deliver my sister's baby, if you need a midwife."

"Thank you, Carmen, but I went to see Dr. Gibbons in town, so hopefully it won't take him long to get to me when the time comes."

Crystal could tell from Carmen's expression that she was pleased to be a part of this news, and she said, "And Jube never said a word to me this morning."

"He knew I wanted to be the first to tell you. Mama is already starting to knit baby booties."

They all laughed. Over cookies and milk, they continued to talk with excitement about everything concerning a baby. Finally Emily said that she had to get back to the cabin. Crystal had offered her

244

and Jube the line shack that the cowboys used during the winter until they could build a cabin next spring.

"A baby will be a wonderful change around here, Emily. Once again, I am tickled for you and Jube." Crystal hooked her arm in Emily's and walked with her outside. "When your time gets close, you must stay either with your mother or with me. It'll be a lot closer than the line cabin."

"Oh, I couldn't do that . . ." Emily pulled herself into the wagon and picked up the reins.

"I insist. But that's a long way off right now."

While they had been visiting, the temperature had dropped like a rock, and now the blue-gray clouds were low and threatening. Crystal tucked a blanket around Emily's feet.

"Now we have two to take care of. I don't want you to catch cold, Emily. Take good care of yourself, and I'll see you soon."

"I promise to do just that. Jube is being so sweet that I don't know if I can stand it." Emily giggled, her curls bouncing against the top of her shoulders.

Crystal waved good-bye as the first October snowflake touched her cheek. Surprised, she stuck out her tongue and tasted the next one. In Georgia, snow was not a common winter experience, but sometimes they had a January ice storm. She shivered when she remembered the bad blizzard of '87 that Rusty had told her about. She pulled the coat tighter around her and watched the snowflakes dropping out of heavy, gray clouds.

By supper time, the snow clung to the ponderosa pine boughs with its first dusting and covered the porch steps. Carmen had stew simmering, and Crystal kept a nice fire glowing in the grate. Rusty, Luke, and Kurt shook the snow off their coats and stomped their feet on the porch before entering the house.

"Soon as supper is over, I'll clear you a path out the front door, Crystal," Luke said, hanging his coat on a peg by the door.

"I'm glad we got the wood cut today," Rusty commented to no one in particular. He took his seat at the table. "Just in case we might get more than a few inches tonight. Looks like it's startin' to come down heavy now."

Once everyone was seated, Crystal asked the blessing, and Carmen proceeded to ladle out steaming stew. Crystal had made cornbread from a recipe she found in her aunt's cookbook. She hoped it would taste good, but from the looks of these hungry men, they wouldn't slow down eating long enough to find out.

She looked around and felt a warm coziness in the camaraderie they all had sitting at the table, with the snow falling continuously and casting its peculiar light in the toasty dining room. While everyone ate, they talked about the day's events, and Crystal noticed how Kurt and Carmen sat close together but not touching. Once or twice, Crystal felt Luke's eyes on her, but when she glanced down the table at him, he grinned. She wished she knew what he was thinking. Her heart would just have to get over him.

"Why don't we sit around the fire after supper and play checkers? What do you think, Crystal? Or would you rather have us just go back to the bunkhouse?" Rusty stuffed the cornbread into his mouth and then wiped his red beard. "With Kate gone, it sure is nice to be around two lovely ladies."

Carmen laughed. "Rusty, sounds to me like you don't want to go back to that cold bunkhouse."

"Doggone straight."

Everyone laughed, and Carmen started clearing the plates. Kurt rose to help Carmen carry the dishes to the sink.

"Let's go sit by the fire. Are there any of those cookies left, Carmen?" Crystal asked as she stood.

"I think there may be a few. Kurt and I will bring them with some fresh coffee. Just let me get the dishes soaking in the sink."

Once comfortable by the fire, Rusty and Luke set up the checkerboard. After a few rounds, it was obvious that Luke couldn't beat Rusty, who was an old pro at the game of checkers. Carmen and Kurt carried a tray of cookies and hot coffee to the parlor.

"I think this would be a good time for Crystal to get out her Autoharp and play us some tunes," Luke said. "What do you all think?" Everyone chimed in with eagerness to hear Crystal play.

"Oh . . . all right." She blushed. "But it's been awhile."

"Quit making excuses." Luke settled down in his chair to get comfortable.

Crystal fetched her Autoharp from the bedroom and began to play. She caught Luke watching her as she sang and played, but she looked away. His look made her nervous somehow.

Kurt dragged Carmen to her feet, and they danced around the big room while Rusty clapped to the beat of the music. When Crystal finally stole a glance at Luke, he was smiling broadly and tapping the toe of his worn boot against the hardwood floor.

Luke thought he was looking into the face of an angel as Crystal strummed the Autoharp with her slender fingers. The firelight created soft shadows on her sweet, oval face, and she appeared to be lost in thought as she sang. When the time was right, he would tell her that he had broken off his engagement to April. He wasn't sure what to say. This morning he'd hedged when she asked him about the wedding plans. But the scene he had with April was still fresh in his mind, and he didn't want to talk about it.

Ever since the pie bidding at the bazaar, he realized that he didn't love April and didn't like the way she tried to lead him around by the nose. Because her father was an important and wealthy man, April seemed to think that everyone should fall all over her. She was spoiled by her father. The deal he'd struck with McBride about owning the land near Blue River didn't seem all that important anymore.

At any rate, he racked his brain about how to tell Crystal that he owned the ranch and she didn't. Luke didn't want to hurt her. Once he told her, she would probably pack up and head back South. But he didn't want her to leave. Just the opposite. He wanted Crystal to stay here, and now that he sat here watching her sing in her sweet, lyrical voice, he found himself wanting to kiss her. He wondered if she felt anything about him in that way. Sometimes women were hard for him to figure.

Luke wondered where things stood between Crystal and Josh McBride. *He can't have her!* his mind screamed. *But I might not have anything to say about that.* What if Crystal loved Josh? Well, he'd wait for the time being and see how it would all play out.

His ruminating was interrupted by everyone's applause at Crystal's music. It was time to get to bed, and he was tired. It had been a long day. He thought of Jube, who had left earlier and was clearly eager to get back to Emily, now pregnant with their child. One day he hoped to have children. It would be nice if Crystal would be his wife. *Now where did that come from?*

His breathing felt tight as he watched her put away the Autoharp. Everyone shuffled to the door, and the men donned their coats to leave. Carmen opened the door, and the bitter chill entered the room. "The snow is getting thick now."

"At least the wind has died down. I'll bring in another stack of wood so you'll have it in the morning." Luke pulled his hat on, ran his hand around the brim as was his habit, and stepped out onto the snow-covered porch.

Rusty was already making his way across the yard to the bunkhouse. Kurt and Carmen were saying good night. Kurt leaned down and gave Carmen a peck on the cheek, and Luke saw a deep flush come over Carmen's face.

Crystal walked to the door and looked out. It was as if some magical fairy had sprinkled fine confectioner's powder on the entire world. "Oh . . . it's so beautiful."

"Good night, all." Kurt headed out. "Stay warm now."

"Good night." Carmen turned to Crystal. "I'm going to go work on those dishes I left soaking." She headed in the direction of the kitchen.

Luke carried in a stack of logs and placed them by the fireplace, then turned to Crystal. "Anything else you need, just holler. I have a feeling it will snow all night long."

"Thanks, Luke. We had a good time just the five of us, didn't we?" Standing this close to him, Crystal felt her heart thumping wildly in her chest.

"It was a fine evening. Good way to start the winter off."

"Luke, I didn't receive the invitation list from April yet for the shower. Will you be seeing her, or do I need to just ride over there and pick the list up?"

Luke pursed his thin lips into a straight line. He shifted from one hip to the other and shoved his hands in his coat pockets. "That's something I wanted to talk to you about." He cleared his throat. "Me and April just don't seem to see eye to eye . . . The wedding's been called off."

His eyes searched hers. Crystal wanted to jump up and down, but she remained outwardly unfazed. "Oh . . . Luke, I am sorry. Do you care to talk about it?"

"Let's just put it this way—we want different things in life. I want a family, and that's not what she wants. She's too enamored with material things and what she can get with her name to give any thought to raising a family. April likes to be in charge of almost everything. Besides, I'm not too crazy about living with her mother and daddy. I guess that piece of land near the Blue River will never belong to me now." His face showed more relief than sadness, which surprised Crystal.

She held his blue eyes with a steady look. "I'm sorry." Her palms felt moist.

"You already said that."

"But I mean it. I know how it feels when you plan for your marriage and then decide that it's not the right thing for you."

Luke shot her a quizzical look. "Does this have anything to do with that feller Drew?"

"How do you know about him?"

"That night after the tornado, you called out his name a few times while you were unconscious."

"I did? I must have been talking out of my head." Crystal was

250

embarrassed. "Well . . . it seems that once I came here, he lost no time in finding someone to replace me."

"No, he's the one who must have lost his senses." Luke still stood an arm's length away, and Crystal found herself wanting to touch the bronze face that held genuine concern for her.

"I'd like to think so." She wondered if he was feeling this strong attraction she was experiencing or if he was just being nice. Then she remembered his kiss the day she'd been crying, and she felt a tingle flow over her just at the thought.

"What about Josh?"

His question startled Crystal. She hadn't given much thought to Josh in a while, even though she liked him. "What about him?"

Luke hesitated. "Well, I guess I was just wondering if you two are an item. He seems to like you, Crystal."

Crystal thought a moment before answering. "Are you asking as a friend, or because you'd like to court me?" *Oh boy, now I've gone and done it. He's going to think I'm brazen and bold.*

"Could be I'd like to know where I stand." He moved closer to her and lifted her hand. "I don't want to waste any more time than I already have. I think you have feelings for me too, unless I'm misreading you. And yes, I'd like to see more of you than just across from the supper table."

Crystal felt her heart miss a beat. Her hopes had been dashed when he became engaged to April. Now here he was caressing her hand with his thumb, and she couldn't think straight. Her hand felt small and helpless in his large one. Her tongue felt thick and dry, and she swallowed the lump in her throat before answering.

"Luke, are you sure it's over between you and April? I never wanted to get in the way of you two." Crystal was still skeptical about his true motives. Until the trail drive, he had always treated her like someone to joke around with but not be serious with.

"Trust me. It's definitely over. And it's for the best, believe me. I think you stole my heart that very first day you arrived, but I just didn't want to believe it. It was me that placed those columbines on your nightstand." Luke's voice was husky as he locked eyes with Crystal. Her heart slammed against her chest. She had just assumed the flowers were from Kate.

Luke's manly scent, mingled with soap and aftershave, was making it hard for her to breathe. At that very moment, Carmen walked in, and Luke dropped Crystal's hand and stepped aside. Crystal's face flushed, but Carmen politely announced that she was going to bed and then left them alone again, for which Crystal was grateful.

"You think about what I said," Luke said. "I best be going. I'll check on you first thing in the morning, in case the snow gets worse."

He opened the door, and snow blew in and sprinkled the hallway floor. She watched him fade into the swirling whiteness until she could no longer see him. Crystal felt her heart beat wildly in her chest. *He does care about me*, her heart sang as she twirled around the room. She could hardly believe it. Luke really liked her, Crystal Clark!

Abruptly she stopped dancing and came to her senses. Something was nagging her. Isn't this what she wanted? Yes, she believed he was attracted to her, but what about his wanting the ranch? Maybe that was what he wanted most of all. *Another thing—he's not a believer.* She could still hear her mother's voice telling her not to become unequally yoked with an unbeliever.

But I don't know for a fact that he isn't, she reasoned with herself. He did attend church, and he did have good morals. But that's all she knew. She just needed to slow down and take this one day at a time, even though her heart was saying something different.

Fingers of ice had formed on the window when Crystal peeked out the next morning, and snow was still gently falling, covering everything in its sight. The outdoors was as dazzling as the bright morning light that broke through the snow-laden clouds.

Crystal had had a hard time going to sleep after Luke shared his heart with her the night before. To think that he had liked her all this time. Still, she wondered why he had not declared that until after she owned Aspengold. *Maybe I'm not being fair about this*, she thought, but the nagging idea stayed with her until she finally fell asleep.

In the morning she slipped on her heavy robe and slippers to start a fire in the main room. She could hear Carmen moving around in the kitchen, and Crystal could smell fresh coffee brewing. Once the fire was going, she stood warming her outstretched hands when Carmen entered with a cup of coffee. She was already dressed for the day with several layers of clothing.

"You are too good to me, Carmen." She gratefully accepted the cup.

"No, señorita. It is you who have been good to me and called me your friend as well."

Crystal dismissed her comment with a wave of her hand. "I would hate to think of living here alone and trying to feed this hungry bunch."

"You know, one day Aspengold will become even larger, and you will have grandchildren to inherit it."

"That's a nice thought, Carmen. I hope you're right."

"The ranch will prosper, Crystal. I just know it. You have worked very hard to see to that, and you treat everyone more than fair."

"Thanks. But you flatter me. A lot of the work on this ranch was done by my aunt and Rusty." Her voice wavered. "But I am honored to call you friend."

Carmen smiled. "Looks like the snow is here to stay for a few days. I'll have Kurt bring in more firewood right after breakfast."

Crystal moved away from the fire, her backside thoroughly warm now. "I'll go change and be right back out to set the table. What shall we do with the weather like this?"

"We can sew those curtains that you wanted in the kitchen. How about that?"

"Good idea. I'm glad I'll have a project to keep me busy."

"When it stops snowing, perhaps I could go spend some time with my mother and check on my new nephew, if that's all right with you?"

"That would be fine. I know you're anxious to see them. A new baby is always irresistible."

Crystal heard footsteps on the porch and hurried to get the door. Rusty, Kurt, and Luke hurried in and made their way to the fire.

"It's bone-chillin' cold this morning, Crystal." Rusty rubbed his rawboned hands together over the blazing fire.

"The thermometer measures three degrees and falling out by

254

the bunkhouse," Kurt informed them, blowing on his bare hands. "I couldn't find my gloves this morning."

"These?" Carmen held up a pair of brown leather gloves.

"Yes, those are mine, thanks." He took them from Carmen's hands, his eyes focusing only on her.

"That boy would leave his head if it wasn't attached. Got your mind on something else, have you?" Rusty teased.

"Aw, leave 'em alone, Rusty. I'm hungry. Breakfast ready, Carmen?" Luke said, but his eyes were on Crystal, who felt her face warm under his gaze.

22

The snow had stopped but blanketed every inch of the valley, and the wind created deep drifts that piled high against the north side of the ranch house and the outlying buildings. The punchers bedded the milk cows in the barn. Rusty and Carmen had teamed up weeks ago and butchered and dressed a few of the Herefords, which were needed for meat during the long winter. Luke and Kurt cleaned the stalls daily and kept the barn swept. Jube mostly stayed near the line cabin with his pregnant, happy wife and checked for any breaks in the fence.

Crystal spent her days sewing bright red gingham curtains for the kitchen windows and poring over a catalog she'd found, while Carmen kept a hot pot of coffee in constant readiness for the men. Afternoons became a highlight of the day with freshly baked apple cookies or cinnamon bread shared with the men when they trooped into the warm kitchen for a little respite from the cold. Crystal looked forward to the break in her day and anticipated each time Luke walked through the front door. By now it was apparent that there was a mutual affection growing between Crystal and Luke, although no one said anything aloud.

In the evenings after supper when the men had grudgingly returned to the bunkhouse, Crystal would read Scripture out loud while Carmen worked on their mending. It was a fine way to end the day, cozied in the horsehair chairs next to the fire with a cup of steaming hot chocolate.

Today the snow had stopped, and the bright sun turned the glaring whiteness into thousands of glittering diamonds. Crystal stepped out into the cold, brilliant day. Rusty, snow shovel in his weathered hands, sliced away at the mound of white stuff to clear a path from the house to the barn.

Crystal had tied a woolen scarf around her hat to keep her ears warm and donned her aunt's heaviest coat, finishing with long handles beneath her woolen skirt. Although it was very cold, she was exhilarated at just being outdoors again. She danced around on the porch, clutching a cloth napkin in her hand.

"Watch yer step now, Crystal. There's ice underneath the path I'm making." Rusty paused to lean on his shovel and chuckled at Crystal's antics.

Crystal half slid down the steps and reached up with her free hand to pat Rusty's red-cheeked face. "Isn't it a glorious day, Rusty?"

"I think you've been cooped up too long, missy. Most women are crank horns after a few weeks of being snowed in." Rusty's bushy eyebrows furrowed.

"You need to remember that I've never seen this much snow in one place." She laughed. "It's an adventure." Crystal suddenly stopped her little dancing gig, embarrassed, when she saw Luke approaching from the bunkhouse.

Luke wore lambskin chaps over his Levi's and a huge fur-lined duster. He was the picture of pure masculinity, exuding confidence even in the way he walked. Though his dark hat was pulled low and a scarf was around his neck, tiny icicles clung to his moustache and eyebrows. Crystal resisted the urge to wipe them away. A bubble of excitement inched its way upward from her chest and landed a beaming smile on her face.

Then her conscience reminded her to think twice about this cowboy. Yes, he had told her it was over with April, but Crystal remembered the earlier day when they were out riding—he told her in no uncertain terms that he *would* have that land to build his own spread. Did he care for her, or was he bent on owning Aspengold? Maybe he thought this was easier than having to marry April to secure the land on the Blue River. Just what were his intentions?

"Whatcha got in the napkin?" Luke asked.

She unfolded the napkin. "This is some dried bread for the birds. Winter is so hard on them. I'll need to order birdseed the next time I'm in Steamboat." Crystal broke the bread into small bits and dropped it onto the ground.

Rusty grunted. "You are just like Kate. Couldn't stand the thought of a harmless creature not being cared for."

"All except chickens," Luke teased. Crystal felt her face flush, warming her cold cheeks.

Luke laughed as he watched Crystal teeter into a slip-slide with every step she took. "If it's skating you want, Crystal, there's gonna be an ice skating party over at the Johnsons' this afternoon, before it gets too cold to be out after the sun goes down." He swiftly reached over and grabbed her elbow to keep her from falling.

"How did you know there was a skating party?" Crystal didn't remember seeing anyone leave the ranch. Her mind was now on the hand that held her arm.

"Someone passed the word to Jube out at the line camp when I rode up there yesterday to check things out. Are you and Carmen interested?"

Crystal clapped her gloved hands. "You bet I am—except for one thing. I can't skate."

"What you don't know, I'll be happy to teach you. There's skates in the barn. I'll fetch a couple of pairs to see if any will fit you. We'll go right after lunch. It may take us awhile to get there, so be sure you and Carmen dress in layers."

"I'll stay here and keep the fires burning till you return." Rusty paused again with his shoveling. "Might even make us some chicken soup. How's that sound for supper?"

"Delicious, Rusty. Can you give me a hand and we'll get the sleigh ready?" Luke winked at Crystal.

"Be right there." Rusty thrust his shovel into a snowdrift and followed Luke.

"Ooh . . . this will be fun. I'll run and tell Carmen." Crystal hurried down the path back to the house. It would be so wonderful to be with friends after being cooped up for weeks—and to be with Luke.

Crystal and Carmen chatted with excitement while Kurt settled Carmen in the back of the sleigh. He then took his seat next to her, covering them both with buffalo hides.

Luke took his time and with care wrapped a quilt around Crystal, tucked it around her legs, and threw a buffalo hide on top. Not until he was sure they all were adequately covered did he flick the reins over the horses, and they lurched forward in a fast trot. The smooth blades of the sleigh glided over the fallen snow, and the harnesses jingled on the wind. The air was pristine with sparkling azure skies, and Crystal watched the breath of the horses filter past her in a puff of white. The glare from the sun reflecting off the snow was so stark that it made seeing difficult, and Crystal had to squint. She snuggled even further under the warm covers.

Crystal glanced sideways at Luke, who was sitting as close as was proper in order for their body heat to generate warmth. She felt a thrill that he was so capable, always taking charge with whatever situation was at hand. She decided that she loved every-thing about him, but she wanted him to be in love with her, not pretending to be in order to secure Aspengold.

In a short time they arrived at the Johnsons', and Luke stopped the sleigh in front of the barn. John Franklin trotted up to help him with the horses and then led them into the barn. Kurt assisted the ladies down and escorted them to where the other guests were gathered, their happy voices echoing in the clearing.

Crystal stiffened when she saw April, but April turned away. She leaned over to whisper something to Beth, who was stand-ing with Bill's arm encircling her waist. Josh broke away from the group to meet them halfway.

"I'm so glad someone planned this little get-together. How've you been, Crystal?"

"A bit cold, I'm afraid, but other than that, all right." Crystal had forgotten how warm and friendly Josh's brown eyes were. She hadn't seen him since before the trail drive except at church.

Josh took her arm. "It's only a short walk to the lake, and the Johnsons have a nice bonfire going. You can warm up there."

Before Crystal could protest, he guided her over to the merry bunch, their boots crunching under the snow. Spirits were high as everyone exchanged warm greetings. Luke, she noted, followed with John, but she caught the wounded look in his eyes before he glanced away.

"Did you survive the snow, Crystal? I was thinking about you stuck there in the house all alone, with the wind howling. Tell me, were you dreaming of Southern nights?" April's smile didn't reach her icy blue eyes.

"Oh, but I wasn't alone. I had dear Carmen with me. And every evening the cowboys would stay after supper and play checkers, or we'd all get together to talk, sing, and just get to know one another."

"I envy you, Crystal. Being in the line camp with Jube, I got a little lonely. I'm glad the snow stopped." Emily pulled her coat tighter about her.

"You're shivering, Em. We need to get you to the fire. Are you sure you're up to skating?"

"Oh no." Emily patted her rounding belly. "I came along for the company. I'll feel much better once I get warm." Emily scooted over to hook her arm in Jube's, who agreed they needed to get moving.

"Standing around won't keep us warm, but skating will," Beth said. "Let's go." Beth led the small group to the bonfire that Mary and Sara were feeding with wood. The fire snapped and popped and shot its flames upward into the sky to create a toasty retreat.

"Did you bring some skates, Crystal?" Josh asked.

Luke hurried over to the makeshift bench that Crystal sat on and placed a pair of skates before her feet. "I have a couple pairs right here for you to try." He more or less pushed his way in front of Josh and started unlacing a pair for her. Josh yanked his skates on and stood there, hands in his pockets. Crystal grinned. She watched as Luke's long fingers quickly worked on the eyelets of the skates. He had nice hands, and she remembered how his hands had caressed Buck's head and forelocks.

The first pair Luke tried was a perfect fit, but he laced them so tight that Crystal winced. "Sorry," Luke said, "they need to be tight around the ankle for support. He pulled her up into a standing position. "Now just stand still a moment and get the feel of them."

Crystal watched all her friends, some already whirling around on the frozen lake, and wondered how in the world she would ever be able to stand, let alone skate.

"I'll take her out, Luke. You get your skates on." Josh grabbed Crystal's gloved hand.

Somewhat unsure of her ability, Crystal followed Josh, her legs wobbling like jelly on a saucer. She leaned over, not trusting herself to stand up straight. She giggled and tried to cover her nervousness, but she was perfectly aware that Luke was miffed as he followed close behind.

Josh was a smooth skater, but he took smaller strides for her sake, and after five loops around the pond, Crystal could pull her chest and shoulders up. To her surprise, she had more balance this way. Mary and Sara were cheering her on by the fire, and Crystal yelled out to them in her excitement and waved, and would have lost her balance if it hadn't been for Josh's steady arm.

Luke skated closely behind them in case Crystal fell. He was fuming that Josh had just taken over. Crystal had never answered him when he'd asked about Josh the night Carmen had walked in on them. *Well, I won't play second fiddle to anyone. I've already told her how I feel.* He watched them laughing at her struggle and was amazed at how fast Crystal learned. Not great, but pretty good, considering this was her first time on skates.

"I'll take it from here, Josh. You can go get rested up or sit by the fire." Luke tapped Josh on the shoulder.

"Crystal's catching on fast. I don't believe she needs your help, Luke." Josh's voice was steady.

"She came here with me, and I intend to skate with her. Do you get that?" he said, poking Josh on his chest.

Josh was red-faced when he spoke. "Who put a burr under your saddle, Luke?" He nodded to Crystal. "I'll see you by the fire, Crystal." He released her hands and skated in the direction of the bonfire.

"Luke! Where are your manners?" Crystal said.

"Well, you *did* come with me, Crystal. Is he courting you, or what?" Luke pulled her around the circle of the lake in easy fashion.

"He most certainly is not. I was trying to let him down gently, as a matter of fact, when you interrupted."

"So where exactly do I stand, Crystal? Or do you want to leave me dangling like you did Josh? Maybe that's why Drew dropped you, since you flirted with all the men." The words tumbled out, and in a heartbeat he was sorry he had said them.

"How insulting! I haven't figured you out, Luke. One minute you're engaged to April, and the next minute you're telling me you want to court me. I find it mighty strange, Luke Weber, that you made a deal with McBride to marry his daughter just so you could have the land on the Blue River. Now that she's out of the picture and my aunt is gone, suddenly you are interested in me. Is it just so you can have Aspengold?" Crystal spat out the accusation, and Luke was shocked by her outburst. She stood on wobbly ankles, her hands on her hips.

"Watch out or you'll fall." He pulled her in the direction of the fire, holding on to her arms with a firm grip to keep her feet stable, while he faced her and skated backward. "If you think for one single minute that I want to marry you in order to own the ranch, you've got another think comin'! I already told you how I feel."

"Marry me!" Crystal squeaked. "We haven't even courted yet."

Luke's shirt collar felt tight around his neck now, and the muscles in his jaw clenched in frustration. As their voices grew louder, a few skaters slowed to watch them.

He wanted to tell her that he already owned the ranch, but this was not the place. So much for the perfect day he had planned. It was ruined, and they hadn't even had refreshments. "Crystal, honestly. You can't believe that . . . Do you think I would stoop that low?"

"I don't know . . . I'm not sure what to believe." Her voice wavered.

"Fine." Luke's voice was flat. "Have it your way." He turned away and skated off, his head down. He stared at the ice as though it held the answers to the questions tormenting his mind.

As he flew past the other skaters, he ignored their waves and greetings. He was wounded to the core. Had these past few months been just something to pass the time? Their time had always been shared when the other punchers and Carmen were around, but he thought Crystal had enjoyed his company. Why in the world did he think Crystal felt something for him? Apparently he mistook the signals she had given him as something else. Maybe she was just a flirt.

And why hadn't that lawyer sent her a post about the ranch deed? Or had Luke promised the attorney that he'd inform her? Why couldn't he remember something as simple as that conversation? He didn't know, but sure as the moon was rising, he would find out.

Luke saw April's large blue eyes look on from the edge of the lake, where she stood talking to Beth and Reverend Alden, but he turned away.

Women, who needs them?

The ride back to the ranch was a quiet one. Everyone was spent from the skating activity and the cold. Luke was glad because he didn't want to have to talk. He kept a good distance between him and Crystal, making certain that his side in no way touched hers. Once they arrived home, he brooded at the table, picked at the delicious soup Rusty had made, and contributed to the conversation with only minimal words. He did not stay for the usual after-dinner coffee but pulled his coat and gloves on and stepped out into the frigid night air. Out here he could breathe.

The moonlight played with the shadows created on the stark snow from the swaying boughs of the ponderosa pines. Luke took a deep breath and sighed. He walked over to the barn and strolled into the tack room, looking at nothing in particular. He lifted a bridle from its perch and felt the smooth leather under his fingers. He guessed he was a lot like a horse without a bridle. Without it, a horse didn't know which way a cowboy wanted him to go, but with the bit between the horse's jaws, the rider was the master and could direct the horse with a slight tug on the reins to go right or left.

Lord, I guess I lost my temper. I'm new at asking for Your help, but where Crystal's concerned . . . I guess I let my stubborn pride get in the way. I reckon I rushed her. I need another chance to make it up to her, 'cause I just went and made a fool of myself and clammed up instead of talking to her on the way home tonight. I guess what I'm asking for is Your direction, like Buck needs from me. I'd be grateful, Lord. I don't want to lose her. Amen.

Peace filled Luke's heart, and he smiled and placed the bridle back on its peg. He realized that his feet were growing numb, and the bitter cold was seeping into his layered clothing. As he stepped out into the cold night air to make his way to the bunkhouse, the solitary cry of a coyote stretched across the countryside, echoing the tranquility he felt in his heart.

23

The next morning passed in a hurry, and after lunch Crystal helped Carmen pack for a couple of months to visit her family. Carmen promised to return in the spring. The two hugged good-bye, and Crystal stood in the sharp wind and waved as Carmen drove the wagon across the snow-packed drive. Kurt had volunteered to follow on his horse for part of the way to make sure she had no problem finding the road that led to the valley into Stillwater, where her folks still lived.

Entering the house, Crystal realized how lonely she would be without her friend. She put on a fresh apron and started measuring out the ingredients for biscuits that would go with the beef stew Carmen had left simmering on the stove. Once Crystal mixed the ingredients, she dumped the lump onto the counter, kneaded it a few times, and formed the biscuits. She placed them on a pan and set them aside until right before supper. Wiping the flour off her hands, she wandered into the living room, at odds on what chore she should attend to next.

Crystal glanced over to the closed door that used to be her aunt's bedroom. She had not entered the room since her death, but now she felt drawn to open the door and step inside. Perhaps she could move her things into her aunt's larger room now.

Months of dust had collected on the bureau and nightstand. Kate's once-shiny, black Sunday boots, now dull, sat in front of a comfortable armchair. Across the bed, an everyday housedress lay as if waiting for the moment it would be worn. A lump caught in her throat, and Crystal almost retreated, but instead she willed herself to walk farther and stand before the wardrobe door. Easing the handle, she pulled the door open and peered inside. Tears sprang to her eyes. The scent of cedar and rose water floated into the air and hung there.

An exquisite sadness enveloped her. Crystal fingered the pale blue gown Kate had worn the night of the party given in Crystal's honor. Her aunt hadn't owned too many dresses and had preferred simple things to the extravagant. Weeping, Crystal clung to the dress and slid down to the floor in a heap. She wrapped her arms around her legs, and her sobbing shook her slight frame. The longing for her aunt was strong, but it also brought back memories of her parents, now gone on to heaven, and the thought made her sob all the more, the sorrow coming from deep within her soul.

"I go to prepare a place for you . . . that where I am, there ye may be also." The sound of Reverend Alden's voice reading Scripture next to the grave at Kate's funeral reverberated in her mind. The verse penetrated her heart and brought her sweet comfort. She knew the Lord cared about all her hurts, big and small.

Minutes passed, and Crystal wiped her eyes on the edge of her apron. She dragged herself up, thoroughly spent from sobbing, and the toe of her shoe caught on something. She looked down and spied a shoe box tied with an old rag and lying on its side.

Carefully she lifted the box and untied the clumsy knot. She felt as though she were looking into someone's private life. Inside the box were two envelopes, one addressed to her. The other one had the return address of a Denver attorney in the upper left-hand corner.

Her heart skipped a beat as she unfolded the letter written to her and recognized her aunt's handwriting.

My dear Crystal, what a joy it is to have you come live with me. God chose not to bless me with children, but He did bless me with a precious niece, and with Luke, whom I consider like my own son. To that effect, I hope you will understand what I have done in regards to the ranch in the event of my death, which hopefully is years from now.

I have had my attorney in Denver, whom I have known for years, draw up the necessary papers to document that I am leaving Aspengold to Luke Weber. Any income from the sale of cattle, though it won't be much, should go to you upon my death. In addition, I would like you to have this columbine pin that your uncle had made for me, because of the flower's beauty everywhere on the ranch. I hope you will wear it proudly.

I am asking that Luke allow Rusty to live as long as he likes at Aspengold. Nothing could please me more than to have you and Luke marry and find complete happiness filling this big house with children. He loves you. I know by the talks we've had, and how he looks at you when you enter the room.

An instant thrill slid down her spine when she read those words. Her aunt and Carmen were right. Luke did love her. She let that thought sink in for a moment and savored the sweetness of its possibilities. She remembered how he had kissed her, and his tenderness to her the night they had buried Curly. Her trembling lips formed a half smile as she continued reading the letter.

May God be your guide for the best future possible. I love you.

Aunt Kate

Crystal bit her lip, stifled the tears that threatened again, and held the beautiful flower pin close to her heart. Oh, how she wished Kate were here. The letter had been dated just two days before her death.

What a shock—Luke owned the ranch! Crystal just assumed the ranch was hers to inherit, because Kate had no other living relatives. Why wasn't she told? Maybe no one knew . . .

She must collect her thoughts. What a hot-tempered little fool she had been, accusing Luke of wanting to marry her to get the ranch. This was one of her bad habits that she needed to overcome, jumping to conclusions before she had all the facts. This changed things. She would have to tell Luke.

Crystal opened the other envelope, which revealed pretty much what Kate had stated in her letter, but in legal terms, with the Colorado seal affixed at the bottom. But where was the deed? It seemed the attorney should have sent it by now. Maybe the snow had delayed the mail in Steamboat. No matter. Her next step would be to see if she could straighten things out with Luke.

But where could she go? Back to Georgia? And see Drew with his new wife? Hardly. But she couldn't stay here now that the ranch wasn't hers. Maybe she could find some kind of work in Steamboat at the general store. The Franklins seemed to like her. And she would have to let Carmen go . . . Crystal could feel her neck muscles becoming tight and her head throbbing.

It was almost suppertime. She must hurry to set the table and stick the biscuits in the oven. But how was she going to face Luke? Crystal's appetite suddenly vanished and was replaced with a knot in her stomach.

All through supper, Crystal watched Luke for a sign that there could be a truce. By the look on his face, that was the farthest thing from his mind. He avoided Crystal's eyes and ate his dinner in silence. She barely picked at her food and kept quiet for most of the meal. Rusty was in the middle of one of his yarns in an effort to entertain them, but neither of them were paying attention.

Rusty dipped himself another bowl of stew and said, "I can't let Carmen's portion go to waste, now can I? Can I refill yours, Luke?"

"I think I've had all I can handle." Luke pushed his chair back to leave when there was a loud pounding on the front door.

Rusty dropped the soup ladle. "Who can that be?"

"I'll get it." Luke left the dining room and opened the front door, Crystal on his heels.

No sooner than he'd swung the door open, Jube burst in, exclaiming, "Crystal—you've got to come quick. It's Em . . . she's in a bad way." He paused to catch his breath.

"Jube, what is it?"

"She's been having terrible pains all afternoon, and I think the baby's coming too early. She's just five months. Please, can you come, and can someone send for the doc over in Stillwater?" Jube's eyes were wide and pleading.

"Of course I will. Now, get yourself some water to drink while I gather a few things. Luke, would you saddle a horse for me while I fetch Aunt Kate's medicine bag and some warm clothes?" Crystal made her way to the pantry and pictured how competently her aunt would have handled all this. The letter was still fresh in her mind, and Crystal knew that Kate believed she would be able to do whatever she put her mind to. Crystal wanted to show Luke that she could handle whatever crisis came her way.

"I'll do that, but I'm coming with you. You might need some help." Luke sprang into action and in two strides hurried out to saddle the horses.

"What's all the commotion?" Rusty scratched his red beard and met Crystal at the pantry.

"It's Emily. She may be in labor. Could you go for the doc in Stillwater—I think he's closer—and then send word over to Sara to come as quickly as she can? It's a long way out to their place." Crystal headed to the door and struggled into her warm coat and gloves.

"You can count on me. You know that."

By the time Crystal stepped outside, Luke was waiting for her. He was leading Bess and had readied a fresh mount for Jube. The three of them quickly left for the line cabin, heedless of the new snow that had begun to fall.

On the ride to the cabin, Crystal went over in her mind everything she knew about babies, which wasn't very much. But she did know that it was too soon for Emily's child to enter the world.

She shuddered. *Please, God, take care of that little baby and Emily. Calm her heart and fears, and help me too!*

In short order they made it to the cabin, even though the snow was thicker now. They threw the reins over the hitching post, and Jube opened the cabin door. Moans escaped the closed bedroom door, and Crystal saw the fear in Jube's wide eyes.

"I'll just go take care of the horses. Let me know if I'm needed." Luke backed out, looking uncomfortable.

Jube opened the door, and they entered the bedroom. Crystal tried to put on a bright face for Emily, who was writhing in pain, her hair damp against the pillow. She stepped close to the bed, took Emily's hand in hers, and patted it. "Em . . . I'm here. I want to help you. How close are the pains?"

"About . . . four minutes. I'm not sure," she managed between gritted teeth. "Crystal, it's too soon. But I can't stop it . . . ooh, it hurts!" She tried to sit up with each contraction.

"Now, just lie back down, Emily, and take some deep breaths. Maybe we can halt the labor. I'll check you out." Crystal made her voice as steady as possible, but in truth she was scared to death. She couldn't help but see the cradle that Jube had set up near the fire, and her heart jerked.

"Jube, why don't you go sit in the kitchen, and I'll call you when I need you." She guided him to the door and patted him on the shoulder. "Try not to worry."

She didn't have to tell him twice, and he sat stiffly next to Luke, who had returned after getting the horses settled.

Closing the door behind her, Crystal squared her shoulders, determined to do whatever she could to help her friend. She wished Carmen hadn't left today. She would have known what to do.

"Emily, I'm going to pull back the blankets and check you now." Crystal was surprised at her own voice. She sounded so in control, but her hands were shaking. Emily nodded and closed her eyes. Pain coursed through her pale face.

Lifting the cover, Crystal drew in a sharp breath. There was blood on the sheets.

Oh, dear God, what do I do now? she pleaded. There would be no stopping this baby, she was sure of that. And there was no hope of its survival. What had Jube told her—that Emily was barely five months?

She replaced the cover, watching the clock tick the minutes between Emily's contractions. Two minutes now. Emily grabbed her hand in a nightmare grip.

"That's right, squeeze as hard as you like, Em."

When Emily's pain subsided, Crystal opened the door and asked Luke to rustle up a pan of hot, soapy water and some clean cloths. "Do you want to help me, Jube?"

Jube stood. "I just can't go back in there, Crystal. Is the baby coming?"

"I'm afraid so, Jube. There's nothing I can do to stop it. Emily's bleeding quite a bit."

Jube turned so white that Luke had to reach out to steady him. Luke pushed him back into his chair. "Take it easy, buddy." Luke's face was masked in concern.

"Luke, after you get the clean cloths, please step into the bedroom. I may need you."

Jube rallied. "I'll get the cloths and water. I'm not helpless." But Luke hurried to heat up the water. "You stay put," he directed Jube.

A piercing wail came from the direction of the bedroom, and Crystal hurried back in.

"I can't do this, Crystal! We wanted this baby," Emily cried.

"Shh . . . calm down. We have to let nature take its course, sweetie." Crystal removed her coat and rolled up the sleeves of her dress. She took Emily's hand again and gave it an affectionate squeeze.

Before long Luke knocked softly on the door, and Crystal called out for him to come in. He carried a couple of worn towels along with hot water in a huge enamel pan and set them on the bureau, then stood next to the bed.

Crystal peeled Emily's fingers from her hand and placed them inside Luke's larger one. "Hold on to Luke's hand, Em." Crystal was in control now, and she stole a glance at Luke, whose eyes peered back at hers.

"Where . . . is Jube? I need him," Emily panted.

"Jube is just fine, Emily. He is getting things that you need. Luke can hold your hand," Crystal said above the rising of Emily's voice.

Crystal stood near the foot of the bed, washed her arms and hands in the hot soapy water, and dried them quickly. It wouldn't be long before the baby would be expelled. *Lord, help me.* When she glanced down and saw how much blood Emily had lost, she mouthed "pray" to Luke, and he nodded his agreement.

Crystal pulled back the covers as far as was decent, ready to receive the tiny form within all the bloody mess. "Push, Emily, push!" Emily cried out one last time and then fell back into her pillows.

Crystal's hands were now covered with blood. She lifted the

tiny baby, a little bigger than her palm, and wiped away the dark, sticky matter. Tears sprang to her eyes, and she looked up at Luke, who was stone-faced, and swallowed hard. Thankfully Emily had passed out. Crystal took a sharp knife that Jube had sterilized earlier and swiftly cut the umbilical cord, then tied it with string.

Tears streamed down Crystal's face. She watched as Luke took the bloody infant from her with care and wrapped it tenderly in a flannel blanket that he'd found in the cradle.

"It was a little girl . . ." Crystal's voice croaked. She wiped her bloodied hands on a fresh towel and looked into Luke's eyes, which mirrored her own pain. He stared back at her, the muscles in his jaw flexing with emotion, and Crystal reached out and touched his forearm.

Whimpering from the bed brought Crystal back to Emily, who had wakened. Kneeling, she took Emily's hand in her own and pressed it to her chest. "Oh, Em . . . I'm so sorry." Crystal chewed her bottom lip to keep from trembling, but Emily just continued to weep softly.

"I've sent for your mother and the doctor. They should be here soon."

"I want . . . to see Jube, Crystal. Does he know?"

"Not yet. Look, I need to clean you up a bit." Crystal wiped Emily's face. "So you just lie still now. Luke will bring Jube in a bit."

As Crystal turned to go, Emily's hand on her arm stopped her. "What was it?"

Emily's sad face was hard for Crystal to look at. "A little girl . . . I'm about to clean her up for you, Em."

Crystal stuffed the lump back down in her throat and reached for the warm soapy water in the enamel pan to reverently wash the tiny bundle that Luke held. She thought she detected a tear at the corner of his eye.

She continued with her ministrations and wrapped a soft blanket around the baby. How delicate and precious. Inside her heart was breaking. *"Be strong for Emily and Jube,"* she could almost hear Kate say.

Crystal brought the baby to Emily, who seemed to be trying hard not to lose control. She pressed the baby to her wet face.

Crystal stepped back to the foot of the bed and was horrified at the blood beginning to pool. She hurriedly tried to staunch the flow and felt so incompetent. Crystal wished she knew what to do next. *Hurry, Doc, please hurry,* her mind screamed.

Luke washed his hands, then handed Crystal fresh towels and averted his eyes as he stepped outside to talk with Jube. She folded the towels and, with a little help from Emily, placed them underneath her hips. Emily's face was so pale. *She just has to make it, Lord. Please stop the bleeding, if it be Your will. Jube needs her,* Crystal prayed.

The sound of voices outside the door interrupted her praying. Thank God the doctor was here now. He could take over.

Crystal was only too happy to relinquish her patient into the kind and capable hands of Dr. Gibbons, who remarked at what a good job Crystal had done thus far for Emily. Most important now was that the bleeding be stopped before they lost Emily too.

Luke took Crystal's arm and led her to a nearby chair in the other room of the cabin. She waited with Luke and Jube and prayed. It seemed like hours, but in truth, it was a short time before the doctor stuck his head out and declared that the bleeding had stopped. The three of them jumped to their feet at the sound of the door.

"She's mighty weak, losing all that blood, but I think with adequate rest, she'll make it," the doctor said, looking over his spectacles at Jube. "You go on in now. She's asking for you, son."

Relief flooded their faces, and Crystal sank into her chair, exhausted.

Crystal and Luke stayed with Emily and Jube the rest of the evening. Crystal offered what comfort she could and fixed them a light supper, although no one had an appetite. Emily sipped a little broth, but after the gentle urging of Jube, who refused to leave her side, she managed to drink it.

Sara arrived while the doctor was giving strict orders for Emily to stay in bed for the next two weeks. Sara now took over and lovingly enfolded Emily in her arms, stroking her hair with tenderness. Sara's sad face and red-rimmed eyes spoke volumes about her daughter's loss to Crystal.

"She needs her rest now, Mrs. Johnson." Dr. Gibbons snapped his bag shut, indicating he had done all he could this day. It was apparent that he wished to speak to the others in private. They understood and followed him out of the room, where Luke was stoking a crackling fire that filled the small room with warmth.

The doctor wasted no time with small talk. "Most people die with miscarriages at this stage, but I was able to deliver the afterbirth to allay infection. Thank God I was able to get here so soon." He ran his hand through his hair.

"I don't know how to thank you, Doc," Jube said.

"No need, friend. I'll come back to check on her later this week. If you need anything, you just send for me." After giving Sara instructions on mixing laudanum for Emily's pain, the kind doctor left.

What a long day, Crystal thought. She had an ache in her shoulders that matched the one in her heart. She thought it best that she and Luke leave the small cabin so that the family could have their privacy, but not until she looked in on Emily.

She was propped up on two pillows, and her smile was very weak when Crystal sat on the edge of the bed.

"Crystal . . . thank you."

"Shh . . . don't thank me, thank God that you're going to be okay. You just get your rest now and do as your mother says, okay?"

"Maybe I'll never have children, Crystal . . ."

"Don't think about that right now. I'm sure you will."

"But why didn't I get to keep this baby?" Tears started filling her blue eyes again.

"Honey, I wish I could answer that. Only the good Lord knows why you lost this baby . . . but I do know your baby is in Jesus's arms right now. You'll have a baby when the time is right, and it will be a healthy baby too. But you're exhausted. I'll pray for you to regain your strength in a hurry. I'm going now so you can get your rest, and we'll talk again later. I'll leave you in your mother's care, and there's no better place to be."

Emily's swollen eyes were already heavy now with the dose of laudanum the doctor had administered. Crystal stood, bent down to smooth the quilt over Emily, and quietly tiptoed out.

Snow had been falling all day and had accumulated four inches more atop the snow that fell earlier in the week. When the snow made the going slow on their horses, Luke began to talk in a quiet voice about life and death and the sadness of it all.

"You know, when Curly died, I started thinking . . . I always knew there was a God, but I didn't know He cared about me in a personal way. I listened to you and Curly talking that night about the stars and God's handiwork, and then the next day Curly was dead." Luke's voice cracked with emotion.

Crystal strained to hear what he said next, sensing his openness to talk about his feelings.

"I couldn't get it off my mind. Then I really started paying attention to what Reverend Alden had to say. It began to make sense. Although Kate always took me to church, she never forced her belief in Jesus on me. I guess she was letting me make up my own mind . . ."

"And did you?" Crystal held her breath.

Luke stopped his horse. Crystal did likewise, heedless of the biting wind and snow.

"Remember the day of the bazaar? That was the day I broke up with April. I had certainly made a mess of things. That very night I asked God to forgive me for my past mistakes and be a part of my life from then on. I figured if it was good enough for Curly, then it was good enough for me."

Crystal's heart quickened. She looked across the distance

separating them and into Luke's piercing blue eyes, hardly able to believe what she'd just heard. "Oh, Luke. That's the best news I've heard in a long time. You will not regret making that decision."

"Well, there has to be more to life besides ranching. But I don't have it all figured out yet. Then today with Emily losing her baby . . . well, it was hard. I had to believe Someone other than me is in control of our lives, or it just plain wouldn't make sense."

"I don't understand everything either, Luke. But that's a good place to start." Crystal nudged Bess to follow Luke as they made their way through the new drifts of snow. While Crystal was thrilled about this new piece of news, it didn't change the fact that she would have to leave the ranch. Her eyes misted over when she thought of leaving Luke, and she felt a knot in her chest. Once he found out the ranch was his, he wouldn't have to pretend with her anymore. He could court whomever he liked.

Crystal was weary by the time they reached the ranch, and it was already dark. The sun had gone down behind the mountain range, and Crystal was cold through and through. Rusty was in the kitchen, keeping supper hot for them.

"How's Emily?" Rusty met them with hot cups of coffee and took their coats while they stood next to the fire.

"She lost the baby . . . " Crystal's voice trailed off. This was her first experience with babies and pregnancy, let alone the death of a baby. Her heart felt heavy, and she turned to heat her backside, noting the sadness flicker across Rusty's face.

"Aw . . . that's just too bad." He scratched his red head. "I kept a little supper hot. I'll dish it up while you two warm yourselves, and then you can tell me all about it."

"Thanks, Rusty." Luke took his hat off and threw his gloves inside it. His forehead bore a hatband mark, and his thick dark hair was matted down. If Crystal hadn't been so sad, she would have made a teasing comment, but she knew now was not the time for lightheartedness.

"I was proud of you today, Crystal," Luke said huskily. "I know that was not something you expected you'd ever have to do."

"Thank you, Luke. I was scared. It was the good Lord that got me through it. I feel so terrible for Jube and Emily."

"You delivered Emily's baby?" Rusty blinked with surprise, just about dropping the biscuits he was carrying to the table.

"Well, let's just say, I did all I could until the doctor arrived, but Luke was a big help. I wish I could have done more."

"She did all that was humanly possible," Luke told Rusty.

They sat at the small kitchen table, and Rusty poured more coffee and poked at the fire a few times while the two of them ate. He reminded Crystal so much of her aunt, always bustling around attending to everyone's needs. That made Crystal think of the letter she had read earlier. *Had that just been today?* It seemed like days ago. Tomorrow, when she was rested, she would figure out where she would go and what she would do.

Luke was quiet, dipping his biscuit in his coffee. Before, this kind of habit would have driven her crazy, but now Crystal thought it endearing. He looked up, and his eyes searched hers. What was he thinking?

Wait until he finds out he owns the ranch.

She would tell him first thing in the morning after breakfast, after everyone else went about their ranch duties. She was too weary to mention it in front of Rusty, because she knew he would ask a lot of questions. Right now she didn't want to talk about that. The only thing she wanted to do was get into her warm gown and robe and just sit by the fire, to be alone with her thoughts tonight.

Luke excused himself and headed off to the bunkhouse, and that made Crystal feel worse. She knew that this was his house, and if not for her, he could be sleeping in a nice, comfortable bed instead of sharing a bunkhouse with Kurt and Rusty.

She and Rusty carried the dishes to the sink. "You just go make yourself comfortable, and I'll clean up the kitchen. That's one thing I'm good at." Rusty started on the plates and scraped them clean.

"Rusty, how well do you know Luke?" Crystal asked.

"Well . . . let's see now, he came here as a fourteen-year-old boy as far as I can remember, and his parents were Kate's closest friends. They lived on the Blue River. Why?"

When Crystal hesitated, he asked, "Is something on your mind besides Emily tonight?" He didn't look up but continued with his chore.

"A lot of things. Were his parents good people?"

"They were for a fact, missy. Why do you ask?"

"He told me tonight that he had asked God into his heart the night of the bazaar."

"Does that surprise you?" He stacked the clean plates on a fresh towel to dry.

"I guess . . . We had a big fight yesterday, and he didn't act so Christian."

"Crystal, you don't go pulling up your carrots from the garden to see if they're growing and then shove them back in the ground, do you? Give him time to grow. His faith is new, not that he was ever a bad person to begin with. Luke wants to do the right thing, and he's a man of his word."

"I guess my own faith has grown since my daddy died and then Aunt Kate. I know I have a lot more to learn too. I don't know why I should expect so much of others when I'm not being the best that I can be either."

Rusty gave her a quick, fatherly hug. "That's human nature, missy. You are doing fine, what with having to find your own way and all. Just let the good Lord above be first, and everything else will fall into place." Rusty set the last dish on the towel. "Now, as for me, that last dish is done. Can't wait for Carmen to get back," he said good-naturedly. "I'm off to bed. See you in the mornin'."

After a restless night going over the day's events and the letter from her aunt, Crystal knew what she must do. Once the men had had breakfast and set about their chores, she pulled her suitcase out of the closet and started packing the most needed items. Later, when she knew where she would be staying, she would send for her trunk.

She would miss the life here that she had come to know. Maybe she should have left when her aunt died.

Crystal picked up the columbine pin and tucked it between the folds of her clothes. She had no animosity toward Luke because Kate hadn't left the ranch to her. Now she just felt embarrassment that she had given orders to the cowboys as if she owned the place and had decided to take over without ever giving legal ownership a second thought. It just never occurred to her.

Her first stop would be Franklin's Mercantile. She would ask Mary if she could use some help in the store and perhaps find a room at the boardinghouse.

Crystal dragged the case into the front room. She would see if Rusty would drive her to Steamboat. Tiny snowflakes began to fall, and it was bitterly cold. She went back to fetch the letter from her aunt to give to Luke before leaving, and she was just getting ready to go find Rusty when Luke knocked on the door and walked in.

"Crystal, I'm going to ride up to the line cabin later and check on Emily—" He stopped dead in his tracks. "You going somewhere?"

Crystal swallowed hard. "I'm going to see if Rusty will drive me into Steamboat this morning."

"Whatever for? It's still snowing." He raised an eyebrow and frowned.

She moved around him with a snap to her step. "It's best that I leave, Luke."

"Crystal, what are you talking about? What do you mean, leave? Permanently?"

She wouldn't meet his eyes. "Luke, I have something for you." Crystal handed him the envelope that held the letter from the attorney. She watched him unfold the parchment and read it. Her mouth went dry, and she waited for his anger to descend on her like a thundercloud.

He shifted his hips, making his spurs jangle softly. "When were you going to tell me?" His voice was stern, but his steady blue eyes were kind. Before she could answer, he asked, "How long have you known?"

"I found out yesterday, right before we left for Emily's. There just wasn't a time to tell you."

"So, you were just gonna up and leave?"

"This place belongs to you, Luke. I have no right here." Crystal couldn't meet his gaze.

Luke took a step closer. "Don't leave . . . I knew about the deed when the trail drive ended in Denver."

"What! And you never said anything?" Crystal's heart was pounding in her ears.

"I wanted to, but I didn't because I figured you'd go back to Georgia."

"But how could you *not* tell me? Especially after I made a complete fool of myself that night at the skating party, saying you wanted to marry me in order to own the ranch." Hot anger flashed over Crystal. She stepped away from him and jerked her coat off the peg, nearly pulling the rack right off the wall.

Luke placed a hand on her arm. "I'm sorry. I thought if you knew the place rightfully belonged to me, you would leave and go back to Georgia and Drew."

"Instead, for months you let me dictate orders to you and the cowboys, when I had no right to?" Crystal was shaking now. Her conscience pricked her. She knew her indignation was not warranted. She knew if she looked straight into his eyes, she would crumble.

Luke took her coat and hung it back on the peg and reached for her trembling hands. His callused hands were warm as he caressed hers. "Crystal . . ." His voice was low and husky. "Please look at me."

Crystal slowly lifted her eyes to look at Luke's pleading blue ones. His nearness made it difficult to breathe. "I'm so embarrassed that I just assumed a role that I was not entitled to. What will everyone think?"

"It doesn't matter what they think as long as we set it straight. They won't care, believe me. They love you, and you have treated us all like family. Just like Kate did. I wouldn't have expected any less." Luke continued to hold her hands. "I never meant to hurt you. I wanted to protect you. Don't you see? I don't care about the ranch, I care about you, and I don't think I could live without you if you left. I realized that fact on the trail drive, and that's why I had to break it off with April. I'm sorry for everything you've had to go through since you came here. And I'm sorry for all your losses you had in Georgia. I'm sorry for that smart comment about Drew too. If you'd let me, I'd like to take away that loneliness you have. I want us to be real partners, Crystal, if you'll have me. I've already been praying about this, and I believe we would have God's blessing."

"Oh, Luke, I'm sorry too," she whispered. "I was afraid that you really wanted Aspengold instead of me. I have judged you wrongly."

His fingers reached up to graze her face, and he pulled her to his chest. Crystal welcomed his embrace and encircled his back with her arms. She was right where she'd always wanted to be since the first day she'd met him. *Thank you, God. You've kept the best for last.*

Crystal pulled back and turned her face up to him, inviting a kiss. Luke was so tall that he had to lean down and lift her up to kiss her. Crystal had waited months for this kiss. A flicker of passion quickened deep within her heart as she returned his kiss. His moustache tickled her upper lip, and she giggled and pulled back for air, breathless.

"You are so beautiful, Crystal, inside and out. I love you and cannot bear thinking of spending one day of my life without you." Luke set her feet back on the floor. His eyes shone, full of love and expectation.

"I love you too, Luke. But you know I can't cook very well. Are you sure about this?" Crystal laughed, but she seriously wanted to know if he loved her with all her flaws.

"That's one of the things I love about you—your honesty and humor. Don't ever change. I love everything about you." He pulled her to him and crushed his lips against hers again. "Don't guess I'll ever get that fried chicken?"

"Together we might have fun learning how to whip up a whole dinner on the church grounds." She reached up to touch his eyebrow with her thumb. "Yes, I think it'll be fun to live in the Wild West."

25

A black-crested, brilliant blue Steller's jay swooped down and perched on the ledge of an open window of the little white church, as though called to be a witness of the ceremony taking place inside. The day couldn't be a more perfect one on this pristine June afternoon. Despite a chilly start, it had warmed to an agreeable temperature. Luke couldn't be happier than he was at this moment. He surveyed the small room and smiled to see so many in attendance.

Guests crammed the pews. Friends, cowboys, farmers of the Yampa Valley, and merchants from Steamboat had driven miles, excited to be a part of this happy occasion. Emily, now expecting again, sat with Jube's arm curled protectively around her shoulders. Luke nodded at them. He was tickled for them and prayed that God would protect this child. Kurt sat with the Johnsons. Everyone Luke cared about was here, except Kate and Curly, and he felt his eyes sting at the thought.

He was surprised to see the McBride family present. April was sitting between her parents, and Josh was next to his mother. Crystal insisted on inviting them. Luke guessed that April didn't want to miss any social event if there were eligible men present. When he had run into her in Steamboat, he'd talked to her, but she had been cool toward him. Luke didn't wish her any ill will. He hoped one day she could find happiness, and he prayed God would change her heart.

The organ music started playing the wedding march, and Luke and Reverend Alden turned to face the back of the church, awaiting the moment Crystal would walk down the aisle.

Carmen entered in a green gown. Hadn't he seen that somewhere?

Even though it was a mild day, Luke was sweating beneath his necktie and vest. His nervousness took him by surprise. He'd waited all winter for this very moment.

He had stayed in the bunkhouse, despite Crystal's offer to move into a hotel, and had spent a lot of time with Rusty, fixing up the log house when weather permitted. Crystal had decided that she and Luke would move into her aunt's larger room once they were married, so Rusty had helped her clean the room and get it ready for the couple. Luke had wanted to make sure that he and Crystal would have free time to get to know each other more and, who knows, maybe start a family.

Now it was all he could do to wait, and he nervously shifted his weight from one leg to the other.

Crystal entered the church door on Rusty's arm, an exquisite vision of loveliness, and Luke's chest swelled with pride as she glided down the aisle toward him. He knew Mary had created the wedding gown from the cream silk fabric he had recovered after the tornado.

He was so glad he had found it now, after seeing what a beautiful wedding dress Crystal and Mary had designed. The columbine broach was pinned on the lace at her throat. She wore the cream hat but had attached a thin layer of tulle that fell over her face. Luke could see her eyes shining brightly beneath it. He smiled widely at her, his clammy hands hanging at his side.

In her hands she carried a bouquet of bright blue columbines held together with cream ribbons. Luke swallowed the huge lump that had formed in his throat. *Thank you, God, for this gift you have given me. I will make you and Kate proud.*

Crystal was barely aware of the approving sighs from the guests. She could not take her eyes off her handsome bridegroom. She walked toward the front of the church, where he stood waiting with the reverend. The love she saw shining in the depths of his blue eyes covered her like warm sunshine covered the wildflowers. He looked so handsome in his new suit.

Her heart was thumping hard against her chest, and she gave him her best smile, though her bottom lip quivered. *Don't cry now.* Thoughts of her parents and Kate threatened to cause her to crumble. She pushed the sad feelings aside, knowing that they would all be happy that she had found the love of her life and a new beginning.

It had been a very long winter indeed, cold and harsh, but the one thing that had kept Crystal's spirits up was looking forward to the future. When the aspen leaves had turned from their scarlet colors and had fallen to the ground, leaving their limbs bare in the winter, she had leaned on God and His promises. In the spring, when tiny green buds had begun to sprout on the aspen trees, it seemed a signal to her of the new inner strength and hope she had gained.

She had come a long way since she came to this rugged land that was so foreign to her, and she loved the people here. Most of them were genuine, honest, and hardworking folks determined to carve out a future for their children. But, even more surprising, she had come to love the land too, and the longings for Georgia seemed to be a sweet memory.

Thank you, God, for bringing me out here to find this strong, faithful man who wants to please You and care for me. I'm so grateful, Lord. For You know the thoughts that You think toward me . . . thoughts of peace, and not of evil, to give me an expected end.

She barely remembered Rusty saying, "I give this woman in marriage," as she handed her bouquet to Carmen, who was crying. Reverend Alden took her hands and placed them in Luke's, and they turned to face each other, hearts bursting with love, ready to speak their vows in commitment to God before His people.

A Sneak Peek

HEART
of the WEST * 2

THE
JEWEL
OF HIS *Heart*

1896
Utica, Montana

I need a wife.

Josh McBride rode down a grassy slope to the sparkling creek, allowing his horse, Pete, a drink while surveying with a keen eye the parcel of land he'd purchased three years before.

It's pretty here—the best spot on God's good earth,

But that didn't keep him from feeling lonely.

He was enjoying the beautiful Montana mountains this morning, and the satisfaction of pursuing his own dream and place in the world instead of his father's. On these solitary morning rides, he treasured the peace and privacy with his Creator, feeling His presence.

He took his bandana from his neck and dipped it into the cold stream to wipe his face. The creek narrowed at this juncture to not much more than a trickle, or Josh might have missed the handful of small blue pebbles that had collected there. Reaching into the icy water, he scooped the pebbles up for a closer look. The sunlight reflected off the translucent blue pebbles, their hue unlike anything Josh had ever seen. Instinctively he knew these were not just blue pebbles or ordinary stones, but what he did not know was how they would ultimately change his life forever.

Josh slipped the handful of blue stones into his leather vest pocket and mounted his horse. He headed back to the grassy rise overlooking the valley, pausing to gaze with pride at his sizable herd of sheep. Suddenly Josh's white and amber dog, Shebe, ran up to gaze at him lovingly, her tongue lolling from the side of her mouth.

"Hey, girl. Looking for me?"

Shebe's short bark was her answer, and Josh laughed. "We've sure been through some lonely times, haven't we, girl?"

"Boss McBride!" A rider below waved his hat at Josh and pushed his horse up the grassy ridge.

Josh called back a greeting to his youngest sheepherder, Andy, and nudged Pete's flanks with his boot heel. He'd left his spurs behind when he rode off his father's cattle ranch. Besides, he and Pete understood each other perfectly. Josh sometimes thought Pete and Shebe understood him better than anyone else, and his affection for his horse and sheepdog ran deep. But still, he wanted a wife. A dog and a horse could not take the place of a companion and fill the lonely space in his heart.

"What's up, Andy?" Josh reined Pete in next to Andy's horse.

"There's a grub-line rider down at the camp. Said he was passing this way from Lewistown. Think he said his name was Charlie."

"Does he want to join up, or is he just looking for a place to light for a few days?"

"I'm not sure, Boss. Reckon you'd better talk to him yourself. He's a bit different, and carrying some strange-looking canvas case with him." Andy folded his arms across his saddle horn, waiting for the boss's direction.

"All right, Andy. I'll follow you back to camp. You have the coffee hot?"

"Don't I always?" he said matter-of-factly.

They ambled along in silence. The worn leather saddle, with Josh's .44 Winchester rifle packed across the front, creaked under his shifting weight. Except for an occasional snort from their horses, it was a calm, still day. A lone eagle soared above the timberline, sending out its shrill call into the bright morning skies. Shebe was not far behind her beloved master.

As they entered the small clearing where the sheep wagon was parked by a bubbling creek, a handsome wrangler rose from a stump, a cigarette dangling from his lips. He wore a floppy hat pushed back at the crown, exposing a shock of long blond bangs that fell across his forehead. He sported a red sash around his neck.

"Howdy." He quickly threw the cigarette down, ground it out under his heel, and walked toward them.

"Hi yourself. What can I do for you? Our camp is quite a ways out for strangers." Josh dismounted, and Andy followed, taking the horses' reins. Josh was careful when strangers appeared, never knowing who to trust when someone dropped by unexpectedly.

The stranger stuck out his hand. "I'm Charlie Russell. Live over in Great Falls, just passing through. I saw your camp and thought a good cup of hot coffee would be mighty nice." His smile was warm and friendly, and he had a sparkle in his eyes.

Josh shook his hand. "My name's Josh McBride. I own the sheep, and Andy here is my sheepherder. Where ya headed?"

"I was over in Lewistown, and now I'm heading home. Crossed the Judith River and saw smoke from your campfire."

"Sit down, Charlie. Andy, how 'bout a cup of java?"

Josh felt an instant liking for Charlie. He was apparently friendly, and good-looking too. *Bet he has a way with the women. He could've talked Crystal into taking off to Montana, had he known her.* Josh was startled by the turn his thoughts had taken. It had been some time since he had given Crystal any thought. He knew that she was happy and that Luke adored her. Josh had finally come to terms with that.

Charlie sipped from the chipped enameled cup Andy had given him. "I may have to sketch you with that friendly dog you have there, Josh. What's her name?"

Josh scratched Shebe's head lovingly as she sat on her haunches next to her master, keeping a keen eye on Charlie. "I call her Shebe. She's my best friend, right, girl?" Shebe barked in happy agreement.

Charlie yanked open the black box he was carrying and pulled out a sketch pad and pencils. Josh started to move away. "No, just sit right there with Shebe. We can just talk. You can tell me about yourself." He flipped open his pad to a clean sheet and outlined Josh and his dog.

"Not much to tell. I'm a sheepherder by way of Colorado, where my daddy is a cattle baron. I wanted to spread my wings and experience something different. Started out with a small herd of sheep that Andy mostly tends now. I have a cabin, but I'm planning on building me a real home soon. What about you?"

Charlie seemed eager to talk. "I'm an artist of sorts. Hung up my spurs in '92 after wrangling since I was sixteen. I used to be a horse wrangler with some of the best outfits around. I once worked at Judith River Basin as the night hawk. From time to time, I drew scenes of wrangling, calf branding, and cattle drives. I guess you could say that I'm a self-taught artist. Once people actually wanted to buy my paintings, well, I decided to hang up my spurs and pursue my dream."

"Self-taught? Well, there has to be talent involved. I could no more teach myself to paint than design a ship that would hold up at sea." Josh fidgeted, shifting to a more comfortable position.

"Hold still, I'll be done here pretty quick."

Charlie's eyes twinkled, and he laughed as he deftly sketched an image that was beginning to emerge as Josh's face, showing him playfully touching Shebe's head as she lay curled at his feet. "Shucks, everything can be learned. I grew up in Missouri and left at sixteen to live out my childhood fantasy, but if it hadn't been for my good friend Hoover, I wouldn't have learned or experienced the ways of frontier life or being a cowboy. He took me under his wing and taught me the ropes." Charlie grinned at them. "Hey! That's funny. He did teach me how to rope." He chortled. "I did a little sheepherding myself for Pike Miller's sheep ranch near Judith Basin, but I didn't stick with it, and he was glad to see me go. But Hoover taught me a lot."

Andy, who was stirring up cornmeal batter, strolled back to where Charlie was adding the finishing touch to his sketch of Josh. "That name sounds familiar . . . Hoover." He walked behind Charlie and looked over his shoulder at the drawing. "Well, I'll be doggoned. That looks just like you, Josh." Andy just shook his head in awe. "I never knew an artist."

"I'm pleased that you like it, Andy. Can't say I'm really making much money at it yet. Anyway, as I was saying, Hoover's a mountain man. He did a little gold mining too, but never struck it big. I lived with him at his cabin at Pig Eye Basin. His latchstring was always out. I think he really loved people, along with his habit of drinking. I could use a drink myself."

"I don't drink." Josh cleared his throat. "So, you won't find one in my camp."

"No matter. I'm about done here. As I was saying, Hoover discovered sapphires near Utica, and I think he's formed a partnership to mine there with some investors."

"Wish I could find gold or somethin' somewhere," Andy said, pouring himself some coffee. "You staying for grub?"

"Is that an invite?"

Josh nodded, rising stiffly to peer at the picture Charlie had drawn. "Pretty good picture. Guess we owe you some beans and johnnycakes. You're welcome to stay."

"That's mighty kind of you, and I think I will." Charlie held out the picture toward Josh. "Here, you can have this."

"No thanks, Charlie. I have nowhere to put it right now. Keep it for your portfolio. Maybe you'll be famous someday." Josh lifted the lid on the pot of beans, and the savory smell wafted out into the chilly morning air. "The beans are close to being done. Andy, flip us some of your johnnycakes to go along with this."

Charlie stuffed the sketch and his pencils back in his canvas case. "Sounds good to me. Is there anything I can help with?"

"Nope," Andy said. "There's some oats over in that there barrel if you want to give your horse a nibble."

"Thanks. I'll do that."

Josh watched Charlie as he proceeded to pour oats in a bucket for his horse. He was an affable cowpoke, easy to talk to. Josh couldn't help but wonder what kind of skills he had as a cowboy, but thought Charlie was at least a pretty decent artist.

The rest of the workday brought nothing unusual. Josh pulled a bleating lamb from a thicket, and it began frantically looking for its mother. Charlie tagged along. He talked the entire time, as if finding the whole realm of sheepherding interesting.

The sun was just beginning to slip behind the purple mountains of Tollgate Hill when Josh and Charlie tethered their horses. Josh removed Pete's saddle while Charlie gave the horses fresh water to drink.

"Mmm . . . I'm about to starve to death," Charlie said when they entered the campsite.

"Good thing, 'cause I'm just about to dish up the food." Andy was flipping johnnycakes on the open fire with a flick of his wrist.

"Andy, you've turned out to be a good cook. I'm hungry myself. Hope there's some coffee to go with it." Josh smiled at Andy.

"Matter of fact, I just made some fresh."

Josh looked at the young man bent over the fire. Andy made him smile inwardly at his eagerness to please. He was a runaway from a stepfather who was meaner than a snake. Josh was glad he had hired him—Andy was worth his weight in gold. Josh had never had a younger brother, only his sister, April, and that was another thing altogether.

Later, Charlie wiped his mouth with the back of his hand. "Pardner, that was some fine eating that I wasn't expecting out here tonight. Thank you, Andy."

"It's my secret ingredient."

301

"And what might that be?" Charlie laughed.

"If I told you, Charlie, it wouldn't be a secret anymore."

Josh chuckled at the two of them. It was getting dark now. He poked the fire, sending orange sparks upward and lighting the faces of Charlie and Andy. He suddenly remembered the blue stones tucked away in his vest pocket. He took another swig of his coffee, set his tin cup down, and pulled out the blue pebbles. Holding them in his palm near the firelight, they twinkled like distant stars.

Andy and Charlie stopped talking when they saw the pebbles in the firelight. Andy let out a soft whistle. "Hey, whatcha got there, Josh?"

"I'm not sure. Found these today in the creek bed when I stopped to let Pete drink. I just remembered." Josh was fascinated with the cornflower blue of the stones as his fingers pushed them around in his palm.

"If you find more, you may be able to build that home quicker than you think," Charlie said. "Remember my friend Hoover that I told you about?" Josh nodded. "Well, these look like the blue stones that he found last year at Yogo Creek. You ought to take those to Lewistown next time you're up that way and have 'em looked at. Could be you're holding your future in the palm of your hand, Josh."

Josh stared at the stones, then tucked them back into his inside vest pocket. He would definitely get them examined by an assayer. He would love to be able to build that house sooner rather than later.

When he'd left Colorado, he had not been on good terms with his father. Jim McBride had told him that if he left the ranch, he would cut Josh out of the will. His father was a mighty powerful and wealthy cattleman. He used his influence to get what he wanted, when he wanted it. Besides, Josh had told his father that he'd wanted to do something different and be responsible for his own welfare. Tempers flared and an argument ensued. Then, when the woman he was really interested in married another man, Josh decided it was time to leave instead of mooning over her and seeing her with someone else.

Crystal. He paused over the image in his mind. The pain was gone after three years, and he decided that it must have been God's will for him. Another plan. Another life. Funny, when he thought about it. His sister, April, had been engaged to the man Crystal eventually married. What a strange turn of events.

He'd struggled in the last three years to make ends meet, and now he was beginning to reap the benefits. Not wealthy by any stretch of the imagination like his father, but he was happy here in Montana and had put the past behind him. He was looking forward to what the future had in store for him.

Maggie Brendan is a member of the American Christian Writers (ACW) and the American Christian Fiction Writers (ACFW). She was a recipient of the 2004 ACW Persistence Award. An active student of Colorado's history, topography, and botany, Maggie has spent years studying both the landscape and the rich folklore of the beginning territory of Colorado.

Maggie has experience in media and print production and has a particular interest and affinity with radio. She also writes reviews for some of her favorite authors, which can be found on her blog, http://southernbellewriter.blogspot.com.

Maggie is married with two grown children and four grandchildren. When she is not writing, she enjoys reading, singing, painting, scrapbooking, and being with her family. She lives in Marietta, Georgia.